Tender Things Shall Die

"A powerful story, tautly written, with quill sharp dialogue."
Estella McQueen, author of *Secrets of The Past*

Tender Things
Shall Die

Tender Things Shall Die

Stephen Edward Reid

TOP HAT BOOKS

Winchester, UK
Washington, USA

JOHN HUNT PUBLISHING

First published by Top Hat Books, 2023
Top Hat Books is an imprint of John Hunt Publishing Ltd., No. 3 East St., Alresford,
Hampshire SO24 9EE, UK
office@jhpbooks.com
www.johnhuntpublishing.com
www.tophat-books.com

For distributor details and how to order please visit the 'Ordering' section on our website.

Text copyright: Stephen Edward Reid 2022

ISBN: 978 1 80341 269 6
978 1 80341 270 2 (ebook)
Library of Congress Control Number: 2022939084

A CIP catalogue record for this book is available from the British Library.

Design: Lapiz Digital Serivices

UK: Printed and bound by CPI Group (UK) Ltd, Croydon, CR0 4YY
US: Printed and bound by Thomson-Shore, 7300 West Joy Road, Dexter, MI 48130

We operate a distinctive and ethical publishing philosophy in
all areas of our business, from our global network of authors to
production and worldwide distribution.

Contents

For Susan

PART 1

I

When Violet Walker turned up on the doorstep of Arman Shaw on the morning of 2nd October 1865, it was the first time in 441 days that he had seen anybody. That morning, like the day before, and the day before that, he had risen while it was still dark. Trudging through thick mud in an unbuttoned nightshirt and heavy black boots he had fed the chickens, pulling his shirt up to cover his nose as the smell of damp hay and rotten eggs hung in the air. The stench still clung to his nostrils as he washed himself with rusty cold water from the pump at the side of his house. On another day he may have heated it and bathed properly. On another day he may not have washed at all. As the night sky turned to blue, he was out front cutting wood. With his right hand wrapped just below the axe head, and his left further up the base, he tightened his grip, relaxing it again just as he began his swing. As the axe gained momentum, his right hand slid back to find the left, bringing both hands together as the axe came slamming down into the log, splintering it to the base and sticking into the stump beneath. He rested a boot on the stump as leverage to help him pull the axe free. He repeated the process several times. On the final log, as his hands came together, he shifted himself into a semi-squat that brought the axe down with extra force. As the wood cracked and split violently down the centre, Arman felt a brief burning sensation in his palm. He looked at his hand and saw a thin dark splinter just below his middle finger. He picked at it with dirty fingernails, scratching at the palm, but it wouldn't budge. He went back into the house, to retrieve a small knife from the kitchen drawer, and that's when he heard the knock at his door. He froze, looking back towards the door, unsure if he'd heard what he thought he'd heard. It was an old house and it creaked and groaned with the changing wind. He waited, and just a moment later, came another knock.

"One moment please!" he shouted at the closed door. He scrambled to his front room, where he retrieved a pair of black trousers from the back of a wooden chair. He still had the knife he intended to use on his splinter clutched in his hand. He switched it from hand to hand as he struggled to pull the trousers on over his boots, jumping up and down to force them up his legs. He hastily fastened the top buttons on his nightshirt and tucked it into his trousers with his free hand. He ran a hand over his thin dark hair, patting it down at the sides and completely missing the stray tuft that stuck out at the back. He ran the same hand through a thick beard, hoping there was no rogue food or spittle there to embarrass him. There was a further knock at the door.

"A moment!" he hollered. His throat was dry. It had been a long time since he'd spoken to anyone but himself. He made it to the door in three huge steps and opened it with more force than it needed, letting a loud icy wind trespass inside.

On his doorstep, unaccompanied, stood Violet Walker, her scuffed boots partially sunk in the soaking mud. Her delicate hands bunched the material of her brown calico dress, lifting it ever so slightly so the hem skirted across the top of the mud. Some of the spatter had stained the white hem and dirtied much of the lower part of the yellow and white floral spray that covered much of the dress. A burgundy and teal paisley shawl lazily slipped from around her chest and she dipped a shoulder slightly to stop it falling free. She had something small tucked under her arm but Arman couldn't make out what it was.

"Good morning, Mr Shaw," she said. "Are you well?"

He cleared his throat and told her, "Yes."

"Are you expecting trouble?" she said.

I

His brow furrowed, confused, then he followed her stare, to his hand which still held the small sharp knife. "Oh," he stumbled, "no. Just a splinter."

"Will you invite me in?"

"Of course," he said, and for the first time in a long while, he smiled. "Come in, please, Mrs Walker."

"Violet, please," she said.

He stood aside and she came past him. Inside, she let go of her dress, letting the bottom tumble over her boots. She redressed her shawl, bringing it tightly across her shoulders and overlapping it at her chest. She orientated herself quickly, turning left into the kitchen where she sat down at the small table. From under her arm, she removed a small book, tied with a ribbon. She placed it on the table in front of her. Arman pulled out a chair and used his hand to wipe crumbs from it before he sat opposite her. She held out her hand. He seemed puzzled for a moment. She nodded at his knife.

"I have good eyes," she told him. "Let's see this splinter."

He handed her the knife. In return, she took his hand and turned it over to inspect the palm. The ease and confidence with which she took his hand startled him but he remained silent. As she examined him, he studied her face. She was a little younger than he was, but only a few years he guessed. Her blonde hair was so light that it appeared white in places. It was clumsily swept back into a bun and mostly hidden beneath a low brim cotton bonnet. Wisps and curls escaped at the sides and circled her ears. Her skin was smooth and pale, her eyes a deep blue, her lips full and wide. He remembered how memorable her smile was, broad and genuine, warming even, but she wasn't smiling now. Her tongue was perched at the corner of her mouth and she held the knife in a peculiar way, almost as if it were a pen, as she inspected his hand.

"It's been a while, Mrs Walker."

"Violet."

"Violet, yes."

She nodded, manoeuvring the tip of the knife under the skin of his palm. A thick droplet of blood emerged at the knife's point. She squinted, moving the hand closer to her face. Arman winced as the knife delved a little deeper. Her hands were slight and soft, at odds with Arman's rough, dirty large hand. Violet briefly stopped to look up at him. He turned his attention away from her hands and met her eyes.

"How have you been, Mr Shaw?"

He nodded by way of an answer, then added, "I've lost track of time a little."

"I'll say," she said, twisting the knife ever so slightly, "we have not seen you for over a year now."

"Time got away from me," he said.

She brought the knife out, smoothly, sliding it out and studying the tip to look for the offending piece of wood. She squinted as she brought it closer to her eyes, the bridge of her nose wrinkling as she strained to see. "Did I get it?"

Arman shook his head to indicate; no. He brought his palm to his mouth, sucking at the blood, hoping to free the splinter with his teeth. She held her hand out once more, impatiently waiting to have another go.

"How's Mr Walker?" he asked.

"Mr Walker?" she replied. "Robert's dead, Mr Shaw."

He flinched, his hand moving, causing her to move the knife out the way sharply. "I'm so sorry. When did it happen?"

"Two days gone," she said.

Arman's mouth opened, lost between shock and silence. Violet returned her attention back to his palm, digging in once more.

"Mrs Walker, I'm sorr—"

"—No apology needed. That's why I've come to see you." One eye closed, her tongue pressing against the back of her teeth, she worked the tip of the knife up and out of the reddened skin. Without taking her eyes from his palm, she placed the knife onto the table. She leaned in a little closer, and with her nails, she slowly extracted the splinter. She held it up, smiling, showing off the micro aggressor. "Such a little thing," she said and wiped it on the corner of the table.

"What happened?" he asked.

Her smile disappeared. "He was murdered, Mr Shaw. A group of travellers came through town, stopping over for the night. One of them got in a fight with Robert and—"

She stopped, unable to continue. Arman leaned forward to comfort her but she moved, just slightly, shifting her body to indicate she didn't welcome it. Arman stayed still. He could see the pain etched across her face. A silence hung in the air as she steadied herself to continue. "We caught him."

"Where is he?"

"Bound at the hands and chained to the oak tree in the village."

Arman's hand covered his mouth in shock. He struggled to find the right words. "Mrs Walker, I'm so sorry."

She lowered her head, looking at her hands. A spot of Arman's blood had found its way onto the sleeve of her dress and she rubbed at it. "I was also sorry to hear about your wife, Mr Shaw. Mathilda was a friend to me when I joined the congregation. I understand why you needed your own time. Your own space. Nobody in town judged you for it."

"I just—" he started, but had nowhere to go. "I didn't cope very well," and he laughed, though soon the laughter became tears that he struggled to contain.

Violet leaned forward and patted his hands. "We've both lost."

Arman regained his composure. He had imagined speaking to Mathilda most days, but he hadn't spoken *of* her to anyone else. He hadn't even realised that he couldn't. "What will happen to this man? Will he be taken into the city?"

She shook her head; no. "We take care of things ourselves, Mr Shaw, you know that. The general consensus in town is that he be executed."

"Executed?"

She raised her shoulders in a throwaway shrug that Arman couldn't decipher.

"Is that what you want?" he said.

"Will it bring my Robert back to me?"

"No."

Violet looked around, her attention drawn to her surroundings. Arman kept a tidy house, at least if the kitchen was anything to go by. She had noticed the small hallway when she came in, with a front room opposite the kitchen and two doors leading to two more rooms. She knew one of them was the bedroom Arman now slept in alone, and presumed the other would have been a nursery had things turned out differently. The house had once belonged to the family that owned the land the village now stood on. When it was later bequeathed to the townspeople, Arman and Mathilda had staked a claim on the house and nobody had objected. Right now, she envied its isolation, just far enough from the town to be alone, but close enough to still be part of the community.

"Vengeance," said Arman.

Violet snapped back to reality. "Vengeance?"

He shrugged, "I don't know. After Mathilda, I wanted someone to blame, so I blamed myself."

"I blame this man. I hate this man, though we have always been taught to forgive. It's easy to hate, it's hard to forgive. Perhaps that's why we preach it to our children. We preach forgiveness but we clamour for vengeance. The congregation seek my permission."

"Your permission?"

She nodded. "If they kill him, then they're murderers, but if I consent, it's justice. Do you follow?"

"Of a sort," Arman said.

"They can't understand why I won't give it."

"Your permission?"

"My permission." ·

"You want to forgive him?"

"No," she said, her voice rising, "Mr Shaw, I want him to die."

He shifted in his seat, uncomfortable. The stinging in his hand irritated him. A thin trickle of blood lingered on the small wound. He stood, going to a kitchen drawer and rummaging around until he found an old handkerchief. He wrapped it round his hand and almost instantly a small blot of blood seeped through to the outside.

Violet's head was down, looking down at her lap. "Did I shock you?"

"No, I..." he trailed off, thinking of the words. "I'm confused. You want him dead. They want him dead. Give them your permission. Give them the excuse they need. This is justice."

Violet rose from her chair, looking down at the book she had placed onto the table. She picked it up and held it out for Arman. He moved away from the sink, reaching out to take it from her. He pulled at the thin red ribbon that was tied around it. The book, pocket sized, bound in deep brown leather with gold gilded letters, was a copy of the Bible.

"Is this for me?" he asked.

"It was Robert's. I thought you might like it."

"Thank you."

"I am certain you already have a copy—"

Arman chuckled. "I've not looked at it for a while."

"Robert underlined some of his favourite parts."

"He did?" asked Arman. "Do you have a favourite?"

"I..." she shook her head. "No, I don't."

"I'm sorry," he said. "I'm not judging. This book holds different things for different people. No two people hold the same Bible."

"I don't know what that means," she smiled.

"I'm sorry—"

"—You keep apologising—"

"—It just means, we're all different. We all walk our own paths. It's understandable if you feel uncomfortable about the congregation wanting to execute a man."

Violet pulled at her shawl, drawing it to her. "Our life here is a very delicate balance. We choose our form of worship. We administer our own affairs. We exercise our own discipline. We are autonomous under God's rule. It is not a life, Mr Shaw, built for the complexity of criminality, do you understand? All our rules, our way of life, are based upon obedience to the principles. An outsider has come in and committed a crime and we're desperately trying to pretend that it is somehow covered by our own rules of governance."

Arman squeezed his hand into a fist a couple of times, stretching his fingers out each time, wincing as he did so.

"It was just a splinter, Mr Shaw, nobody has cut your hand off."

"It stings," he said, shaking his head. "Mrs Walker? Why did you come here today?"

"Do you miss the congregation, Mr Shaw?"

He nodded. "But I've been apart from them so long. Every day away makes it that much harder to go back."

"They would welcome you back, Mr Shaw. Absolutely so."

"Perhaps it would depend on the circumstances," he said, before repeating his question, "Why did you come here, Mrs Shaw?"

"Because the men of this town wish to commit murder and use me as an excuse," she said. "They think me cold, perhaps heartless, because I don't cry for vengeance. I cry for Robert, and Robert's never coming home again." No more tears now. She stared at Arman, resolute, strong. "If they won't take him to the city, if they insist that they can administer justice, then let them administer justice. Give the man a trial, a fair trial, and if he is found guilty, then administer the punishment. Punish him for his guilt, however you see fit."

"Any trial, Mrs Walker, would just be for show, wouldn't it?"

"Perhaps."

"Then why—"

"—defend him, Mr Shaw."

And there it was. Her reason for coming. After a year apart from the town, this would be his return. As agitator. He shook his head, a silent refusal.

"Please, Mr Shaw, you are a fair man. You are a just man. You are apart from this village but you are a part of it. They will accept you because you're one of them. Defend this man, and I will know that justice has been served. Then I can accept their punishment. Please, Mr Shaw, for me."

She had said "for me" like he owed her something. But he owed them nothing. He had very specifically stayed out of their way all this time because he didn't want to be part of their, or any, society anymore. Her logic was so deeply flawed and he could think of no way to explain it to her. The people of the town would find this man guilty and they would execute him regardless of Arman's defence, no matter how spirited or persuasive he might make it, and then what would his position be in the town? Would he still be tolerated as one of their own? This was not his house. This was not his land. He was here by the mercy of the congregation, and if they turned on him, then he could lose what little he had in this world. There could be no winning in this situation, only degrees of losing.

"Mrs Shaw—"

"—Violet."

"Violet, please, I very much want to return to the congregation. But with this, the people would turn on me—"

"—they've agreed not to," she said.

"Whatever agreement you think you have with the congregation, it's not worth the paper it's not written on, Violet, you must understand—"

"—Mr Shaw, I am asking for your help. I need you."

"There must be someone else that—"

Violet interrupted him, almost spitting the words out, "—there is nobody else, Mr Shaw! They are a *mob* and they want blood."

"I can't help you—"

"—What would Mathilda want you to do?"

Arman stopped, visibly shaken. He stared at Violet and she held his stare. "She would..." he started, but stopped.

"If she was here, and I had come to see you, asking for your help, to find peace following the death of my husband, would she turn me away, or would she implore you to help me?"

Anger boiled inside of Arman, but he kept it under control. Violet seemed so helpless standing before him. So alone. He recognised his own angry grief in her demeanour, in the way she spoke, and sometimes, in the silence when she didn't.

"She'd tell you to help me, wouldn't she?"

"What would Robert want *you* to do? Would he want this charade of a trial, or would he want vengeance?"

"He can't get vengeance, Mr Shaw, but I would take comfort in peace. Will you give me peace?"

"What if I win? What if I prove his innocence?" he asked.

"Then you will have proven his innocence, and I would not want to punish an innocent man."

Arman nodded. A little over a year ago he had lost all sense of right and wrong, all sense of his place in the world. Looking back, he couldn't be sure how he made it through each day. Many times, he had contemplated how easy it might be to give up. But he hadn't. He had chosen to live. It's what Mathilda would've wanted, just as she would want him to help Violet now. If she were still here, she'd know the right thing to say. She would guide him.

"Mr Shaw? The congregation is turning against me. Not you too, I beg you."

Arman looked at the Bible still held in his hands. He flicked through the pages, catching fleeting words. He could see places where Robert had underlined in pencil, sometimes words, sometimes sentences or whole passages. Arman became aware that he couldn't remember the last time he had read it.

"Which part has caught your eye?" she asked.

"The Book of Job," he said, closing the book and the conversation. "Is he guilty, Violet? This man. Did he do it?"

"He did. There are witnesses."

"Lord help me."

"Will you do it, Mr Shaw?"

"I would be a miserable comforter if I did not."

"Is that a quote from Job?" she asked.

"Return to your home, Violet," he said. "I shall see you in the morning."

II

The water had mostly cooled by the time Arman got into the bathtub, though as he lowered his aching frame down, it still felt like burning. As each part of him disappeared under the water, he breathed in, deeper and deeper, until eventually he held his breath completely. Finally, as he shifted his position, and found comfort, he exhaled in a drawn-out breath. He could see his ribs jutting out, the flesh eaten back by low appetite and toil. His wiry chest hair stuck tightly to his skin as the water splashed over it. He watched his chest rise and fall, rise and fall. He closed his eyes, dipping his ears below the surface of the water and entering another world. The sores and strains that peppered his fingers, hands, his back, melted away with the gentle sway of the water. He stayed in long enough for his fingers to prune and the water to become cold.

He laid out his clothes on the bed, choosing outfits that had been living untouched in a bottom drawer for over a year. Trousers; grey and pressed, a white shirt with starched collar, a charcoal grey woollen waistcoat and his black overcoat. He retrieved his bowler hat from the top of the wardrobe, wiping off a thick layer of dust from around the rim. He dressed slowly, assessing himself in front of the cracked mirror in his bedroom. Everything felt both too large, and yet constrictive and itchy, like he was wearing clothes that belonged to someone else. He scratched at his thick beard and contemplated shaving it off. It was wildly unkempt, sprouting haphazardly across his gaunt face. He wished the hair on his head was as thick, but time had left him thinning significantly on top. He decided to leave the beard. Perhaps he could get it shaved in the village.

The walk wasn't long, no matter how slow he tried to go. Much of it was downhill, and at times, he had to break into a trot as the incline proved too much for him. There was a long stretch of the path that had a drop either side, where thick spirals of thorns and branches threatened to tangle with anyone unlucky enough to lose their footing. Within the half hour he could see the small village spread out beneath him. Though they claimed it was coincidental, the village was laid out like a cross, with two intersecting roads. Twelve houses were spaced out along the roads, with only the turning to the church free of homes. Behind the church lay a small graveyard, and beyond that the crops and the animals, each area separated by wooden fences. Even at this early hour, he could see people tending to the flock. At the criss-cross of the roads was a gated garden, surrounded by flowers and small trees, but with a grassy space in the middle where wooden benches were spaced out. At the opposite end of the village to the church was the oak tree where Arman could just about make out a chained figure huddled beneath. Surrounding the tree were several stumps, the remains of trees that had been felled following rot. Only the oak survived.

Arman avoided an incline that would've taken him down to the nearest house, convincing himself that it was too steep. Instead, he took the longer path, winding round the outside of the village. The long grass, wet with morning dew, scraped across his trousers and he was relieved when it flattened out and he came upon the traditional way into the village, where a wide wooden archway decorated with fresh flowers, mostly light-coloured lilies, formed an unofficial entrance. To the side, a carved wooden sign read;

You are entering the village of
HOPE
"I was a stranger and you welcomed me."

Arman wondered how many strangers had been welcomed here of late. He found a smile from somewhere deep inside, took a breath, and stepped through the archway. Ahead of him lay the road to the garden, to his right the church, his left the oak tree. The first person to see him was Phoebe Everly and her round face lit up when she saw him. She put the washing she had been sorting back into the basket and sprung from her garden to the path to greet him.

"Arman Shaw!" she threw her chubby arms around him and squeezed hard. "Mr Shaw, it's been too long!" She released him and took a step back, eyeing him from head to toe. "You're so thin. Do you not eat up there on the bluff?"

He laughed, but didn't answer. "It's good to see you," he said instead.

"Mr Everly and I wanted to come and see you, but Niall suggested we give you your space. We were both so sorry to hear about Mathilda."

"Thank you," he said.

"What brings you back, Mr Shaw?"

He stuttered over a response, unsure if he should begin his return to the village by lying to the first person he met. The decision was taken out of his hands by another voice, joining their conversation.

"Does he need a reason?" said Niall, striding over and shaking Arman's hand. Niall was older than Arman, but looked ten years younger. He was always "Niall" and never "Mr Terran". He insisted to everyone, even strangers, that they address him informally. Niall was tall and broad, his shirt sleeves rolled back to reveal strong forearms. If you mentioned it, he would say that the land kept him in shape. His thick white hair was pushed back and tucked behind his ears. His smile seemed genuine and Arman returned it.

Within minutes, a small crowd had gathered, welcoming back Arman to the congregation. They all offered condolences for Mathilda and Arman lost count of the amount of "thank you" and "that's very kind of you" statements he made. There was some gentle ribbing of his time away and several of the women noted his thinner figure and thick beard. There were one or two questions about the reasons for his return, but each time, it was Niall that cut them off, diverting the conversation back to pleasantries. Arman couldn't help but notice Violet Walker's house, just beyond the gathering and further down the street. Its door was closed and there was no sign of Violet.

Rufus, a likeable enough father and husband, was the first person to allude to the murder of Robert Walker. "We've had some terrible business of late." A few people around him nodded and mumbled something along similar lines.

"There's time for that," said Niall, then repeated himself, "There's time for that. Now, are we keeping this big shaggy beard, Arman?"

Arman scratched at it, a smile on his face. He shrugged, and his indecision was picked up on by Evan, who stepped forward and slapped Arman on the back. Evan, easily the oldest man in the congregation, doubled as both a barber and a cobbler depending on the situation. Niall wrapped an arm around Arman, steering him away from the small crowd, and along with Evan, they headed towards a house along the road leading away from the church. Arman waved his goodbye to the others, promising to catch up with them all. His gaze drifted from the waving congregation and back over to Violet's house. Arman wondered again why she hadn't come out to meet him.

Evan's house had a front room that had been converted into a workshop, where a workbench on the far wall took up most of the space. Three pairs of shoes were spread across the workbench, in various states of ill-repair. Evan had a chair in the window with a table beside it. On the table, he placed a bowl of warm water and some soap. Inviting Arman to take a seat, Evan produced a towel from nowhere, expertly draping it around Arman's neck before he prepared the soap. Niall took a seat on the opposite wall, crossing his legs and letting out a long sigh that caused Evan to stop what he was doing.

"Everything well, Niall?" said Evan.

He nodded, maybe a touch too long, certainly long enough to indicate that maybe everything was most certainly not well. Evan took him at his word, turning back to Arman. He placed the soap on the table and picked up a pair of scissors, attacking the beard with practised vigour.

"She came to see you, didn't she?" said Niall.

Arman kept his head facing front, for fear of coming foul of Evan's scissors, but he managed to tilt it ever so slightly, enough for his eyes to find Niall in his periphery. "She did," he said. The sound of the scissors snip-snip-snipped through his ears and he had a strong urge to tell the barber to stop, to leave him be, but he didn't. Evan manoeuvred Arman's head to the side, taking Niall from his sightline. "I'm not very comfortable with it," he said, and when at first there was no response, he wondered if Niall had even heard him. As he was about to repeat himself, Niall spoke.

"We are God's people, Arman. Whoever takes a human life shall surely be put to death."

Evan had placed the scissors back on the table. He used a brush to apply the soap to Arman's face and neck. Each man stayed silent as Evan finished with the soap and placed it on the table by the scissors and bowl. He wiped a razor across his forearm, tilted Arman's head back, and slowly ran the blade up his throat.

"I know," said Arman, belatedly.

"Keep still, keep still," muttered Evan as he worked.

"We don't need many rules here, Arman, or many laws. The congregation self-governs extremely effectively. But when we're faced with the most egregious of sins, of crimes, we cannot shirk our responsibilities."

"Did you consider taking him to the city?" asked Arman.

"We did consider it," replied Niall, "but the congregation made a vow when we settled here, Arman, with founding principles, one of which was that we would form an organised society as we saw necessary. Passing our problems onto somebody else would weaken us as a society."

Arman went to speak, but stopped, as Evan held his head tightly, administering a long stroke from the base of his neck to his chin, the stubble scarping free with a grinding noise. He waited until Evan had made his movement, wiping the blade before the next round. "Are you against a trial then, Niall?"

"Arman, hand on my heart, if there were doubt of any kind, any kind at all, I would be the first one calling for a trial. But this man killed Robert Walker in front of witnesses. His guilt is absolute. Any trial would be just for show."

"Perhaps so," said Arman, "but for Mrs Walker's sake—"

"—you think it's in her best interest to stretch this out? To make a show of it?"

"She feels, however right or wrong, that an execution without a trial is murder."

Evan stuttered for a second, just nicking Arman below his lower lip. The old man winced and took a step back. Arman's hand jumped to it involuntarily, dabbing at the blood. Evan, flustered, scrambled with his towel and wiped away a trickle of blood that ran down Arman's chin. "Apologies," he said, then, chastising, "I said to keep still."

Arman nodded and Evan continued, Evan moving the razor a tiny bit slower than he had been, his hand not as steady as he'd like.

"What would you have us do, Arman?" asked Niall.

"I don't know," he said, then, "perhaps respect her wishes. Give her her trial, even if the result of which is a foregone conclusion. Would it be such a nuisance to give her some peace."

"Still, still," said Evan as he worked.

Arman's eyes found his barber's and he whispered, "I am still."

"Did you know," said Niall, "Violet Walker was the last to join us? Other than newborns, she was the last to be baptised into the congregation."

"I know."

"She didn't just marry Robert Walker, she married his beliefs, taking them as her own."

"Yes." Arman did know that, though he wasn't sure of its relevance. His lip stung, but he resisted the temptation to touch it. Evan's hand still shook, and Arman kept an eye on him as the razor turned his rough skin smooth. He had had the beard for a year and he wondered if he'd recognise himself in the mirror afterwards. He half-turned to Niall and asked, "How's it looking?"

"I think I preferred the beard," replied Niall with a grin.

Arman laughed, causing Evan to jump and momentarily stop the shave. He waited an appropriate enough time, when he was sure the joviality had stopped, before he readied himself to continue.

"The old man is *this* close to cutting your throat, Arman!" said Niall.

Evan stopped and looked over at Niall disapprovingly. Niall waved a hand at him dismissively and after a pause, he turned back to Arman to continue.

"How would it go?" asked Niall, "We'd need a judge, I presume?"

"And a man on each side, arguing the case."

"I don't think there's much to argue," said Niall.

"Still," said Arman. "Someone to argue guilt, someone innocence. And then the judge rules and the matter is over."

"Need it take long?"

"Not at all. A few days perhaps. Each man prepares his arguments and presents them."

"And how would you go about preparing an argument for a guilty man's defence, Arman?"

"With your permission, I would speak to those that witnessed it, as would, I presume, the other man, and make sure that what happened, was what happened."

Niall laughed, slapping his hands down on his thighs.

Evan finished the shave and took a step back to admire his work. He fumbled on the nearby mantelpiece and found a hand mirror, which he passed to Arman. Arman inspected his smooth face. He looked older, the lines on his face more visible. It didn't quite seem right, but he couldn't put his finger on why.

"Can I be the judge?" asked Niall. "In the trial? That way, if it all goes wrong, I've only got myself to blame."

"I don't have any objection," said Arman, "but perhaps we should let Mrs Walker confirm it. This is all for her."

Niall ground his teeth, sucking in air like it was poison, "All for her."

"Because she's one of us," said Arman.

"Us?" asked Niall. "Like you and me? Where have you been, Arman? Not among the congregation."

"Niall, you know —"

"—I know. I know. Even with your prolonged absence, you will always be one of us, Arman. Violet Walker, however, I couldn't say. I'm not sure, even as Robert lived and breathed, that she was ever really one of us. But still, I will speak with her. What are the next steps?"

"I will talk to the congregation," said Arman, "begin my preparation. You speak to Mrs Walker, agree on a judge and a man to argue for guilt. Then the judge can set a date for events to take place. Does that sound suitable?"

"It does. Absurd. But suitable."

Arman rose from his chair, once more shaking the approaching Niall's hand. Arman caught sight of the mirror now lying flat on the table. Something still seemed wrong. He saw his reflection but didn't recognise himself.

III

It started on Monday evening when three travellers came to the village. They were on horses and had a wagon with them. The men were called Fred Decker, Don Hope and perhaps Roy or Ray Howard, or Howarth perhaps, perhaps something different. Strangely, nobody definitively recalled the name of the third man, who by every account was a non-assuming gentleman of indeterminate age and appearance. Don Hope had made a great deal of the fact that he had the same name as the village, and jokingly claimed some kind of proprietorial rights. To this fact, everyone agreed. They had asked to stop for the night and made great pains to insist that they would be no trouble and would ultimately be just passing through. Niall had allocated them some land behind the church and they had seemed agreeable to this.

The village had been mostly assembled in the centre gardens and Edmund Haynes had been playing his guitar while his sister, Esther Haynes, had sung hymns. Alma Dryden, who lived with her husband, Philip, and young sons, Bradley and Bertie, recalled Esther singing "O the Deep, Deep Love of Jesus," and "Lift Up Your Hearts!" The two Dryden children, both young enough to still be struggling with basic words, ran around the living room, chasing each other and giggling. They had been introduced to "Mr Shaw" but had mistaken his name for "Mr Shoe" and ran around, unrestrained and without reprimand shouting out "Mr Shoe! Mr Shoe!" Philip, a pipe perched precariously at the corner of his mouth, told Arman that he hadn't witnessed anything out of the ordinary.

Olive Kirby, whose house was furthest from the church, back towards the oak tree, remembered everyone joining in for a rousing rendition of "Abide With Me". She, like several other people, would note that one of the travellers, Don Hope, joined in with them and was particularly energetic, and though not gifted with a great voice, made up for it with enthusiasm. Olive, who laid out a plate of shortbread and a tall glass of milk, fussed about her living room, apologising for the mess. A slew of dried herbs hung bunched together from a thick length of string that ran across the window end of the room. Arman sat in a musty, mint draught and wondered why they weren't hung in the kitchen.

Euphemia Hall, who served Arman a buttermilk scone and some tea, and insisted on being called Effie, recalled a general feeling of goodwill regarding the evening. Effie, her hands hugging a pregnant bump protectively, shouted through to her husband, Benjamin, reading in the adjoining room, and he agreed with her, though had nothing to add. "The problem started," she whispered, though Arman wasn't sure why, "just after breakfast the following day." Arman waited for more, but after a prolonged silence, she added, "At least, that's what I heard."

The following morning, sometime just before sunrise, there was a commotion in the church. Several people mentioned hearing raised voices. Phoebe Everly, who was up and tending to her vegetable garden, looked up and saw one of the travellers, Fred Decker, emerge from the church clutching his hands close to his chest, perhaps "concealing a weapon" but definitely "covered in blood". Phoebe, serving macaroons topped unexpectedly with an overbearing almond icing, poured Arman more tea as she struggled to remember certain details. When asked why she thought Fred Decker might be concealing a weapon, she presumed, though wasn't sure, that he had "something in his hands. Or maybe it was nothing." Eamonn Everly, sitting next to his wife and wondering why she wasn't topping up *his* tea or offering *him* some of the macaroons, felt the need to tell Arman that he'd, "Seen nothing. Not a thing." He had then laughed to himself and said, "I probably wouldn't

have noticed if I'd seen poor Robert actually being murdered."
As Phoebe threw him a scornful look, he added, "Apologies Mr
Shaw, that was inappropriate."

Miles Faber couldn't sleep, and was at his bedroom window,
waiting for the sunrise. He also saw Fred Decker emerge from
the church, clutching something tightly which he "presumed
to be a knife or weapon of some sort", but "might have been
nothing", and appeared to have blood on his hands and chest.
In the general disarray of the next few minutes, the travellers
attempted to leave. Miles, still in his underclothes, ran from his
home and tackled Fred Decker as he attempted to mount a horse.
They both fell to the ground and "scuffled something fierce".
Miles, now sat in his cold kitchen, clawed at his own shirt to
demonstrate to Arman where he had grabbed Fred Decker.
Arman noticed that Miles' shirt was buttoned incorrectly. There
was no offer of cake or tea in this house. Arman wondered if
Miles fed himself, let alone worried about entertaining visitors.
By this time, having heard the commotion, Vincent Law came
out and assisted Miles in subduing Fred Decker. Miles told
Arman that Vincent was "still pulling on his trousers when he
came running out!"

Neither Miles nor Vincent saw what happened to the other
travellers, but Roman Farley, who insisted that Arman eat
a second slice of his wife's honey cake that she'd made the
previous evening, said that the men "rode out of the village
without looking back". By this time, "Most people were up and
at their doors or out onto the street." Roman Farley, overweight,
slumped down in a chair in front of the fire, struggled to
remember more. He drummed fat fingers on the armrest of his
chair, staring into the fire as if an image of clearer events might
present itself. Arman thanked Roman for speaking to him and
left before a third slice of cake was offered.

Inside the church, Bernard Ogden witnessed the crime, and
was with Robert Walker until the end. Arman had been welcomed

into the Ogden house, with Bernard's wife, Joan, offering him tea and the largest piece of lemon cake, his fourth or fifth sweet serving that morning. At some point he'd lost count. He didn't like to say no, despite his rising wave of nausea. The room was dark, the curtains were open but the light outside was partially blocked by an outhouse built too close to the front of their house. The couple had sat together on the sofa, her clutching his hand in her lap. Both smiled. Both seemed eager to help. Arman, as he had done many times that day, explained why he was there.

"Just to tie everything together," he said. "I'm not trying to stir up a hornet's nest. Nobody's questioning the man's guilt. Violet Walker has requested a trial be held, in order for us to say we showed due diligence and didn't rush to punishment without looking at the facts. It's fallen to me to offer a defence, if you will."

"A defence?" said Joan, her smile wavering for the first time.

"To say he didn't do it?" added Bernard.

Arman shook his head, "Nothing like that. Every trial, even ones such as this, need to hear both sides—"

"There's another side?" asked Joan.

"Again," said Arman, "it's just a formality, to show we've not rushed to judgement."

"You're trying to prove his innocence?" asked Joan.

"No," said Arman. "Yes, of a kind. His guilt is beyond question, it's just—"

"—what if you succeed?" asked Bernard.

"Yes," added his wife, "what if you succeed?"

"Succeed?" asked Arman.

"What if you prove his innocence?"

Arman took a moment, looking from Joan to Bernard, trying to choose his words carefully. "Well, I don't think there's much question as to his guilt. I mean to say, you saw him do it, yes, Bernard?"

"I did."

"So there we have it—"

"—So why try to say he didn't do it?" asked Bernard.

Arman took a sip of his tea. "Lovely tea, thank you." He shifted in his seat, nervously looking for the right words to placate the Ogdens. "Violet Walker wants a trial—"

"—Yes, you said that," said Joan, impatiently.

"And we all know he's guilty," said Arman, "but in order to stage the trial, and assign punishment, we need to show that we've at least offered a defence of some sort. A counter-point. An irrelevant formality. It would be very helpful for me if you could just go over what happened once more."

Joan's smile had left her face a while ago and not returned. She looked down at her lap, while her disgruntled husband recounted his story once more.

"We were in the church," started Bernard, "discussing the upcoming harvest festival. We had gone through to the back room, to see how we might organise the donations. We had—"

"—at sunrise?"

Bernard's eyebrows raised, a question in their own right.

"Had you pre-arranged to be there that early or was it just a coincidence that you were both up?"

"Mr Shaw—"

"—Arman, please—"

"—I thought you wanted to hear my story, not call me a liar."

Arman held his hands up, "That was not my intention, Mr Ogden, apologies, I just want to make sure I understand fully."

"We had arranged, at the previous evening's festivities, that we would meet early, before the morning service, to discuss the harvest festival. We are, as you surmised, early risers."

"Apologies, please continue."

"We heard a noise, from the main church. We exchanged a look—"

"—a look?—"

"A look, Mr Shaw, because we both heard it. We went back into the church and saw the traveller, who I would later find out to be called Fred Decker, attempting to steal the gem from the box that houses the Holy Relic."

"He was using a knife? To pry off the gems?"

"Yes," said Bernard. "Well, we both shouted at him. Robert made for him and went to subdue the thief. A fight broke out—"

"—do you remember who started the fight?"

Bernard shook his head, "It happened very fast, Mr Shaw. There was shouting and then they were tussling. I wasn't sure how I could help. They ended up on the floor, and at some point this Fred Decker used the knife to stab Robert in the neck. Robert was silent but the man, Fred Decker, was in hysteria. He ran from the church. I went to Robert, to help him, but..."

"But it was too late," said Joan.

"The bleeding wouldn't stop," said Bernard, his voice beginning to shake at the recollection. "It just...gushed out. I couldn't do anything."

"I'm so sorry," said Arman. "And I don't mean to prolong your pain, but could I just ask, did you see Fred Decker stab Robert Walker in the neck?"

"He didn't stab himself, Mr Shaw."

"I know, but did you see it?"

"It all happened very quickly," said Bernard, adding confusingly, "I didn't, but I did, do you understand?"

Joan put her arm around her husband, and brought her attention round to Arman, chastising him with her eyes. "I hope you've got what you came for. Perhaps you may leave us now."

Arman nodded, replaced his tea cup onto the saucer and stood. Joan and Bernard stayed seated, so he made his own way to the front door. Once outside, he let out a long breath and puffed out his cheeks. He had a fear that he may bring up any one of the several slices of cake he had eaten. Across the street, Herman Blyth was on his knees in his garden, picking out weeds. He saw Arman and waved. Arman waved back. Herman groaned as he got to his feet, shifting his weight away from a bad right leg. He had been afflicted since a teenager with a weakness on his right side. He propped himself up on his garden gate.

"How've you been, Mr Shaw?" asked Herman. His voice was gravelly deep and he spoke slowly, as if considering each word before he said it. "Busy morning?"

"You could say that," replied Arman, walking across the street to shake Herman's hand. "Violet Walker has asked for a trial for this Fred Decker fellow, and I've—"

Herman held up his hand, "—Niall filled me in, Mr Shaw. It's a thankless task."

"It is," agreed Arman.

"It was agreed that I would be your opposite number, Mr Shaw, proving the evidence for guilt. Hope that doesn't put us at odds?"

"Not at all," said Arman, smiling, "you're a fair man and a fine choice, Mr Blyth. I don't think the man's guilt is going to be up for much debate."

"Call me Herman, please," said Herman. He let go of the fence, resting his hands on his hips. He looked up and down the street, seemingly lost in his own thoughts for a moment. His smile faded away, the deep lines on his face etching an image of weariness and age. Still looking off into the distance, he said, "So sorry to hear about your wife."

Arman nodded. "Is everything well, Herman?"

"Something like this casts a large shadow. I'm not relishing delivering a punishment on someone, regardless of the certainty of their guilt."

"How will it be done?"

"The punishment or the trial?"

"The execution," said Arman.

"Execution, hmmm," said Herman, "that will be by axe or by poison. The final choice will be by the prisoner, Mr Decker. Niall thinks it removes our complicity if he chooses his own death."

"You don't agree?"

Herman shrugged, "I have no idea, truthfully, I don't. But Violet Walker deserves her trial, if that's what she needs to find her peace. But after, I wonder if Hope will ever be the same."

"You think Mrs Walker deserves a trial?"

"Do you not?"

"It's just Niall seems—"

"—Niall seems to have a grievance of some kind with the widow. He's still judging the misguided girl she used to be, and the life she used to lead, and not the woman that Robert trusted and married. But Niall isn't entirely alone. There's talk..."

"Talk?"

"Amongst others around the congregation. They whisper amongst themselves. They don't like the way she grieves, if you can picture that. And I suppose this business with 'finding peace' rather than punishing the man that everybody knows killed her husband, well..."

"What do *you* think, Herman?"

"How long did you take away from the congregation, Mr Shaw? Grief takes many forms. Let the lady have her peace."

They exchanged friendly goodbyes, as Arman left to return to his home. He had politely declined Herman's offers of food. He missed his house. He missed the solitude. Almost everyone had been friendly, and none but the Ogdens seemed to judge him for his questions. But the sudden reintegration into society, or maybe it was the excessive cake, had left him feeling sick in his stomach. He wasn't used to smiling for this long. He would head home, get some food and perhaps a nap, then return to the village this evening. There was talk of a candlelight gathering, in the garden, telling stories or perhaps singing hymns once more. The idea of such a display didn't excite him, but he still felt hopelessly out of touch, and hoped that spending more time amongst the others may better facilitate his return to normality.

He left the village with no fanfare, just quietly exiting and joining the winding road that would lead him home. Some of the thick brambles from the incline either side of the path had sprung up and spread across the main path but Arman sidestepped them easily enough. Within the half hour, he was back at his house, feeling like he'd been away for days. He decided on a nap before getting any food. Still in his clothes, he lay on his bed, listening to the silence and embracing the stillness that lived all around him. Maybe if he could just rest for a short while, grab a few minutes. When he woke up, it was dark. He could hear his sheep moving restlessly outside. He sat up, rubbing at his temples. A headache had formed and wasn't easing up any. It was time to return to the village.

IV

It was late when Arman returned to the village. There were candles placed in a circle around the garden, with the amber flickering light illuminating Esther Hayes, perched on a step and singing a hymn that Arman didn't recognise. Around her sat a half dozen of the congregation singing along. They sang with heart, but not too loud. This was an evening of reflection, not celebration. Sylvia Farley had set up a table in front of her house and was making drinks for people. The whole village seemed to be out, mingling, chatting and enjoying the evening air. Arman moved between them, smiling at some, exchanging pleasantries with others. The ones who hadn't offered their condolences about Mathilda earlier, did so now. Niall approached Arman, giving him one of the two glasses of lemonade he was carrying.

"Courtesy of Sylvia Farley," he said. "Tastes dreadful, but I daren't complain."

Arman thanked him and took a sip of what turned out to be, as pointed out, an awful glass of lemonade. He winced, the bitterness biting hard.

"Told you!" laughed Niall. "How's the argument for the defence coming along? I've been hearing some things."

"What things?" asked Arman.

"The Ogdens feel harangued. I think that was the word they used."

"I think the Ogdens and I have a different idea of what harangued means."

Niall laughed once more, but this time it felt more forced. He took a sip of his drink, grimaced then tossed the liquid to his side, letting it splash onto the dirt. Arman followed suit, disposing of the bitter liquid. "Harangued or not," started Niall, "people are talking. They're not sure why you're trying to defend this man. Before you say anything, I know, I know, but I don't think you'll ever change their minds."

"I don't want to defend him," said Arman.

"I know. I really do. Violet Walker's desire for a fair trial comes at a cost, and not for the guilty man. It comes for you. No matter what we say, there are some people in this village who think you want us to set free a murderer."

"That's just ridiculous."

"Arman, I know that! But there'll be plenty of eyes trained on you during this so-called trial. Stay strong." Niall slapped him on the back, a conciliatory gesture.

Arman nodded, acknowledging him, then sidled off, mingling amongst the others. He moved past the garden, away from the church and towards the oak tree at the end of the street. Only a few of the villagers were this far down the street, some in couples, some in groups. Beyond the last house, just up ahead, Arman saw the figure of Fred Decker, sat back against the tree. He moved closer, approaching from behind and finding a nearby stump where he sat down without being noticed. It didn't take him long to realise that he wasn't the only one quietly watching Fred Decker. Away from the candlelight of the village, just beyond the tree, Arman saw Violet Walker. The stump she sat on was directly opposite Fred Decker, facing him from around fifteen feet away. She stared at her husband's killer. He didn't look back. His eyes were down, studying the ground at his feet. Arman could only really just about make out the barest details of Fred Decker from here. He looked tall, over six feet he guessed. He had shoulder-length dark hair and broad shoulders. He had large ears and a big nose, but strong cheekbones and from this distance, seemed quite striking. Violet watched him from the darkness. Arman could really only make out the vagueness of her shape. Every now and again she rocked forward slightly and the moonlight caught her eyes.

"Are you awake?" she shouted at Fred Decker.

At first there was no response. They were just far enough from the main activities of the village that it had felt quiet. Violet's voice had cut through that. Now, the only sound Arman could really hear was Fred Decker's silence.

"Are you awake?" she repeated.

It seemed like no answer would be forthcoming, but on the cusp of being asked again, Fred Decker responded with a simple, "Yes."

"You killed my husband," she said, and though it wasn't a question, it felt like she was looking for an answer. She was met with silence. From nearby, one or two of the villagers had picked up on her voice and were headed that way. Nobody went to her, but a few sat nearby. "Fred Decker, is it?"

"Yes," he said, his voice deep but soft.

"Fred Decker, you killed my husband. His name was Robert Walker."

Arman wanted to stand up, to say something, to tell Violet to stop, to tell her that no good could come of this. He was poised on the edge of his stump, caught in indecision. It wasn't his place. Perhaps one of the villagers may go and comfort her, lead her away from this. But no such luck. Arman hadn't noticed when, but at some point Violet had stood up. She didn't move any closer, but Arman feared that might change soon enough. He looked around for support, but all he saw was an ever-growing group of gawkers.

"Why did you kill him, Fred Decker?" she said, loud, but not shouting. This felt like pain, not aggression. "Why did you do it?"

Silence, or at least silence from Fred Decker. Arman could hear the whispers from the villagers. Everyone seemed to have an opinion, but only in hushed tones to like minds. Nobody was stepping forward to comfort Violet, to stop this. Arman cleared his throat, ready to say something, but he had no words. He wasn't the person to stop this. Did she not have close friends

31

here somewhere? He looked around the villagers, some in moonlight, some anonymously lost in the darkness. Perhaps as many as ten or fifteen people lingered nearby, ghoulishly taking in the show. Arman tried to find Niall, or even Herman Blyth, in the group. He looked for somebody stronger than himself.

"Fred Decker!" slightly louder, but still not shouting. "Why did you murder him?"

Arman's hands were propped on the corner of his stump, caught between seated and standing, desperately trying to find a way to defuse the situation.

Violet's voice wavered, "Why did you do it?"

Arman's heart ached to hear her desperate questions. He cleared his throat once more, then said "Mrs Walker" in the hope of drawing her attention. She didn't seem to hear him, so slightly louder, he called "Mrs Walker" once more. She turned her head in his direction, considering him but not saying anything. This would be a great place for one of her friends, preferably a female friend, to put an arm around her and lead her back home. But nobody moved. Arman, desperate, said, "Violet, stop."

Even in this light, he could almost see her considering his words. She broke away from his gaze, lowering her eyes and staring at the ground for the longest time. Then, almost to herself, barely above a whisper, she said, "Why did you have to kill him?"

Arman had barely heard it himself, but he noticed Fred Decker's movement. He raised his head to look at her.

"I was defending myself," Fred Decker said.

There was a rumble of whispers and movements in the villagers watching on. Violet had lifted her head to look back at Fred Decker. Though she surely couldn't make out any detail in this light, she seemed to study him.

"No," she said, shaking her head, then once more, "No."

"He attacked me," said Fred Decker.

Violet took a single step towards him, a decision-making process surely working its way through her head. Arman willed her to walk away. She was shaking her head, internally denying Fred Decker's accusation against her husband. She paced back and forth in the small area around her stump. Even from here, Arman could hear her breathing becoming laboured as she fought back tears. She eventually stopped pacing, dropping down to her knees and resting her head against the ground. Arman looked away, just for a moment, so he didn't see her grab it, but when he looked up, she had a palm-sized rock clenched in her hand and she was covering the short distance between herself and Fred Decker. He went to say something, but she brought the rock round in an arc and hit him hard in the face. Again, throwing her arm back as if about to punch him, she pounded the rock into the side of his face and he slumped over. She raised it again and Arman was on his feet and covering the ground. He heard someone from the congregation shout out to "Kill him, Violet!"

Arman got to her and grabbed at her arm, stopping her mid-swing. She fought against him, a guttural growl erupting as she twisted in his grip. Arman felt strong arms around his waist, pulling him away, and he and his unknown attacker both fell backwards into the dirt. Arman landed hard, feeling a jabbing pain in his shoulder. Free of Arman, Violet swung the rock high and began to bring it down once more, but this time she stopped, hovering it in the air over the fallen figure of Fred Decker.

"Do it, Violet!" another voice, the same taunting suggestion.

Arman tried to say, "No," but the wind had been knocked out of him by the fall. He struggled round to try and see his attacker, but whoever it had been had broken free and moved away, losing himself in the assembled villagers. "Stop," said Arman, though he doubted anyone could hear him.

Eventually, far too late, a number of the women came forward to comfort Violet. One of them took the rock from her and tossed it away. Violet's legs seemed unsteady, and suddenly she found arms either side of her to keep her on her feet. They led her away as she began to sob. Herman Blyth, who would be Arman's opposite in the trial very soon, came to Arman and held out his hand. Arman grabbed it and Herman helped bring him to his feet.

"Are you hurt?" asked Herman.

Arman rolled his shoulder a few times. Nothing seemed broken, but he would bet he'd have a bruise by the morning. He shook his head, unable to properly comprehend what had just happened.

"Maybe it's time to head home, Mr Shaw," said Herman. "Can you walk?"

"Yes," said Arman, still looking confused, unable to decipher all the faces nearby. He could hear people grumbling, none too discreetly cursing his name. He couldn't make it all out, and he wasn't sure who his aggressors were, but he didn't feel safe standing in the darkness of the village. He became aware of another man to his rear and he turned his head to see Niall behind him.

"Are you injured, Arman?" asked Niall.

Arman shook his head.

"Do you need any help getting home?"

Arman shook his head; no. He looked over at the still slumped figure of Fred Decker chained to the oak tree. The slumped form stirred, a groan emanating from somewhere deep.

"Someone should probably see to him," said Arman, nodding towards the fallen man.

Niall and Herman exchanged a look, their smiles falling away for a moment.

"Don't worry about him, Arman, someone will take care of his wounds," said Niall.

Arman nodded once more, still disorientated by everything that had happened. He felt a hand slap his back, seemingly friendly, but also a reminder to get moving. Arman muttered his farewells and started back through the village, heading for the winding road home. He kept his head down as he walked, gently massaging his shoulder as he went. He daren't look up, he was too afraid to, because he feared what he would see. He would see angry faces, accusing eyes, wondering why he had stopped Violet Walker from giving Fred Walker the judgement he deserved. The road home never felt as long, and on the way, his mind replayed the whole situation again and again, except in his head, he left Violet alone and every future he envisioned was a lot brighter because of it.

V

He got to the village early the next morning, hoping not to see too many people before he got to Violet's house. Phoebe Everly tended her vegetable garden and when she saw him, she gave him a polite, if decidedly cold, smile. He waved at her and moved on. Violet's house was near the church. He opened her white gate and walked down the path lined with tulips and roses to her front door. He knocked gently, not wanting to wake her if she wasn't up. There was a long pause. He readied himself to knock again, before deciding against it. If need be, he'd come back later. As he turned to go, he heard her voice from the other side of the door.

"Who is it?"

He turned back, pressing his mouth close to the door. He didn't want the neighbours hearing him and coming out. "Mrs Walker? It's Arman Shaw."

After another long pause, he heard movement. He took a step back and the door opened, just an inch. Violet looked through the gap, almost as if she expected an imposter to be standing there.

"It's early, Arman," she said.

"I know," he replied, "Sorry. I just wanted to talk to you."

She looked tired, with dark circles under her eyes. The hair tied back into the bun seemed even more unruly than usual, with strands sprouting at the back and sides and a few sweeping across her face. She unlocked the door and held it open for him. He looked up and down the street before he entered, as if attending a clandestine meeting. Violet wore a long dress, a sombre brown, with a grey cardigan over the top which seemed too big for her. She overlapped the sides and wrapped it round herself with crossed arms.

"Tea? Coffee?"

"Coffee, thank you, Mrs Walker."

"Violet," she told him.

She moved through to a kitchen at the back and Arman stayed in the living room. It was small, with an old rug that took up much of the floor. Bright sunshine, fresh from rising, swept in through the window, giving the room a yellow glow. There was a small table by the wall and two armchairs spaced evenly apart either side of it. On a mantelpiece sat a framed photo of an old couple he took to be Violet's parents. He picked it up, studying it, looking for a family resemblance. A rattle of crockery signalled Violet at the door, carrying a tray of coffee and milk. Arman noticed a bandage on her hand. He turned the photo round to show her what he was looking at.

"Your parents?"

She shook her head, "Robert's."

She placed the drinks down on the table and took a seat. Arman replaced the photo on the mantelpiece and sat in the armchair opposite. As Violet added milk to her coffee, he took his black from the tray and took a sip. Violet stirred her drink, letting the teaspoon rattle noisily around the cup for longer than necessary.

"How's the hand?" he asked her.

She looked at the bandaged hand, turning it over palm side up. She made an odd expression, half squinting, half grimacing, and said, "Bruised. But then, I've only got myself to blame."

He sipped his coffee.

"Isn't this the part," she asked, "where you tell me that I'm not to blame?"

He nodded and shrugged, unsure of how to respond. Violet smiled, happy that he wasn't offering empty condolences.

"I would've killed him, had it not been for you."

Arman didn't know if he should apologise or not, so he stayed quiet. He got the feeling he wasn't meant to say anything yet. He drank his coffee. He watched her as she struggled to meet his eyes. She fiddled with her hand, fingered at her bandage.

"They wanted me to kill him," she eventually said.

"They did," he agreed.

"But you stopped me. Why did you stop me?"

He put his coffee back down onto the tray, taking his time, doing it carefully, as if making too much noise might ruin the moment. He perched on the edge of his armchair. "I don't know," he said, then, "a hundred reasons."

"You live by yourself for over a year, comfortable in your own company, content. And out of the blue I turn up and ask you to re-join the congregation. To do me a favour. To help me out," said Violet. "Because I ask you to come and do something that nobody wants you to do. I ask you to come and do the impossible. And I return the favour by acting like a fool."

"I don't blame you, Mrs W...Violet."

"You don't?"

"Last night, I saw a woman in pain, suffering, unable to deal with grief. Nobody came to help you. They sat there, watching you, goading you, waiting for you to kill a man. I felt a responsibility, with nobody else acting, of stopping you doing something you'd regret. And I'm reasonably certain now that everyone in the village hates me. But if I had to do it all again, I'd do exactly the same thing. Maybe I'd step in earlier."

Violet's shoulders hunched, her whole body seeming to fold in on itself. Tears came, fast and violently, streaming down her cheeks. Arman moved from his chair and knelt in front of her, taking her hands in his and holding them as she sobbed. "They hate me too," she managed to sputter out.

"Nobody hates you, Violet."

"They all hate me. I'm not one of them. I married into this. I'm not one of them. I'm the *wife* of one of them. The widow. They have their rules, they have their ways, and I'm always on the outside."

"Nobody hates you," he repeated.

She sniffed hard, fighting back the tears and composing herself as best she could manage. "They loved Robert. Not me."

"Violet, what happened that morning? He had a meeting in the back room of the church with Bernard Ogden to talk about the harvest festival?"

"The two of them were in charge of it this year. I think they just wanted to get it right. Robert worked best in the mornings."

Arman nodded, still kneeling, still holding her hands. He smiled, hoping she'd smile back, and she did. He had an overwhelming desire to hold her close, to press his cheek to hers, but instead he patted her hand and got to his feet.

"Thank you for the coffee, Violet."

"Thank you for saving me, Arman," she replied.

He let himself out. The sun was up and the sky was clear and blue, but a cold wind whipped all around him. He turned and headed towards the church. He passed Alma Dryden on the way and they exchanged pleasantries. The church had large, wooden double doors, and one was closed and the other open outward. It was empty inside. He stood in the open doorway, savouring the peace, savouring the space. The church had been the first building built in Hope. It was built in wood, fifteen feet high, with enough space for every member of the congregation to fit inside. There were five rows of pews, with a centre aisle leading to a step, which took you up to a simple altar. Behind the altar was a large window, looking out at expansive green fields beyond. A door to the right of the altar led you to a back room, which had begun life as a room for private council, but had transitioned into a storage room at some point.

Arman took his time, taking in the space, reacquainting himself with the atmosphere. Though a simple built building, he felt the church carried with it a gravitas that he couldn't fully explain. He felt a reverence, but presumed it was just down to a life spent in servitude of God. He imagined the path of Fred

Driver, sneaking up the aisle, taking the steps up to the altar. Just behind, on a small table, lay a box, encrusted with a gem. Inside lay the Holy Relic. Bernard Ogden had said that Fred Decker had been using a knife to pry it free. Arman picked up the box. It was light. He couldn't see any scratches or scuffs. No sign of any knife marks dug into it. He tucked his fingers around the gem, feeling it give a little. He pulled, but not too hard. He was almost certain it would come free with very little exertion. The box itself was small and light, why hadn't Fred Decker just taken the whole thing?

He imagined a shout, coming from his side and startling Fred Decker. Robert Walker had emerged from the side room and instantly challenged him. They fought on the floor and as Bernard Ogden stood helplessly to the side, Fred Decker fatally stabbed Robert Walker in the neck. Somebody had cleaned the church since then, but there was still a large dark stain on the wooden floor. Robert Walker had died here. Fred Decker had become hysterical, to use Bernard Ogden's words, and had fled the church, still clutching the knife and covered in blood. Arman tried to imagine it, but he could only do so in fragments, like trying to recollect a dream from long ago. He put the box down, careful to place it exactly where he had picked it up from. He moved to his side, heading into the back room through the open door. The space was small, with odds and ends piled up against each wall. Arman couldn't imagine how they would've organised this room for a harvest festival. Wouldn't it have made more sense to pile the offerings up around the altar? He would love to clarify some comments from Bernard Ogden but was reasonably sure he wouldn't be welcome there anymore.

He left the church, contemplating how he might go about summing up everything that had happened into some kind of a defence. He moved along the side of the church, staying close to the wall as he walked round to the back. Between the church and the fields beyond were small piles of rubbish, waiting to be sorted and destroyed, or repurposed in another part of the village. A set of chairs, some with three legs rather than four, others missing a part of the back, were stacked clumsily on top of each other. A short wooden fence, broken into hundreds of pieces, was piled up haphazardly. Much of it was stained with what Arman presumed was blood. It must have been destroyed as Robert and Fred fought and now it had been discarded. It was a problem for another day. Arman looked out across the fields, considering his next step. Mathilda was buried in the graveyard nearby, but he didn't want to visit her. Not yet.

He didn't want to, but he would need to speak to Fred Decker. He had seemed in a bad way the previous night and Arman wondered if somebody had tended to his wounds and possibly given him somewhere to sleep and recover. Moving away from the church, he passed by the gardens and saw the oak tree down the street. When he saw the figure on the ground, slumped over at the base of the tree, he stopped in his tracks. He looked around, watching the villagers going about their daily lives. Nobody seemed to be reacting to the lifeless body just a stone's throw away. He broke into a light run, moving past the confused locals and heading straight for the tree. When he got there, he found Fred Decker sprawled across the ground, blood crusted across his face and pooled under his head. He was still chained, round his waist and round the tree. Nobody had seen to him since Violet Walker attacked him last night. He knelt down, turning Fred Decker's head, checking for signs of life. He was breathing, though his mouth was covered in blood and dirt. His eyes flickered open and he looked up at Arman. He had a wound on his left cheekbone, desperately close to his eye that had swollen his eyelid nearly shut. The wound was black and red and smeared with mud and a white patch of skin flapped at its side.

"Fred Decker," he hissed, "do you hear me?"

Fred Decker stirred though didn't respond. These villagers, who bowed to their god and preached of love and respect and forgiveness, wanted this man to die. Eyes were on him now. He could feel them, burning into him as he knelt at Fred Decker's side. He had promised Violet Walker a trial. He had promised they would pass judgement and it would be fair. But Violet had done this to Fred Decker. Violet could act however she pleased but Arman, returning to the congregation after so much time away, was under intense scrutiny. His life, or his future when this was all over, would be determined by how he acted in the coming days, in the coming weeks.

He turned around to face the blank, gawking villagers, and he shouted, "Will somebody help this man?!"

VI

Alma Dryden reluctantly answered Arman's call, slowly heading towards him. Her two young boys, Bradley and Bertie, ran around her in dizzying circles, brushing against her long dress as they giggled and screamed. She shuffled forward as if in a daze. She snuck glances back at the other villagers, each standing still and watching as she approached Arman and Fred Decker. She got within a few feet and caught sight of Fred Decker's wounds. She recoiled, grabbing at her mouth. Both small boys stopped in their tracks. Bradley found a hiding place behind his mother. Both his small hands grabbed at the back of her dress. Bertie stood at her side, open mouthed and staring.

"Boys," said Alma calmly, "go home."

Bradley turned and ran but Bertie stayed, fascinated by the injured man on the floor. Alma grabbed at his collar and pulled him away.

"Bertie!" she hissed at him. Bertie fought her for a moment, straining to get away from her grip. Eventually, he tired of fighting and decided to listen, turning and sprinting away to catch up with his brother. Alma turned back to Arman.

"He needs help," said Arman, calmly. "Can you help?"

Alma composed herself, looking back towards the other villagers for an approval that wasn't coming. She took a deep breath and stepped forward, taking a knee beside Arman. They exchanged looks and he nodded a thank you to her. She turned Fred Decker's head towards her, examining his facial wound. Her thumb teased at the white patch of loose skin on his cheek. As she intently examined Fred Decker's face, a voice behind her made her jump.

"What's going on?" Niall strode towards them, a growing anger spreading across his face.

Arman, expecting confrontation, got to his feet to ward off the town elder. He looked down at Alma and said, "Carry on."

"No," snapped Niall, stopping beside them, "do not carry on, Alma. What are you doing here, Arman?"

Arman studied Niall's face, hoping to work with him rather than antagonise him further. He held up both his hands, almost apologetically. "He's not been seen to since he was attacked."

Niall looked in exasperation between Fred Decker, Alma and Arman. He threw his hands up, turning around and looking back towards the village. When he turned back, he seemed calmer, but still irritated by everything he was seeing. "Arman, I despair. Tomorrow morning we will hold this trial of yours—"

"—it's not mine, It's Violet Wal—"

"—and we will put this man to his death! So what does it matter what state he might be in today? It's still a lot better than the state he'll be in tomorrow, Arman."

"It is our responsibility," said Arman, "to care for this man, until the trial passes judgement on him."

"Arman, this man murdered one of our brothers. He tried to steal from us and he stabbed Robert Walker in the neck and left him to die in our own church. We are going ahead with this abomination of a trial, to satisfy your, or Violet's, needs, but as far as I and everyone else in Hope is concerned, he is guilty, and will remain guilty even while you stand up in front of us all and insist that he is somehow, uncomprehendingly, innocent of such a crime."

Arman rested his hands on his hips, trying to turn his own growing anger into something manageable, something able to placate Niall before this escalated beyond help. He looked down at Alma, still cradling Fred Decker's face, and wished he had the answer. She looked back up at him and asked, "What should I do?"

"Nothing," interjected Niall, "you should do nothing!"

She hesitated, looking back to Arman for a response.

"Don't look to him!" Niall shouted at her.

Arman took a step closer to Niall, going against his own better instincts to diffuse, and stared him down. Without taking his eyes from Niall, he said to Alma, "Alma, don't move. That man needs your help."

"Alma," warned Niall.

"Alma," said Arman calmly, "this man needs help, will you help him?"

She nodded, slowly turning away from both men to attend to Fred Decker. Niall went to grab for her, to push her away from Fred Decker, but Arman moved forward and laid his hands on Niall's shirt. Grabbing him harshly, he pushed the older man back against the tree and held him there.

"Don't you touch her!" Arman shouted at him.

"What are you doing?" spat Niall back at him. "He's a murderer! He murdered Robert Walker and he's going to get what's coming to him! Do you hear me!?"

Arman released his grip and Niall shrugged him off, stepping away from him, calmer, more composed.

"Hear his case," said Arman, "find him guilty, then kill him. Until we do those three things, in that order, we need to care for him, because that's what we do. Our very foundation of life is based upon forgiveness and respect and love."

"What do you know about our way, Arman? Nobody has seen you in over a year?" said Niall. "And Violet Walker? She was a heathen until Robert Walker took her in."

"Then tell her," said Arman. "Tell her that she can't have her trial. Tell her the congregation has spoken and stop wasting my time! Get it over with!" Arman snarled at him, rage that had barely been concealed before, bubbling to the surface. "I'm trying to do the right thing, Niall, I truly am."

Niall scratched at his chin, his fingernails scraping against day-old stubble. He sighed, because the right words were in short supply right now.

"Niall? Let's do this properly and then put it behind us."

Niall nodded, an acquiescence born of frustration. "But not here. And not by her," he pointed at Alma. "Let Violet stitch him up."

"Niall, you can't ask a widow — "

" — Arman, we're all dancing to her tune at the minute. She made this latest mess and she can clear it up. That's all I shall say on this matter. Tomorrow we judge this man. Today is yours and Violet's business."

Arman exchanged a look with Alma. She nodded agreement, and Arman joined her by Fred Decker's side. They helped get him to his feet, each with an arm around him, propping him up. They moved slowly, Fred Decker taking small steps. They walked agonisingly slowly through the village. Violet's house was the other side of the village and it seemed like they must pass everyone else on the way. Maybe that had been Niall's plan? Nobody said a word, either hostile or friendly. A few turned their backs as the trio walked slowly by. Just past the gardens and Fred Decker stumbled, falling to his knees. Nobody came forward to help. Arman knelt down, getting a better grip. Alma did likewise on her side. They got him up and got him moving again. A trio of ravens circled briefly overhead, "cawing" loudly, as if taunting the group below.

Quiet, so as not to be heard by any of the villagers, Arman said, "Thank you, Mrs Dryden."

"They'll never forgive you, Mr Shaw," she said back without malice.

They reached Violet's gate and stopped. Her door was already open and she stood there, shocked. Arman and Alma waited for her cue. She hurried from her door, opening the front gate and moving to Alma's side, she shifted Fred Decker's weight onto her own shoulder.

"Thank you, Mrs Dryden," she said.

Alma smiled, politely, and backed away from the small group. She walked backwards, hesitant to turn back to the rest of the village. Finally, she closed her eyes, catching her breath and then turning to re-join the others. She was comforted by a neighbour, Sylvia Farley, with a motherly arm around her that let her know that nobody blamed her.

Inside Violet's house, she hurriedly swiped away some clothes from an armchair and she and Arman lowered Fred Decker into it. His head lolled to the side, dazed.

"He needs patching up," she said.

"I'm sorry to bring him here," said Arman, "Niall insisted."

"And you followed," she said, though any rebuttal was lost as she disappeared to fetch some supplies. After some loud clanging in the kitchen, she returned with a bowl of water, rags and bandages. She began to wipe at Fred Decker's face, clearing away the blood and the dirt as best she could. The water in the bowl quickly swirled red and brown. He had small cuts and scratches on his forehead, but it was the wound beneath the eye that was the deepest. As Violet dabbed at it with a cloth, Fred winced. His eyes found focus and he looked at her as she worked. She stopped, staring back at him. "I won't apologise," she said.

"Thank you," Fred Decker said, softly.

"Don't," she said, her teeth finding her bottom lip as she struggled to keep her composure. "I'll need to stitch up that wound."

Once again, she hurriedly disappeared, finding the supplies she needed. Arman knelt by the armchair and Fred Decker looked at him. "Do I thank *you*?" he asked.

Arman shook his head, "Mr Decker, this town will try you, and most definitely execute you very soon."

"So who are you?"

"My name is Arman Shaw. Violet Walker, the widow of the man you murdered, asked me to defend you in that trial."

"That does seem thankless," said Fred Decker.

"It is."

"Sorry."

The apology hung impotently in the air for the longest time. It was Arman that broke the silence. "To defend you, I'll need to hear your side of the story. If you have one."

Fred Decker shrugged.

"I might need more than that," said Arman.

"Where are you from?" asked Fred Decker.

"Why do you ask?"

"You said your name was…Arman, was it?"

"Yes," nodded Arman. "My father was Iranian, my mother English."

"What brought you to Hope?"

"That's…a story for another day. We don't have a tremendous amount of time and so far, I have nothing to work with. You told Mrs Walker last night that you killed Robert Walker in… defence? Is that true, Mr Decker?"

"Yes," he said. "He attacked me—"

Violet re-entered the room carrying her medical supplies. Fred Decker stopped speaking when he saw her. She took a step into the room and said, "Please continue. You were saying?" Greeted with nothing but silence, she continued, "You were attacked? Oh, poor you."

"Violet, please," said Arman.

"No, please, let him continue, apparently this was all my husband's fault. Is that what you're saying? Did he stab himself, Fred Decker?"

"Violet—"

"—no, Arman, he said—"

"Violet!" a shout this time, and it stopped her in her tracks. "You will stitch this man's wound and then you will leave us in peace while I speak with him. Is that clear?"

She sucked air through her teeth, but stayed silent. She maintained the silence as she crudely stitched up his cheek, ignoring his winces. She finished the job off and wiped it clean with the dirty water. The second she was done, she got to her feet and stormed off, leaving the two men alone in the room.

"How does it feel?" asked Arman.

"It doesn't matter," said Fred. He pressed his fingertips to the wound, tracing a line around the stitches, picking at the white flap of dead skin to the side.

Arman watched him, curious, wondering how he could defend this man, how just a few days ago, those hands had plunged a knife into the neck of an old friend of his. How Robert Walker had bled to death on the floor of the church that he had helped build. If Arman had been part of the congregation, a proper part, would he be like the others, clamouring for this man's death? Would vengeance blind him to his duty as a servant to God? Since Violet Walker had turned up uninvited at his door, he had alienated almost everyone in the village. He had been alone by choice before, but now it was through his actions. What would Mathilda say to that? She would call him a fool. She would blame him, and she would be right.

"What do you want to know?" asked Fred, shaking Arman from his own thoughts.

"What happened?" asked Arman.

Fred Decker told him his story.

VII

Arman woke early the next morning. He stripped down and washed at his sink. He had laid out fresh clothes the night before and following a simple breakfast of porridge, he got dressed. Black trousers, white shirt, black cotton waistcoat and his charcoal coat. He took his time walking into the village, happy to watch the sun rise as he went. By the time he arrived in Hope, the sky was blue and the air was cold and fresh. There was already activity around the garden, but Arman decided not to investigate too closely. Today, he just wanted to focus on the job at hand. He glanced towards the end of the far road and could make out the shape of Fred Decker tied to the tree once more. Niall would have insisted.

He reached the church, where one of the doors was already opened. Niall and Herman were already inside and they greeted him warmly enough when he came in.

"Did you want to give us a hand, Arman?" said Niall.

From the backroom, they retrieved some wooden chairs. One was put up to the side of the altar, presumably for Niall to sit on as the judge, thought Arman. They placed a chair either side of the step up, one for Arman, the other for Herman.

"Would you like a drink?" asked Herman to Arman.

Arman said, "Thank you, Herman. No."

"I was going to sit up here," said Niall, indicating the chair by the altar.

The step up meant he would be looking down on the rest of them. Arman had no objection. Herman asked Arman if he'd like to pick a side to sit on and again, Arman said he had no real opinion either way. Herman claimed the chair on the right-hand side, giving Arman the seat on the left. Their two chairs were angled, half facing the altar, half facing the pews.

"I thought we'd put some of the key people on the front row," said Niall, "in case we need to call upon them."

"Good idea," said Herman.

Arman nodded.

"Everyone else can go in the rows behind," added Niall.

Arman was happy to stay quiet, let them organise it how they saw fit. He was enjoying the civility of it all, even if it was just for his benefit. And with Niall taking charge, it made his job a lot easier. But there was something bothering him and he wasn't sure when he should mention it. Eventually, as Herman was about to start a conversation on another matter, Arman interrupted to ask, "Where will Fred Decker sit?"

Niall and Herman stopped dead in their tracks, exchanging looks. Herman clearly wanted to defer to Niall, looking at his friend for help.

"We didn't think there was any need to have him present," said Niall.

"But we're arguing for his life," said Arman. "And what if we need to clarify anything with him? Will we have to walk down the street to go and see him at the tree?"

"I don't think there'll be much arguing today, Arman," said Niall. "And does it seem appropriate for the widow Walker to have her husband's murderer sat comfortably, at the scene of the crime?"

"What if we covered him?" asked Herman.

"Covered him?" asked Arman.

"We don't want Violet Walker to have the pain of seeing him at the site of her husband's murder. Perhaps he could sit up there, on the other side of the altar, but, covered somehow. With a blindfold, maybe?"

Arman nodded, "I would have no problem with that."

"I would," said Niall. "Do we all agree that I have the final say on how this trial will be conducted?"

Herman nodded. Arman took a moment, but then he too conceded, nodding for Niall. It had been agreed that once it all started, Niall would lead proceedings.

"That man is not welcome in this church. If it becomes an absolute *must* that he be listened to, then we shall answer the problem at that time. But not before. He stays outside."

Arman agreed. This was not a fight worth fighting. He wasn't even sure how he might go about the task ahead of him, and he didn't see a point in antagonising any further. "So," he said, "rules?"

Niall sat down in his chair, rolling his shoulders and straightening his back. He cleared his throat. "Herman will make the case for guilt. Then, Arman will make a case for innocence. You may politely ask questions of each other, and similarly, you may address the congregation relevant if necessary. Once you have both finished, and there are no more cases to be made, or questions to be asked, then I will make the final decision. If that decision is guilt, then Fred Decker will be offered a choice of death; axe or poison. Does that sound reasonable?"

"It does," said Herman.

"It does," said Arman, then, "and who would swing the axe?"

"Cecil Garfield. Begrudgingly he has agreed. He has the strongest swing. I don't wish to cause anyone undue suffering. Likewise, if he chooses potion, then Olive Kirby will make the concoction."

Both Arman and Herman agreed once more. Everything was very civil. Arman wondered if it would remain so once their various arguments started.

"Mary Wheel will be here presently," said Niall. "She has kindly offered to make notes of proceedings for entry into our official records. I pray that Hope never sees another crime of this like, but it's still important to document these things."

As before Arman and Herman both nodded. What else was there to do? All this seemed incredibly reasonable. It was hard to equate the gentle preparations with the fact that they would be holding a trial for murder very soon. There was a knock at the door, and all three men looked towards it. Mary Wheel entered the church. She was short and round, with a pleasant face and a thick, shoulder-length head of hard white hair. She fiddled with her glasses, squinting as she studied each man present.

"Am I late?" she asked.

"Not at all, Mary," said Niall.

She shuffled into the room. Arman didn't know her age but guessed she must be in her eighties, or perhaps early nineties. Under her arm, she carried a notepad that had a small sleeve for a pencil.

"Where do you want me?" she asked.

"Where's best?" asked Niall. "Perhaps the back of the room, so you can see everything that's going on. What do you think, Mary?"

"And I'm writing down everything that happens. And everything everyone says?" she asked.

"That's right, Mary," said Niall, patiently.

She chuckled to herself, "I hope you're all going to speak slowly," she said.

Arman looked to Herman, who just gave a small shrug in reply. Niall disappeared for a moment and returned from the back room with a high-backed wooden chair, which he took to the back of the church, behind the pews, and placed in the corner. Mary thanked him, moved to the back of the church and took her seat. She spent an age shifting from buttock to buttock, trying to find the most comfortable position. She opened her notebook to a clean page and took out the pencil, poised to write.

"Before we begin," said Niall, "do any of you have any questions or concerns regarding proceedings?"

"What was that?" said Mary, looking up and over the top of her glasses.

"I asked if anyone had any questions," said Niall.

"No, all is well," said Herman.

"Arman?"

Arman considered it. He had plenty of questions. But for now, he shook his head and said, "No. Not right now."

Niall took the step down, standing in between Arman and Herman. "Let's get this over with and move on with our lives," he said, then, "Let's begin." He walked down the centre aisle, to the double doors. He unbolted the one closed door and swung it open, stepping outside. With a wave of his arm, people began to flock forward. Niall instructed everyone to sit where they pleased, but to leave the front row on either side of the aisle free for people who may be called upon to talk. When they arrived, he put Phoebe Everly, Miles Faber and Vincent Law on one side. On the other, he put Joan and Bernard Ogden. Violet arrived, dressed in a long black dress, with matching dark bonnet. Niall took her elbow, treating her as though she may break into a thousand pieces should his touch be too strong. He led her to the front, next to the Ogdens. She thanked him and he returned to the front to usher in the remaining members of the congregation.

Cecil Garfield, all curly dark hair and muscles, lingered by the door throwing glances back towards the oak tree some hundred metres away. Niall followed his gaze, though didn't know his intentions.

"All well, Cecil?"

"Should somebody stay," said Cecil, "out here to keep guard? In case he tries to escape?"

"I don't think he's going to eat his way through a steel chain, Cecil," joked Niall.

But Cecil remained still, his furrowed brow doing all the talking.

"If escape had been possible," said Niall, "I imagine he would've done it in the night, as we slept. Or when he was briefly untied to be treated for that head wound of his."

"If you're sure," said Cecil.

"I am," said Niall. He slapped Cecil on the back by way of confirmation.

Cecil took one last look into the distance, making sure Fred Decker wasn't running for the tree line, before bringing his lumbering frame into the church. He sat at the back, in the corner in front of Mary Wheel and her poised pencil and notebook. Niall took a step outside. The village looked deserted. He thought to himself how peaceful it looked. It reinvigorated him, reminding him why they had chosen this land in the first place. But before he could ever enjoy it again fully, something had to be done about the blight which had befallen it. He closed both wooden doors. He walked back up the aisle, smiling as he passed various people. He took the step up to the altar, shifting his chair ever so slightly and sitting down. All eyes turned to him.

"Good morning, everybody," he said, and plenty of people returned his greeting. "For the record, which Mary Wheel is kind enough to be filling in today, it is October 4th, 1851 and we are here to judge Mr Fred Decker, accused of the cold-hearted, cold-blooded murder of our brother, Robert Walker. In the front rows we have the key witnesses; Phoebe Everly, Miles Faber, Vincent Law and Bernard Ogden. Beneath me is Herman Blyth, arguing for guilt, and Arman Shaw, for innocence. We will first listen to Herman, then Arman as they each make their case. They may politely ask questions of each other, and also of those present. Following their respective turns, it will be my decision regarding judgement and, if appropriate, punishment. Does anybody have any questions?"

There were murmurs, but nobody spoke up. Niall waited, happy that this wasn't going to be needlessly stretched out by inanities. "This is a new thing for our congregation. None of us have any experience of this. Trouble has come into our paradise and we must face it. But my word will be final."

Arman sat quietly, listening. He looked around the room, observing everyone's rapt attention. He wondered if they were deliberately avoiding looking his way. He wondered how they might look at him once this was all over, regardless of which way things went. He couldn't imagine ever being welcome in Hope again. His attention snapped back to Niall as he seemed to be set to begin.

"Herman Shaw," said Niall. "Could you tell us what happened on the morning of September 30th?"

Herman stood, and did.

VIII

Herman slowly got to his feet, as if the very act was a ponderous part of his case. He nodded at Niall then slowly turned to face the congregation. He took his time scanning their faces, clearly relishing his moment. "Good morning, everyone. You all know me and my family, and I know you and yours. I'm both honoured and horrified to be standing up in front of you today to be deliberating upon the guilt of an exceptionally guilty man."

Arman wondered if there was such a thing as an "exceptionally guilty man". Surely, you were either guilty or not. Perhaps he might use the term "exceptionally innocent" in his argument, though he doubted it would get much traction with the congregation. He watched everyone's faces as Herman spoke, keen to gauge their reaction. They hung off his every word.

"The travellers came to our village on September 29th and we greeted them, perhaps warily, but as guests. We gave them permission to stop with their wagon and make a camp for the evening. Amongst the men were Fred Decker, Don Hope and a man we believe was called Raymond Howarth, though there is some doubt upon that last name. In truth, he was a forgettable fellow and different people have different recollections of his name. It is not relevant. That night, while Edmund and Esther Hayes entertained the congregation with song, one of the travellers, Don Hope, joined our celebration and was warmly accepted. Do we agree on this, Mr Shaw?"

Arman, who had been concentrating on the congregation, turned his attention to Herman. He believed that they would be given the chance to politely question each other, but he hadn't expected to be called upon to back up the other's version of events. He wished he'd been listening more carefully.

"I believe so," he said, "based on what I was told."

Herman smiled, as if he had gained a victory. He turned that same smile to the congregation, continuing, "The next morning, as many still slept, one of the men, Fred Decker, crept into the church and attempted to steal the gem from the box containing the Holy Relic. However, as he attempted the thievery, he was interrupted by Robert Walker and Bernard Ogden, who had been in the back room making preparations for the upcoming harvest festival. All good so far, Mr Shaw?"

Again, Arman hadn't expected to be called on in such a way. He shifted in his seat as the eyes of Herman, Niall and the congregation fell upon him. "Well," he started, "of a kind."

"Of a kind? Are we disputing the facts already, Arman?"

"Do we know Fred Decker 'crept' into the church?"

"This seems like an odd point to contest, Mr Shaw," replied Herman.

"At some point that morning, with Robert Walker and Bernard Ogden in the back room, Fred Decker entered the church."

"Are we not arguing the same point?"

Arman could feel the stares from many eyes burning into him. He had hoped not to argue over small details. "No," he said. "He *crept* into the church. He snuck in. He *tip-toed* in. The church doors were open. He just came in, we don't know how. Shall we just agree that?"

Herman laughed, a mocking laugh, then turned to Niall with his hands up in exasperation. Niall let out a long sigh, giving Arman an ambiguous glance. Arman presumed he was being silently chastised but wasn't entirely sure on what point. Herman turned to the congregation, smiling, and said, "It might be a long day, everyone." There was some muted response, but nobody was in the mood for laughing. Herman turned back to Arman again, "And the rest of the facts?"

Arman looked nervously around the church then back to Niall for judgement, asking, "Wouldn't it be better if Mr Blyth made his case and then I made mine? If he just wants me to agree to every aspect of his case then that doesn't leave much for mine."

Herman looked to Niall and Niall nodded. Herman made an exaggerated roll of his eyes. "I think everyone is eager to hear your version of events, Mr Shaw. For everyone else here today, I shall tell them the rest of the undisputed facts."

Arman bristled, but stayed quiet.

"Robert Walker shouted at Fred Decker and immediately went to challenge him. The only witness to this fight, Bernard Ogden, tells us, and we have no reason to dispute his recollection, that a fight ensued in which Fred Decker stabbed Robert Walker in the neck. Fred Decker rushed from the church and Bernard Ogden rushed to his fallen friend. Robert Walker died on that church floor, of the massive blood loss from that stab wound."

Arman looked over at Violet. She sat emotionless, looking forward. He looked up at Herman, as if expecting him to seek approval once more, but he did not.

"Fred Decker, still clutching the knife, ran from the church. Phoebe Everly, out in her garden that morning, saw him, covered in Robert Walker's blood, holding the murder weapon. Isn't that right, Mrs Everly?"

Phoebe, on the front row next to her husband, Terrance, nodded her confirmation.

"Miles Faber had woken up early after a troubled night's sleep. He was at his bedroom window when he saw the same thing. Am I correct, Mr Faber?"

"You are," said Miles, turning towards Arman and re-affirming, "that's right."

"The village was waking up and so were Fred Decker's travelling companions. They managed to collect their things exceptionally quickly, almost as if they had been expecting to make a quick escape. They tore through town with their horses and wagon and attempted to take Fred Decker with them. But Mr

Faber, with reactions that we should all be applauding, dashed from his home and was equal to them. He tackled Fred Decker, stopping him making an escape. Is that all as it happened, Mr Faber?"

"Yes," said Miles firmly.

"And he was soon joined by Vincent Law. He responded to the fracas by running from his home and helping Miles to detain the murderer. Am I correct in stating this, Mr Law?"

Vincent cleared his throat and said, "Yes, that's what happened. My boy, Dominic, was right behind me and he played his part too."

"Meanwhile, according to Phoebe Everly, his cohorts made their escape from Hope and never looked back, happy to condemn their companion to whatever fate awaited him. Is that as you recall it, Mrs Everly?"

"Yes," she said, "they headed out of the village."

Herman took a moment, looking out across the congregation, palms up in a shrug. "I'm not sure what else I could tell you. This is what happened, as seen by people we know and trust. You may twist words here and there to create another narrative, but at its core, this story is irrefutably correct. Anyone that says different is a liar."

That one was just for him, thought Arman.

"I'm certain that we're all very new to this kind of thing," said Herman. "None of us have experience of trials and the law, but we know what's right and wrong. We took our time to make this fair and I feel confident to say that we succeeded. I am happy to listen to Mr Shaw give us his version of events. Part of me, I will guiltily admit, is eager to hear what he has to say. Remember, Mr Shaw wasn't there. Phoebe Everly was there. Miles Faber. Vincent Law. Bernard Ogden. They were there. Thank you."

He sat down and received a round of applause from the congregation, except from Arman himself, Niall and Violet. Violet was still, facing forward, seemingly lost in her own thoughts. Arman thought back to her standing on his doorstep. He thought of her in his kitchen, asking him to deliver a fair trial. So she might find peace. So that she might find justice. Is that what she really wanted? He wondered if he might also get a round of applause when he was finished. He almost laughed at the absurdity of it. He wished he could stop time and talk to her. Take her aside from this and ask her if this is what she really wants. But time had run out. Herman had finished his brief argument, if you could call it an argument. He had succinctly told everyone what they already believed. Now Niall was thanking him and he was sitting back down again and Arman was aware that more and more eyes were turning to him and in the briefest of moments he would have to get on his feet and stand in front of this congregation of his friends and defend the indefensible. He fantasised about standing up and affirming his belief in Herman's version of events, watching everybody breathe a huge sigh of relief and then he could slink back to his home in the hills and let the villagers of Hope exact any justice, or punishment, that they felt was necessary or appropriate.

Niall turned to face Arman and said, "Well, Arman, did you want to begin?"

"Yes," he replied, though truthfully he did not. He rose to his feet. He looked down at his shoes, brown and scuffed. He regretted not cleaning them more thoroughly this morning. Everyone's eyes were on him. "Good morning, everyone," he said. There were a few responses, some nods, but as expected, nothing more. "It's nice to see you all here, united under one roof, though I wish it were in happier circumstances. It's been some time since I've spoken with you. I'm ashamed to say that once Mathilda passed away, I stole myself away from the congregation and lived a solitary life. With the benefit of hindsight, I can see that my isolation probably did me more harm than good, and that if I had welcomed the loving warmth of those around me, in my brothers and sisters in this congregation, then maybe the healing process could've begun quicker." He wasn't sure he meant that. He had needed that time alone. No kind words or pitying gestures would ever bring Mathilda back. But right now, he felt like a moment of contrition may help quell people's anger towards him. In essence he was using his wife's death as a cheap ploy to win some people over, and he hated himself for it. "Violet Walker came to see me. She shared with me the awful news of her husband, my friend, Robert Walker's passing. She told me that they had captured the man responsible. She told me that following a fair trial for this man, she would accept the judgement and respect the decision of the congregation. She didn't just want vengeance. Vengeance would not bring Robert back. She wanted us to do our duty by God. To show this man a kindness that perhaps he didn't show us. To judge him fairly. And then, perhaps, she could find some peace. I felt honour bound to fulfil her wishes."

Some of the looks that had been centred on Arman had moved to the back of Violet's head. She was still non-responsive. Even Niall looked over at her, as though expecting her to add something. When it was clear that she would not, he turned back to the congregation. Arman rubbed his hands together nervously, scratching at his palms with his nails. There was only so long he could get by on past sympathies and honouring a widow. At some point he must start a defence of a killer.

"Many of the things I will discuss are similar to the events that Mr Blyth told you. But maybe things aren't quite as they seem. Perhaps the tale of cold-blooded murder is cloudier than we're comfortable with. Our moral indignation works best in black and white, but there may be a grey area we move into, and it may make our judgement harder. If we find this man guilty, he will almost certainly be put to death and we will all have to live with that. Right now we are all angry, but anger passes. All I ask is that we treat this man fairly, and consider all the elements before we commit. Let's go back to that morning..."

IX

Arman wasn't used to this much attention and it made him nervous. He presumed everyone could see the persistent shake in his legs. He dug nails into his palms and wondered what he was doing. He had heard Herman retell the events. He had spoken to the witnesses. He had spoken to Fred Decker. Of all versions, Fred Decker's version stood out, but he wasn't sure how much of it he would use. It was one thing to alienate these people, it was another to tear a whole community apart. He decided, just to get things going, that he would start simply. "At some point, on the morning of September 30th, Fred Decker entered our church, through the opened doors, as he was allowed to, as anyone is allowed to. He told me he was there to pray. He is a religious man and he sought to pray in peace."

"He was there to steal from us!" cried Herman, rising to his feet.

Arman threw his hands up in annoyance, turning to Niall. Niall looked away, so Arman turned to Herman. "I let you speak, now let me."

"What was that?"

All eyes turned. It took Arman a while to realise it was coming from the back of the room. Leaning round the side of Cecil so that she could be seen was Mary Wheel.

"What was that, Mary?" asked Niall.

She shouted back, "I asked what Mr Shaw was saying."

"I was saying that Fred Decker told me he came to the church to pray."

"Today?" she said.

"No," said Arman patiently, "to pray."

"Did you get that, Mary?" asked Niall.

She let out a brief, "Uh-huh."

"We were told," continued Arman, "that Fred Decker was using his knife to pry off the gem from the box of the Holy Relic. But the box has no scratches on. No marks of any kind. And the gem, far from being deeply embedded or stuck in, can be easily pulled off. I tried it."

"I don't understand this," said Herman from his chair. "He was caught in his attempt. Bernard Ogden saw it with his own eyes. He could have just that moment picked it up, not yet realised it was flimsily attached and presumed he'd need his knife. The knife was in his hand. The box was in his hand. What are we fighting over here, Mr Shaw?"

"Sometimes things aren't as they seem," said Arman. "And since we're talking about holding the balance of life in somebody's hands, I thought it best to check our facts. The boring, mundane, day to day truth of life is that sometimes we don't always see what we think we're seeing. Context and memory and misunderstandings play a huge part in how we view the world."

Herman scoffed, shouting, "I suppose Bernard Ogden didn't see Fred Decker stab Robert Walker in the neck with a knife!?"

"No," said Arman, "he didn't."

The congregation seemed stunned and a few, Merry Ramsey, Terence Everly and Philip Dryden, got to their feet to protest loudly at Arman. One of them, and Arman couldn't be sure who, cried, "This is madness!" Herman snorted once more.

Arman shook his head, "He didn't. Ask him."

The congregation looked to the front row where Bernard sat with his wife, Joan. He turned to face them, a nervous look on his face.

"Mr Ogden?" said Herman.

"My husband knows what he saw!" cried out Joan Ogden, squeezing her husband's hand.

"Mr Ogden?" said Arman, calmly, "you saw them fighting, didn't you?"

"I did," said Bernard confidently.

"But you didn't actually see Robert Walker get stabbed, did you?"

"It was..." he stopped, thought about it then said, "Everything was just so fast."

"I know," said Arman. "I believe you. You saw them fight. But we spoke, and you told me what happened, and you said you never saw Fred Decker stab Robert Walker. Am I right?"

"Yes," said Bernard.

"That proves nothing," said Joan, beside him. She turned to face the rest of the congregation and repeated herself, "That proves nothing!"

"It proves nothing. Mr Blyth would like it to have proved Fred Decker guilty, but it doesn't do that. It is the absence of evidence, Mrs Ogden."

"What evidence?" asked Mary Wheel from the back of the room.

"No evidence, Mary," said Niall to her, "Arman has no evidence."

Arman took a sharp intake of breath, irked by Niall's rephrasing. He turned towards Mary and asked, "Can you hear me fine, Mrs Wheel?"

"Yes, thank you, Mr Shaw," she replied.

"Are you sure? You're stuck behind Cecil Garfield there and he's a big lad."

"I'm well, Mr Shaw," she said.

"What does this all prove?" asked Herman.

"A fight broke out. Bernard Ogden said Fred Decker was trying to steal. Fred Decker said that he was there for no such thing. He said he came to pray. Fred Decker is a religious man from a community that is less strong than ours. He had snuck away from his companions to come to our church, and he believed he was alone. Upon hearing voices, he made a hasty attempt to retreat. In doing so, he knocked over the box containing the Holy Relic, and it was in picking it up to replace it that he was found by Robert Walker and Bernard Ogden."

"What stories are these, Mr Shaw?" asked Herman.

"I wonder if anybody would be kind enough to show me the knife he used," asked Arman, looking between Herman and Niall. Met with silence, he waited a moment then asked again, "The knife?"

"We never found it," said Niall.

"I'll come back to that," said Arman. He could feel his heart thundering in his chest. "Seeking solitude, and prayer, Fred Decker came to our church. Hearing voices, and not wanting to offend anyone by his presence, he went to leave. He knocked over our Holy Relic, and when he picked it up, he was confronted. Nobody asked him what he was doing. Nobody spoke to him. Robert Walker charged at him and attacked him. He thought he was an intruder, intent on theft. Any one of us may have done the same thing. Fred Decker defended himself. He fought back. The two men, as Bernard Ogden witnessed, fell to the floor. Bernard Ogden was in shock. He told me that he didn't know what he should do. Everything was happening so fast. Fred Decker said that as the two of them flailed on the floor, they crashed through the small wooden fence we had set up to store the offerings for the upcoming festival. A piece of the wood went into Fred Decker's hand, embedding itself in his palm. Another piece went into Robert Walker's neck."

"I'm sorry," said Herman, "are you saying this was all an accident?"

"Fred Decker saw the blood pouring from Robert Walker. Also seeing the blood, though not the impact that caused it, Bernard Ogden rushed at him. Fred Decker began crying and screaming. He had his own blood running down his hand and Robert Walker's down his front. In hysterics, he left the church, which was witnessed by Phoebe Everly and Miles Faber.

"He didn't have a knife?" asked Herman sarcastically.

"What's that about a knife?" asked Mary, shouting from the back.

"We're talking about Fred Decker's knife, Mary," said Niall.

"No," said Arman, "Mrs Wheel, we're not talking about Fred Decker's knife."

"We're not?" she asked.

"Mrs Wheel!" snapped Arman, "You didn't seem to have any trouble hearing Mr Blyth when he was speaking!"

"Arman Shaw!" shouted Niall, slamming his hands down on his armrests. "Will you control yourself!"

Arman lowered his head, finding no refuge in the five buttons running down his creased white shirt. The button at the bottom was on the cusp of coming free. He looked at it, wondering if he should fix it now. He could hear his own breathing getting faster. Rumbling in the background, the congregation uttered their annoyance at him. "I apologise," he said.

"What was that?" she said.

He lifted his head, "I apologise. I spoke out of turn. I'll try and speak a little clearer for you."

"Shall we proceed?" asked Niall.

Arman wiped at his forehead, running his sweaty hand though his hair. He whistled out a breath. "I was just saying—" he trailed off, trying to recall where he had stopped.

"—you were just saying that Bernard Ogden is blind," said Herman, "and imagined the knife that stabbed Robert Walker."

Arman clicked his fingers several times, an unconscious habit as he recalled his train of thought. "Phoebe Everly in her vegetable garden said she saw him leaving the church, 'covered in blood' and 'clutching something to his chest', was it?' Is that right, Mrs Everly?"

"It is," she said, "I believe he had a knife."

"You believe so," he said, "now that we're talking about a crime with a knife, but when we spoke, you said you recalled just seeing him clutching something to his chest. In fact, you told me that it 'may have been nothing'."

Phoebe didn't respond.

"And Miles Faber," continued Arman, "just waking up and looking through his icy window, saw Fred Decker across the street, clutching something to his chest, perhaps holding a weapon, perhaps not. That's what you said, wasn't it? Perhaps not? Is that right, Mr Faber?"

"I see fine through my window," said Miles.

"I'm sure you do."

"You implied that I don't. You implied that I was groggy. You implied that my window was iced up—"

"—Was it iced up?"

"A little. But I could see clearly enough," said Miles.

"That's fine," said Arman, "but you did say that you were not sure if Fred Decker was holding something, didn't you?"

Miles nodded, "I'm pretty sure he had a knife."

"Or," said Arman, "with his own hand injured, Fred Decker clutched it close to his chest in his other hand. Cradling it as it bled."

"I know what I saw," said Miles.

"You do? You didn't yesterday."

"I couldn't remember."

"But you do now?"

"It was a knife," insisted Miles.

"Prove it," said Arman.

"What was that, Arman?" Mary's voice calling out from the back.

Before Niall could speak, Arman repeated himself louder, "I said 'prove it' to Miles Faber. Fred Decker didn't get away. He didn't flee into the woods or make it to his horse. He was stopped, by Miles Faber. He and Vincent Law restrained him and he was tied to the oak tree at the end of the street. He didn't swallow the knife. He couldn't have hidden it. If there was a knife, we would have seen it. We would have taken it. Quite probably, with the anger we chased him down with, we might even have used it."

Niall's hand came crashing down on his armrest, startling Arman. "Enough! Tempers are getting a little frayed here. I suggest we all take a break. Perhaps return after lunch when cooler heads may prevail."

"But I'm still—"

"—Enough, Arman. We break for lunch. I believe Effie Hall has made a beautiful spread that we can all enjoy."

Arman went to resist once more, but stopped himself. Nothing he could say would make them continue just yet. Everyone rose to their feet, some stretching, others heading straight for the door. Arman stood back slightly, letting the people on the front row of the pew shuffle out. As he went by, Herman gave him a pat-pat on the side of the arm. It seemed like a friendly gesture but he didn't know for sure. As he turned to leave, Niall moved a step closer and placed a hand on the small of Arman's back.

"Would you mind if we spoke?"

"Certainly," said Arman.

The two of them stood at the base of the altar, watching silently as the rest of the congregation filed out. When they had the church to themselves, Niall indicated they sit. Each man sat at the end of the front row, either side of the aisle, the space between them like a chasm. Arman felt uncomfortable. He wasn't sure what Niall wanted to discuss with him but he was fairly certain it couldn't be good. He could hear the sound of the congregation outside. They were chatting and laughing and eating, sounding like they didn't have a care in the world. He suddenly wished he could join them.

X

Niall had his eyes closed and Arman didn't know if he was praying or sleeping. He looked around the empty church, happy for the moment of peace, though Niall's silent presence was an elephant in the room he couldn't ignore. He looked to the floor beneath the altar and thought of Robert Walker dying on the floor. He used to look at the altar and think of Mathilda. They had married here. They had planned to baptise their children here. But life has a way of mocking your plans. Mathilda could never have children. Or maybe it was Arman that couldn't. She always just blamed herself and Arman, in his cowardice, took no blame. As he sat there, he felt shame for being weak and shame for seeing the church for its tragedy rather than its joy.

"What's on your mind, Arman?" asked Niall, his eyes opening, his head turning across the aisle.

"I was thinking of Mathilda."

"What would she make of all this?"

Arman let out a little laugh, "Imagine her reaction if I spoke for her?"

Niall laughed, nodding, "You're right. I apologise."

"But if she *were* here…"

Niall let out a loud, "Ha!" and smiled.

"If she were here, the chances are we'd both be calling for the head of this man. Whether through accident or cold-blooded murder, Fred Decker caused the death of our friend. It would maybe bring out our most vengeful sides."

"But you're not vengeful now?" asked Niall.

"It's not the same," said Arman. "Violet Walker is right. Vengeance can't bring back what we love. It's an impotent gesture that lessens us and gives nothing in return."

"But punishment," said Niall.

"I never thought our life here would involve punishment, for anyone. It's a coward's answer, but an honest one. I'm happy to leave punishment up to the cities. To others. To people who make a living with such things."

"The others will be returning soon," said Niall. "Can I ask you something?"

"Yes."

"Let's say we agree this was all some terrible, tragic accident. What would you do with this man? Let him go?"

"Yes."

Niall nodded, though didn't immediately respond. He looked ahead, at the large window, and beyond where the sun lit the fields up in lush greens. "And what if you're wrong? All your beliefs of this man's innocence, of this being an accident, come from the man we're accusing of Robert's death. Is there a chance he would say absolutely anything to avoid his fate?"

"Yes."

"Yes," agreed Niall.

"There's something else," said Arman. But he stopped, his teeth grinding together. "There's an aspect to the story that I'm omitting, for the sake of those still left alive." Arman looked down at his feet, wanting to tell Niall everything but knowing he shouldn't.

"Go on."

Arman shook his head, "No. What he told me convinced me of his innocence, but I can't tell anybody. I think the evidence, without this one missing piece, is compelling enough. For me it makes all the difference, but nobody else needs to know."

"I don't know what to tell you, Arman," said Niall. "For nothing is hidden that will not be made manifest, nor is anything secret that will not be known and come to light."

"Let God judge the secrets of men," replied Arman.

"When this is all over, will you come into the congregation once more?"

"When this is all over, I am not sure they will want me to."

"Have faith," said Niall. He turned his head at the sound of approaching people. They were returning from their brief lunch. Niall stood, a smile on his face as he greeted the returning congregation.

Arman moved to his seat in front of the pews, though he didn't sit. He stood and waited. He had found a rhythm just as they broke for lunch and now he didn't know how to restart. He waited until everyone was sat down and the last of the chatter had subsided.

"Shall we continue?" said Niall.

"Thank you," said Arman. He looked over at Mary, almost obscured behind Cecil Garfield on the back row. He wasn't going to win any friends by shouting at an elderly woman for doing her job. When he spoke, he spoke slowly, clearly and loudly. "I hope you all had a nice lunch," he said. "I don't want to waste your time by repeating myself. I believe Fred Decker when he told me this was an accident. A misunderstanding that turned tragic. He never had a chance to explain himself. Bernard Ogden told us that. He said they shouted at him and Robert Walker attacked him. I don't believe a knife was involved. Bernard Ogden, the only witness, didn't see a knife. The two people who saw Fred Decker emerge from the church, Phoebe Everly and Miles Faber, told me that they weren't entirely sure what Fred Decker had in his hand, if anything at all. Miles Faber has since said he was sure it was a knife, but yesterday he wasn't sure. Who knows how he might feel tomorrow? However we look at it, we do have the remains of a bloody wooden fence in the rubbish behind the church, but we don't have a knife."

"I know what I saw!" said Miles.

Arman held up a hand, partly to quieten him, partly to let him know that he'd heard. "I know," he said, and argued it no more. "There is a man tied like an animal to a tree just 150 yards from where we worship. He has a wound in his hand. He has a wound on his face from being attacked. He awaits our answer. Life or death. Are we so certain that we know what we know, that we're happy to murder a man? For judgement is without mercy to one who has shown no mercy. Thank you." He sat down.

"Thank you, Arman," said Niall. "Are you two gentlemen finished with your arguments?"

"Yes, thank you," said Herman.

"Thank you," said Arman, again.

"Violet Walker?" asked Niall. She looked up at him but said nothing. "Before I decide upon guilt, or innocence, did you want to say anything?"

"No," she said, softly.

It was Mary that spoke, her loud, shrill voice cutting through the silence to ask, "What was that?"

"She said she had nothing to add," said Niall, not taking his eyes from Violet, who had bowed her head. He finally looked away, turning his attention to the congregation. "I am sure you all understand the gravity of the decision I must make. Both Herman and Arman have raised some excellent points, but now it is up to me to make that final decision. I would like some clarification on a few key points, if you don't mind?"

Nobody objected. Niall took his time, at first seemingly lost in his own thoughts then he singled out Bernard Ogden on the front row. "Bernard, can I ask you, could Fred Decker have been returning the box having knocked it over? Is there a chance that, in the heat of the moment and now in hindsight following the death of our friend, that there was a misunderstanding?"

"No, he was trying to steal it."

"You're certain?"

"With the knife?" interrupted Arman.

"Arman, please," said Niall, silencing him. "Bernard, was he stealing the box, or trying to pry off the gem on the top? Or could there be a chance that, through no fault of your own, bad timing and circumstance intervened to make it seem like a simple gesture was actually a criminal attempt?"

Bernard looked at his wife, then back at the expectant Niall. "He was trying to steal it."

"You're sure?" asked Niall.

Arman stood up, "Mr Ogden, you said before he was trying to pry off the gem with a knife, was that not true?"

"Arman!" Niall snapped. "We're all on the same side here. Bernard, was he stealing the box, the gem or simply trying to return it having perhaps knocked it over? Bernard, a man's life rests in the balance."

"How many times do you want him to say the same thing?" asked Joan, getting to her feet.

Arman joined her, standing and snapping back, "Perhaps if he could manage to tell the same story twice then that might be a start."

"Arman, please!" shouted Niall, "If you can't control yourself then I'm going to have to ask you to wait outside."

"I'm sorry, gentlemen," said Bernard, "my memory of that morning is clouded by the fact that my very dear friend, Robert Walker, perished in my arms at the hands of that animal. Innocent people do not fight you. They do not stab you or try to escape the scene of their misdeeds. Innocent people don't have to be subdued by two men. Why are we arguing over these petty details?"

The congregation erupted into applause. One by one, they rose from their seats, clapping louder, the sound echoing around the small space. Arman looked on in disbelief. Joan had sat back down and had her arm proudly around her husband. He had turned in his seat to face the rest of the congregation, to take in their approval. Finally, he stood and addressed everyone. "That man killed Robert!"

Arman looked over at Niall, but his look wasn't returned. Niall looked blankly out at the cheering congregation instead.

He wasn't banging his armrest. He wasn't shouting for quiet. Arman looked at Violet, quietly just sitting there. He wished she'd say something. She'd thrown him to the wolves and he wondered if she realised, or cared. Bernard turned to him, a wry smile on his face.

Arman stood and shouted at him, "Why don't you tell them why you were really here that morning?" But he didn't answer. Nobody answered. They cheered and applauded. Arman walked to the corner of the pew, almost close enough to grab Bernard. He pointed an accusing finger and repeated his question, "Tell them why you were really there!" Bernard recoiled back, as if avoiding Arman's touch. In the step he took back, he backed into his wife, Joan, and she tumbled to the floor. The people around were in disarray, unsure what happened. A few people seemed to think Arman had physically lashed out at Bernard and they started to shout at him. Arman became confused as the people around him threw insults his way. He looked around for help, but none was there. Instead he felt hands grabbing at him. He jerked free, but was soon in the grasp of an assailant behind him. He was grabbed around the waist. He tried to wriggle free, but the grip was vice-like. He was dragged down the aisle, his flailing legs kicking out to try and get free. He could barely turn his head to see who had accosted him. The crowd still hollered and clapped. He was thrown towards the door, striking his face against the oak door frame. He blacked out, just for a second, but long enough to be disorientated when he found himself face down in the dirt outside the entrance to the church. He spat the dirt out of his mouth, struggling to get up on all fours. He coughed, finding it hard to catch his breath. He could feel the sun on his neck, the breeze on his cheek. The furore from the church was only just coming back into focus, the noise deafening. He didn't think he'd suffered a cut on his head but he couldn't be sure. His head throbbed. He couldn't think straight. It took him a second to find his bearings, to look back towards the church.

His attacker, Cecil Garfield, stood in the doorway, his oversize frame taking up almost the same space as one of the double doors. He shook his head in disgust at Arman, staring at him, almost willing him to fight back. But Arman didn't. He stayed on all fours, helpless. Cecil Garfield closed the door and Arman fell back down to the dirt.

XI

Arman waited. He took a seat on one of the benches in the centre garden. It creaked as he sat down. He touched at his head, checking for a cut that he knew wasn't there. Just a bump. A painful one. He sat back, closing his eyes, enjoying the warm breeze that swirled around him. If he could just stay like this, he'd be fine. But he would eventually have to open his eyes. To stand up and face the others. He wasn't in any rush to do any of those things. He had to fight every natural urge he had not to return to his house. He had lived in solitude before, he could do it again. What did he care what happened to Fred Decker? Or Violet Walker? Or anyone for that matter? Why was he staying around when he was so clearly not wanted? He felt an obligation to wait and find out what the verdict would be, though he suspected he knew. He opened his eyes, letting bright sunshine wash in. He turned to his right, out towards the oak tree. All he could see of Fred Decker was a pair of legs stretched out from behind it.

He heard a commotion and his heart sunk. Here they came. The doors were open and the congregation were spilling out. He looked up, not making eye contact, but not looking away either. Nobody seemed to be going back to their houses. Evidently, there was a lot to talk about upon the streets of Hope. He detected movement in his peripheral vision, though decided to wait to see if whoever it was was stopping or passing by. Whoever it was, was stood right in front of him.

"Niall said he was guilty," said Violet.

"Of course he did."

"May I sit?"

Arman nodded.

Violet sat on the bench next to him and said, "I'm so sorry."

"Sorry for what?"

"Everything," she said.

"I never really got to finish my argument in there," said Arman. "Though I'm not sure it would have made any difference."

"No," she said.

"If it was just you," he said, "deciding his guilt, what would you have chosen?"

Violet stayed silent. She looked down at her hands and Arman didn't ask again. They both looked up when Niall came out of the church and started walking down the street, past them and onwards towards the oak tree. Arman wordlessly rose to his feet, slowly following after him. Violet watched him leave. Arman wasn't the only one following Niall. Many of the congregation were doing the same. Up ahead, Arman watched as Fred Decker found his way to his feet, watching as everyone approached. Arman stayed behind Fred Decker, out of his sight and away from the others. Niall stood in front of the accused man, with many of the congregation behind him.

"Fred Decker," said Niall in a clear, loud voice, "you have been found guilty of the murder of Robert Walker and sentenced to death."

Arman moved to his side, moving on the outskirts of the group, finding a spot where he could see Fred Decker's face.

"What?" said Fred Decker. "No. No. I was defending myself." His face crumpled with defeat, looking around all the faces in front of him and finding no sympathy, no mercy. "Please, you can't do that. You can't do that! I didn't do anything!!"

"You have the choice of poison or axe. Whichever you choose will be administered tomorrow morning at sunrise."

"Poison or axe?? What are you doing??!"

"You don't have to decide now," said Niall, though his voice was being drowned out by Fred Decker's protestations. "We shall prepare both."

"You'll prepare both?!" shouted Fred Decker. "What are you doing?"

"Sorry," said Niall, and walked away.

"Sorry? Did you say 'sorry'? Sorry you're going to murder me?! Don't you walk away from me! Don't you walk away from me!" Fred Decker lurched forward, the metal chain pulling taut as he struggled against it. "Sorry?!"

Niall had gone, sheepishly finding his way home. The other members of the congregation soon followed. Some stayed to watch Fred Decker as he shouted and screamed and pulled at his chain, but when he started shouting at individual people they soon fled to the safety of their own homes. As quick as they had formed around him, they had gone. Soon, all that remained was Arman, Violet still on the bench and Fred Decker, exhausted, out of breath, and fallen to his knees. Violet left her seat and slowly began heading their way. Fred Decker turned his head and found Arman, standing off to his side.

"What did you do?" he asked.

Arman took a couple of steps closer, "I tried."

"You tried?"

"He did," said Violet.

She stood on the other side of Fred Decker and he had to turn his head to look at her. He shook his head. "A lot of good it did."

"I'm sorry," said Arman.

Fred Decker laughed. "Everybody's sorry that they found me guilty and sentenced me to death. Sorry won't save my life tomorrow morning when they make me drink poison or get my fucking head cut off."

Violet visibly recoiled.

"I apologise," said Fred Decker. "And I'm sorry you had to find out about what I saw in the church."

"What?" said Violet, confused.

Fred Decker looked back at Arman, "You didn't tell them?"

"Arman?" asked Violet.

"Why didn't you tell them?" said Fred Decker.

"You asked Bernard Ogden why he was really in the church that morning," said Violet. "What did you mean?"

Fred Decker looked at Arman, repeating himself, "Why didn't you tell them?"

"Tell them what?" asked Violet.

"It wouldn't have done any use," said Arman.

"Tell them what??" asked Violet, raising her voice.

"It wouldn't have done any use?" said Fred Decker, "How do you know that? How do you know it wouldn't have been any use?"

"They threw me out before I could complete my argument," said Arman.

"Will somebody tell me what you're talking about?" asked Violet, trying to stay calm.

"I went into the church that morning to pray—" started Fred Decker.

"Mr Decker, there's no point now telling—" interrupted Arman.

"—to pray," repeated Fred Decker, continuing, "and I heard voices from the back room. I went to see who was there. I didn't want anybody to think I was sneaking around. But when I got to the door, it was just open an inch and I saw—"

"—Mr Decker, please—" said Arman.

"—I saw one of them pressed against the wall, and the other behind him. They had their trousers down and they were—

"—Fred!" snapped Arman.

"They were..." Violet's mouth had fallen open in shock.

"I backed away, as quietly as I could, but I knocked into some stupid box that fell to the floor. When I went to pick it up to return it, they came out the room. They were angry and shouting and one of them attacked me."

Violet turned and ran. They could both hear her tears begin before she disappeared from their sight. Arman shook his head at Fred Decker.

"Don't you judge me," said Fred Decker. "Why didn't you tell them?"

"Because they don't believe you. They don't believe any of your story. They don't believe the stuff they can comprehend. If I'd have said something that fell so completely out of their field of reference then they would've found you guiltier quicker. They'd have stoned you to death. And maybe me too."

"It would've been a tragedy to be stoned to death. Then I would've missed out on all the poison and decapitation coming my way."

"It wouldn't have made any difference," said Arman.

"And now we'll never know. Unless, maybe, I could tell them in the morning when they come to kill me."

"The only thing you'd do is bring shame to the woman you widowed. Nobody's about to change their mind on your guilt because of what you think you saw."

"Oh, what I *think* I saw," laughed Fred Decker, shaking his head. "You people."

"I believe you," said Arman. "I believe your whole story. And I told them that story. I told them the facts of what happened and they forcibly removed me from there when I tried to argue."

"Sounds like a fair trial."

"You were never going to get a fair trial," said Arman. "I'm sorry."

"Please," said Fred Decker, "no more apologies. I'm apologied out."

"Do you mind if I join you?" said Arman, and when there was no objection, he sat down on the floor near Fred Decker. The sky was looking dark and Arman wondered what time it was. The day had got away from him. He looked over at Fred

Decker, who now had his eyes closed and his head tilted back to rest against the tree. Arman wondered what it was like knowing you were living your last night on earth.

"Is there any hope," asked Fred Decker, "that they won't go through with this madness?"

"I don't know," said Arman. "I don't think so." While Fred Decker still had his eyes closed, Arman observed him. The cut on his face was swollen, with a dark purple smear taking up almost half his face. His clothes were stained with dirt and dried blood. He still had a cut on his palm, the blood of which had run down his forearm and dried in a sticky mess. He smelled bad, having spent the last few nights in the same, dirty clothes, chained up. Arman thought about asking Niall if they could at least let him bathe and change his clothes. He doubted he would get much charity from Niall.

"What's it like, living here?" asked Fred Decker out of the blue, still with his eyes closed.

"I can't remember," said Arman. "I've lived outside the village for over a year. I didn't see a soul in all that time."

"How come?"

"My wife died and I..." Arman wasn't sure. He thought about it and eventually decided, "I just didn't feel sociable. It felt like I had a lead weight in my stomach, and the idea of having to smile and talk to people and pretend to be okay, and to carry on with my life, seemed impossible."

"How did she die?"

Arman didn't tell Fred how Mathilda had become ill. That her mind wasn't working properly. How she began to forget things. How she would forget who he was and panic when she saw him. He didn't say that he would find her near the house, wondering, dazed, with a look in her eye, like a child who had lost their mother. He didn't say that she would have moments when it would all come back, and she would just cry and cry and eventually, when the moments of clarity started to become less and less regular, she would ask Arman to end her life. Beg him to end her life. Instead of saying any of that, he just stayed quiet while Fred waited for a response. In the end, he told him the only truth that mattered. The only truth that had clung to him like a weight around his neck. The truth. "I killed her," he said.

XII

Arman woke while it was still dark, though he could tell it was almost dawn. He breathed in the cold, crisp air and propped himself up onto his elbows. He had slept under the oak tree, on the uneven, dirty ground. He wiped away earth from his arm and shoulders. He rubbed his palms into his eyes. There was stillness in the air. A calm. He knew it wouldn't last. He turned and saw Fred Decker, sitting up, wide awake.

"You didn't sleep?" asked Arman.

"It's hard to sleep when you know what's waiting for you when you wake up," he said. "I thought time was limitless, but here we are. The last day. The last morning, at least."

"What have you been doing?"

"I was hoping to think back over my life. To cherish the memories of my loved ones. My parents. My friends. Lovers. Lost moments. Wonderful times. But mostly, I've been trying to decide on poison or axe."

"Did you decide?"

Fred Decker nodded, "Maybe poison. Though I'd be remiss if I didn't at least ask you if you could maybe free me? I mean, this chain looks pretty sturdy, but still…"

"They've been watching us," said Arman. "Nobody's obviously standing guard, but Cecil Garfield, over there, the house at the crossroad by the garden, keeps regular checks. So does the house opposite, Merry Ramsey's curtains have been twitching since I woke up at least."

Fred Decker gave a resigned shrug. "What about you? What would you choose?"

"Axe or poison?" asked Arman.

"Yes."

"The axe would be swung by Cecil Garfield, a man I'm growing to dislike more and more each day. So I don't know

84

if I'd want to give him the satisfaction. Maybe poison. I would hope it would be quick."

"Well, we can hope," said Fred Decker with a wry smile. He picked at the wound on his palm, wincing as he poked at the skin. "I was hoping I'd have been rescued by now."

"You seem calm," said Arman.

"All the turmoil's going on inside. For now," though even as he said it, Fred Decker's eyes reddened and he breathed in sharply, holding back tears. His attention was drawn to something behind him. He arched his neck round, looking back towards the village, where a few people had begun to emerge. The sky was getting lighter, with muted blues blossoming from the darkness. "Not long now," he said.

"No."

"I've been meaning to ask you something?"

"Yes?"

"I kept hearing about some box I was supposed to have been stealing with a relic inside?"

"The Holy Relic," said Arman.

"What is it?"

Arman smiled, looking back towards the village. "It is a ring supposedly worn by Saint Margaret of Cortona. It was gifted to the congregation before I joined."

"I have so many questions."

"Another time," said Arman.

"Another time."

"Can I do anything for you?" asked Arman.

"No," said Fred Decker. "Though I'll probably think of something important just after I get my head cut off."

They were interrupted by three people approaching; Niall, Cecil and Olive Kirby. Olive had blonde hair, on the cusp of grey, and it flowed over her shoulders. She wore a long cream dress, with a thick, cotton shawl wrapped tightly around her.

She seemed almost childlike next to Cecil, who was towering over her, his wide shoulders filling a heavy overcoat.

"Good morning, Mr Decker," said Niall. "Morning, Arman."

Neither Fred Decker nor Arman responded. Niall waited, just a second for a response, before continuing. "Following a fair trial, you were found guilty — "

" — a fair trial?" said Arman. "Did that happen after Garfield forcibly removed me?"

"Arman, let's not go down this road."

"And it was you that night, wasn't it, Garfield? When I tried to stop Violet beating him to death. You were the one that wrestled me to the ground."

"What if I was?" said Cecil sternly.

Arman turned back to Niall. "You got what you wanted. Kill him, but let's not make speeches about fair trials."

Cecil took a step forward, but Niall placed a hand on his arm, stopping him.

"Again, Garfield? You're running out of places to throw me. I suppose it will be out of Hope itself next?" said Arman.

"You don't belong here," said Cecil.

"Please, gentlemen," said Niall. "Mr Decker, have you chosen between poison or the axe?"

"What if I don't choose?"

"Then we will choose for you," said Niall. "Axe or poison is better than the mob tearing you apart, young man, trust me."

Fred Decker looked Cecil up and down and said, "Are you the one swinging the axe?"

Cecil shifted uncomfortably, nodding by way of response.

"Do you have steady hands?" asked Fred Decker.

"My hands are fine," he said.

Fred Decker seemed to consider it before turning his attention to Olive. "Are you...the poisoner?"

Olive visibly blushed. "It'll be quick," she said.

"Quicker than an axe?"

"I don't..." she trailed off.

Niall took a step forward and knelt by Fred Decker's side, "Have you chosen, Mr Decker, or would you like me to choose for you?"

"I get the feeling you'd like the axe," said Fred Decker, "so I'll choose poison."

Niall nodded, "Poison it is. We shall have it ready by sunrise. Is that acceptable, Olive?"

"Yes," she said.

"Olive, was it?" said Fred Decker. When she nodded in agreement, he said, "Olive, have you done this before?"

"No," she said it softly, barely able to meet his eyes. "But it should act fast. Painless. I hope."

Niall led Cecil and Olive away. Fred Decker and Arman watched them in silence as they left. More villagers had woken up and the streets were beginning to come alive. The sky was getting lighter, the silence becoming chatter, the world awaking. Fred Decker gritted his teeth, trying to hold back tears. Arman moved closer, bringing a hand to rest on the back of Fred Decker's neck. They brought their heads together, their foreheads touching, and finally Fred Decker cried, big, shoulder shaking tears, running down his cheeks. Fred Decker moved his head to Arman's shoulder and sobbed. Arman could feel the hot tears trickling onto his neck. Arman opened his eyes and noticed villagers forming, some alone, some paired or in groups, around them. Before long, Niall had returned with Olive. Cecil was nowhere to be seen, which Arman was thankful for. Olive carried with her a vial with light yellow liquid in. Arman wondered what terrible concoction lay within. He whispered into Fred Decker's ear and then he pulled away.

Fred Decker looked up and around at the surrounding congregation. At its centre stood Niall and Olive. He wiped away his tears and got to his feet, standing up straight and facing his executioners.

"If you wish to make peace with God, please do so now, Mr Decker," said Niall.

Fred Decker coughed, clearing his throat, and though he struggled to speak without crying, said, "This is not justice. This is murder. You are murderers, killing an innocent man. Do you understand? Do any of you understand?"

Arman looked around the congregation. Their faces stared blankly back as Fred Decker shouted. Near the back of the group, just behind Sylvia Farley and her husband, Roman, stood Violet. She was dressed in black, with a dark shawl around her head so that just her face was visible. She briefly looked up and caught Arman's eye, but then quickly looked away. Arman turned back to Fred Decker. He had stopped talking. His legs were shaking with nerves.

Prompted by Niall, Olive came forward and stood in front of Fred Decker. She seemed to study him a moment, then spoke quietly. Arman strained and could just about hear her when she said, "It should be quick. Just seconds."

"What's the best way to take it?" said Fred Decker.

"Quickly," she said.

She took a cork from the top and handed it to him. Fred Decker held it in his hand, just looking at it. He swirled it a little, sniffed it, and held it close to his mouth. "You're not just killing me," he said, "you're killing yourselves. This...is...murder."

Somebody shouted out to, "Drink it!"

"You first," said Fred Decker and then he chuckled, just quietly to himself. He raised it, as if in toast, and then drank it all and tossed the empty vial aside. His reaction was immediate. He dropped to a knee and gasped for air. He grabbed at his head, holding it between his hands and he screamed, a ghastly, wailing scream. He tried to stand, but his legs gave way and he fell back to his knees. He tried to scream again but this time had no breath. His hands released his head and he reached out, as if to grab some unknown saviour. His raspy breath escaped him and he struggled to take in another.

Arman took a step forward, as if he may help, but stopped himself. What could he do? He looked around at the congregation. Some looked away, horrified. Others studied him emotionlessly. Other seemed to revel in his suffering. Niall seemed shocked, but didn't look away. Violet Walker was in tears.

Fred Decker gasped for oxygen. He collapsed onto the floor, immediately curling up into a ball and clutching at his chest. His breathing was fast but forced, and it rasped and rattled through his throat with a reluctance that everybody could hear. Patches of dark red skin were forming on neck and face. He began to convulse, though he fought against it by trying to curl himself into a tighter ball.

Some of the congregation had fled. Others backed away, scared by the wretched display in front of them. Niall looked to Olive for answers but she seemed just as horrified as the others. Arman wondered if anybody would do anything, but people only moved backwards, not forward. Arman strode across to where Fred Decker struggled on the floor. He scurried around on his knees in the dirt until he found a thick stick. He grabbed at Fred Decker's head and tried to get the stick into his mouth. Fred Decker's teeth were clamped tightly shut. He hadn't seen her move, but soon Violet was by his side. She grabbed at Fred Decker's jaw, helping to open his mouth just a little, just enough for Arman to get the thick stick in between his teeth. Fred Decker immediately bit down upon it hard, indenting the thick wood with his teeth. His eyes were open and wild, staring upwards at Arman in despair. The whites of his eyes seemed yellow, though a thick redness was forming around the outsides. Arman tried to hold him but Fred Decker bucked and twisted and contorted himself out of Arman's grip.

Cecil stepped out of the crowd. He had gone home and retrieved his axe and it swung at his side. "Enough!" he shouted.

"No!" screamed Arman, holding up his hand as if that alone may stop the advancing axeman.

Fred Decker hungrily gulped in as much air as his constricting chest would allow, but his lips had already turned a ghoulish blue and it seemed like he couldn't manage it much longer. He was on his back now, his leg somehow tucked under the other and twitching intermittently. Violet had a hand resting on his chest as it quickly rose and fell.

Cecil stopped, clutching his axe now in both hands and waiting for some unknown signal to finish the job.

"No," repeated Arman.

Cecil stood his ground, but advanced no further. The axe, tightly gripped in his left hand now, rested threateningly in the palm of his right. It looked like he might spring forward at any second and deliver a nightmare blow.

There were tears in the congregation. Some screams. Arman briefly looked up but it all seemed like a blur. He turned back to Fred Decker and wished he could do something. Fred Decker's body jolted out straight, then contracted back in, then jolted out. Violet took his hand. The worst of the convulsions seemed to be slowly calming down. Fred Decker had once again found himself curled into a ball, rasping for breath. Nobody spoke. The sound of the condemned man's desperate breathing, wheezing in and softly whistling out, was the only sound. His eyes were dark and motionless. But for his chest, his body was still. He still lived, though nobody yet knew what horror the rest of that life might look like.

PART 2

I

The shack built at the end of the street, past the oak tree and just short of the tree line, was five feet high, six feet wide and four feet long. It had been a hasty build, outfitted with a straw mattress and pillow, with a canvas that hung down across the narrow doorway. There were no windows. From the street, you couldn't see inside. The rain that thundered down hit the roof with a thud-thud-thud repetition. Olive approached, a satchel grasped in both hands. She wore a large bonnet, tied tightly under her chin, which deflected much of the rain. She stopped several metres away from the shack. The smell, of faeces and death, simmered on the periphery of the shack like an invisible shield, warning people of what lurked inside. Olive shifted the satchel to one hand and with the other she raised her scarf to cover her nose and mouth. Even before she reached the entrance she could hear his breathing, the heavy, gasped wheeze in and the desperate groan as he exhaled painfully. She steadied herself, and swept the canvas to the side, the smell intensifying. She grabbed at her scarf, pressing it tighter to her face.

Inside, Fred Decker lay on the mattress, a thin cotton sheet wrapped around him. The shack wasn't wide enough for him to stretch out, but even if he could, he wouldn't have. Whatever pain coursed through his body caused him to curl himself into a ball. His head turned as he sensed someone enter and he struggled in the poor candle light to make out who was there. Olive knelt on the ground, tucking her legs beneath her and placing her satchel on the floor. She took her time unbuckling it, in no hurry to face the consequences of her actions. She produced a vial of red liquid which she shook for several seconds.

"This should help," she said softly, "with the pain."

His eyes were bloodshot, his pupils black and large. Purple rings surrounded them. His skin, blotchy, in dark red and grey patches, caused him to rub at it with his palms. Seeing the vial in Olive's hand, he went to speak, but all he could manage was a guttural wail, unable to move his mouth properly. Olive brought the vial to his lips. His lower lip, swollen, hung to the side and as she poured the liquid, much of it dribbled onto his chin. She dabbed at it with the corner of her scarf.

"Sorry," she said, "sorry." She tipped the last of the vial up, unsure how much had gone in. Unsure if it would do any good. Once done, she returned it to her satchel. "Sorry," she said again, as she stood and left. Outside, as the canvas fell back across the entranceway, she let out a large gasp and pressed her lips tightly together to control her emotions. She looked up and saw Arman sat on a tree stump near the oak tree. He was watching her and sipping at a mug of coffee, oblivious to the rain pouring down.

"Morning, Mrs Kirby," he said.

"Good morning, Mr Shaw," she said. She walked to him, putting her satchel down and moving to a nearby stump. The height of the stump caused her to do a little hop to properly get on top. Her feet only just touched the floor.

"Just about made it," joked Arman.

She smiled. "Do you remember when they cut all these trees down?"

"Yes," he said. Though it seems like a long time ago now."

"I'm at the age now," she said, "where everything seems like a long time ago."

"I know the feeling."

She bit her lip, turning her head to the rain just enough to feel it caress her face. Her lips curled to a smile, just a little, but enjoying the rain on her face. Abruptly, she lowered her head, shielding herself from the downpour. "Mr Shaw, I don't know what happened. I didn't do it on purpose. I promise."

"I know," he said. "Nobody blames you."

She turned to look back towards the shack, "Nobody?"

"What happened?" asked Arman.

She shook her head, "I'm just not used to making...poison. I've spent my life working with medicines. Pick me ups. Just simple things. Niall asked if I could make something deadly. He said otherwise the axe would be the only option and I..." She struggled to control her rising emotions, taking a second before she spoke again, "I thought it would be inhumane to use the axe."

"He was wrong to put you in that position."

"Yes," she said, "I think he was."

Arman nodded towards the shack and said, "Take care of him, Mrs Kirby."

She nodded. "What will you do now?" she asked.

"Go home. Probably stay there. I had dreamt of returning to the congregation one day, but after everything that has happened...It's not the same place I left behind."

"It could be."

"Come let me know if that day ever comes," he said with a smile.

"I know you think the village turned on you," she said, "and perhaps they did. But it won't last. Everyone is angry. Everybody has been made helpless by everything that's happened. But they will move on. In time. They won't blame you."

"Thank you, Olive." He got to his feet, shivering at the cold. He went to her and they embraced clumsily, her position on the stump causing him to bend awkwardly. "Can you get down from there?"

She laughed. "I'll wait until you've gone so I don't embarrass myself," she said.

He left her alone and walked back past the oak tree. The rain was keeping people inside their homes and Arman was thankful. He considered visiting Violet, even stopping at her door, but he never knocked. He turned and headed out of Hope and started the walk home.

On his way he thought of Mathilda and how helpless she'd been at the end. Mathilda had asked Arman to help her end her life and they had briefly considered coming to Olive to ask for a quick way out. Ultimately, they had decided against it. They had felt it would be unfair on Olive to ask her to do such a thing. They also didn't want to make anybody else complicit in their sin. Now, walking away from Hope, walking away from Fred Decker, Arman felt the burden of responsibility cling to him once more. Mathilda's moments of clarity, when her world aligned briefly, but correctly, in her mind had been emotional moments, marred by tears and pain. She had worn Arman down with her pleas for him to intercede, though her pleas for mercy were eventually replaced by anger at his inaction.

The ground squelched messily beneath his shoes as he walked briskly down the narrow, twisting path. The sky was grey and foreboding and the rain was heavy. Arman hunched his shoulders, trying to shield himself as best he could from the downpour. Several times he stopped, considering returning to Hope. It felt like there was still too much hanging in the air for him to walk away, but similarly, he couldn't envision being a part of it anymore. The indecision gnawed at him and he cursed himself. The rain had eased off as he came off the winding trail and took the long gravel path to his home. Once inside, he made a fire, taking his time to build it up, and stacking several thick logs on top to keep it burning into the night. He stripped himself down, peeling soaking wet clothes from his white, goose-bumped skin. He went into the bedroom, standing on his toes to reach a high shelf where he kept a stack of blankets. He took a thick wool blanket that had been made by Mathilda, woven with greys and blues, and he wrapped it tightly round himself. He dragged the rocking chair from a spot by the window until it was next to the fire. It was close enough that his skin pricked with the heat. He watched the orange flames as they danced in front of him. Staring at the fire, everything else fell into darkness. He slouched down, and in time, he slept. And dreamt.

An empty village. Its garden withered and dying. Its streets empty, the dust and dirt blowing lazily along its paths. Doors were locked shut. Windows closed. Half-built houses lined the streets. Others were more or less intact, but damaged, missing parts of their walls, some without a roof or door. The only movement was a gentle sway of the branches of the oak tree, which danced to the tune of the wind as it quietly worked its way through them. It had been many years since people had lived here. It lay on the outer reaches of a vast landholding, forgotten and unloved. This was the world the congregation came to. Arman remembered Mathilda's face that day because she hadn't stopped smiling. She had held his hand tightly, her small hands lost in his. Her long red hair swept back into a bun at the back. She had worn a long maroon dress that flourished out around her ankles. She had hugged Niall and thanked him for helping find such a wonderful location for the congregation to start their new lives. Everyone had excitedly started to make plans, to claim houses or plots of land to build upon. The destitute building at the far end would make an excellent church. Herman Blyth had suggested a large window that would show off God's beautiful creation that lay beyond, and all had agreed. Mathilda's emerald eyes, wide and wild and full of joy, imagined a world away from the rest of society, away from sin and corruption, from poverty and filth. Her eyes, that shone, that couldn't hide their emotion. How they bulged. How they bulged with Arman's hands around her neck. How she lay there, years later, in their old bed in their new home, naked, entwined, trying not to struggle as Arman's hand squeezed harder. Her arms spread, reaching out and grabbing at the corners of the bed, bracing herself, trying not to struggle as they gripped tightly at the cotton sheets. How she tried to tell him that it was okay, but it was too late, because his eyes were closed, and he was shaking almost uncontrollably, but still, still, he kept applying pressure, right up to the very end. It was then, with her last breath struggling free, she muttered a single word before she died.

"No."

He awoke with a scream, his own, piercing the silence, causing the fire to flicker. He sprung to his feet, kicking back at the rocking chair. He slammed an open-palmed hand into the stone wall above the fireplace, again and again, screaming, crying. His open palm became a fist and he hit the wall, twice, three times, four, long after the skin had peeled away and the blood ran down his forearm. He kept hitting it even as he felt bones break in his hand. The violence slowed, his laboured breathing coming under control, the palm open again, against the blood-splattered stone. His hand trembled. Flaps of purpled skin hung loosely from the knuckles and beneath lay a deep red mess, loose bits of stonework peppering his wounds. What wasn't cut open, was red or bruised, sore to the touch. He held it at the wrist and stood naked, in front of the fire as the heat surrounded him. He screamed and screamed and eventually dropped down to his knees, doubling over, clutching his broken, bloodied hand close to his chest. He lay down, curling himself up into a ball, feeling the cold floor pressed against his cheek, his shoulder, his arm, his leg. The world around him was a dark blur, a void he was happy to climb into. All there was was the loneliness, the guilt, the pain, and before him a fiery damnation that burned and licked its way into a hellish vision of his future.

II

Sunshine blasted in through his bedroom window and let Arman know that he'd overslept. His hand had ballooned in the night. He lay in bed, holding it in front of himself, turning it to get a good look, examining it. He had crudely wrapped a bit of cloth around it the previous night, but it didn't cover the dried blood and extensive black and purple bruising. He tried to move his fingers. His thumb and little finger were stiff, but still worked, but the three in the middle barely responded when he tried to wriggle them. He got to the edge of his bed and swung his legs out. He hadn't realised how much he depended on his right hand until he couldn't use it. He got to his feet and dragged himself to the kitchen. A bowl of water sat on his kitchen table. He sat down in front of it and began to unwrap the cloth from his hand. The dried blood had made it stick to his skin, and as he tugged harder, he tore off some loose flaps of dead skin that had been hanging free. He gritted his teeth. Free of the cloth, he plunged his hand into the water, breathing in hard to fight back a scream. He tried to make a fist, but his fingers wouldn't respond. He pulled the broken hand free of the water and studied it. He could see the bone jutting under the skin at an unusual angle in at least two places. He placed his injured hand flat on the table, palm down. He placed his other hand over the top, covering as much as he could. He took a few quick, short breaths, and then brought his good hand down hard onto the broken one, pushing the jutting bones back down. He screamed and grabbed at the broken hand, clutching it tightly against his chest. His eyes watered and it took him a minute to get his breath back.

"Idiot," he hissed.

There was a loud series of knocks on his front door and he jumped, startled. He got to his feet, moved through his kitchen and opened his front door. It was Cecil Garfield. He filled the open doorway with his bulk.

"What?" said Arman.

"Got something for you," said Cecil. The large man took a heavy step backwards.

Arman leaned out of his front door and his heart sank. In a small wooden cart, with two back wheels and two front handles, was the slumped body of Fred Decker. Arman looked up at Cecil, expectantly.

"We tried," said Cecil. "We built him a shack. We gave him somewhere to sleep. We gave him medicine. But he just... wheezes. And coughs. And he smells bad. Children were too scared to go down that end of the village. Nobody wanted to treat him. Nobody could stomach the smell. I offered to finish the job off, but Niall said he'd suffered enough."

"What's this got to do with me?"

"We don't want him in the village. We're not going to kill him anymore. You wanted him alive. Here's your chance."

"What are you talking about?" said Arman.

Cecil shrugged and turned his back to Arman, taking a few steps before he stopped and looked back. "If it were me, I'd put this man out of his misery. Nobody would judge you. Nobody would even know. Just say he succumbed."

"Wait!" Arman called after him, but Cecil lumbered away, back down the path he had just trodden. "Cecil!" Cecil tossed a half wave over his shoulder but never stopped and never looked back. Arman stood, motionless, at his front door for the longest time. He looked at Fred Decker, cramped into the cart, an arm and a leg flopping over the side. He wheezed, brutally, regularly, and Arman found it a haunting sound.

"Mr Decker?" he said. "Fred?" But he got no response. He looked back inside the house then back out to the cart, trying to get his brain to make connections that weren't there, trying to think of a plan. He looked at his hand. Several times, he went to take a step, but each time he stopped, riddled with indecision. He closed his eyes, taking solace in the darkness. When he opened them, the world was still there waiting for him. He took a step out and knelt down by the side of the cart.

Fred Decker moved his head, just slightly, but towards Arman, his eyes opening and trying to focus. He opened his mouth, but the gurgled sound that escaped his throat was lost in his swollen tongue and lips.

"Mr Decker, I can't..." Arman trailed off. He looked round for help that he knew wasn't there, struggling to get his mind to make informed rational decisions. He couldn't just leave him out here. Could he? He looked back at his narrow door. Even if he had the full use of his hands, he was almost certain the cart wouldn't go through the gap. He looked out, past the chicken coup that nestled noisily at the side of his house. Beyond that, just twenty yards or so was a small shed with wide, double doors. If he could get him in there, he could try and make it comfortable for him. He got to his feet, using his good hand as leverage, and headed back into his house. In the room at the back, the room that would've been a nursery but had ended up as a storage room, he found what he was looking for; a thick length of rope. He brought it back outside and wound it tightly around each handle of the cart. He took the slack and wrapped it several times around his good hand, until the rope bit into his skin. Then he pulled. It didn't shift at first. Arman's teeth gritted together and he let out a primal grunt as he used more force. The cart shifted, just a little, but enough to break free of the wet mud beneath that it had been slowly embedding itself into. Again, feeling the thick rope cutting into his hand, he pulled at the centre, and it pulled the cart a few inches. A third time, he puffed himself up and pulled ferociously. This time, the rope came free of the handles and Arman fell awkwardly into the dirt. He lay there, on his front, the gravel on his face, puffing out air and deciding if he should get up or just stay there forever. Even from the ground, with his face burning under grazed, sore skin, he could hear the wheezing coming from the cart. He clumsily got to his feet. His good hand had a thick, red rope burn straight across the palm. He wound the rope once more around the cart handles, knotting them as best he could. Again, he wound the rest around his hand and braced himself. A light rain had begun to fall. Arman pulled. The wheels on the cart turned an inch, then an inch more, and moved forward. Arman stopped, almost out of breath already.

In all, it took Arman just under four hours to move the cart to his shed. Inside, he got the cart in enough just to close the door. From the house, he retrieved some blankets which he laid over Fred Decker. He used an oil lamp from the house and propped it up on a wooden chair with a broken back that he'd rescued from a rubbish pile round the back of the house.

"Are you hungry?" asked Arman, to no reply.

He returned to the house an exhausted man. His broken hand was unusable and the other was criss-crossed with rope burns and blisters. His limbs and back ached, and he wondered if he'd even be able to move in the morning. That was a problem for then. He prepared a simple vegetable soup, finding peace in the rhythmic stirring of the watery mixture in his one and only pot. When it was ready, he sat at his kitchen table and ate quietly. Tomorrow he would go to the village and confront Niall. This wasn't his problem. It was unfair that he should be liable for somebody else's mistake. He was being punished.

He finished his soup, refilled the bowl and went out to the shed. At the door, he could hear the laboured breathing beyond. He could smell him from here. He took a deep breath and went inside, making sure to leave the double doors open to let in as much fresh air as possible. Already, the whole shed reeked of death. He moved the oil lamp to the floor and pulled the chair to the side of the cart. Fred Decker turned to face him, his blurry red eyes trying, and failing, to focus properly.

"I made soup," said Arman. "It tastes horrible, but, still…"

He lifted the spoon to Fred Decker's lips, trying to angle it to find a way in. Fred opened his mouth, eager for the food, but much of it went in and spilled out again.

"That's fine," said Arman, "all is well." He tried again, this time trying to get the food more centred, away from the drooping lip. He managed the full spoonful and Fred swallowed hungrily. He repeated it again three or four times to various degrees of success. The fifth drooled out down Fred's chin and Arman didn't have a cloth to wipe it up with, so he used his sleeve.

Fred made a noise, his lips pressing together, struggling to make a coherent sound. Beneath the slurred noise, you could almost make out a word. "Pppad."

"Pad?" asked Arman. "Bad? Are you saying the soup is bad?"

Fred's lip curled, almost imperceptibly at the corner. The closest he could come to a smile.

"It is bad," said Arman, "but you're spilling most of it anyway, so let's not complain just yet." He finished the rest of the bowl off. He had almost got the hang of it by the last spoonful. He used his sleeve to wipe at Fred's lips. "I apologise, that you're stuck in the cart. Tomorrow, I'm going to go into the village to ask for help. To get them to find you somewhere to stay."

Fred responded but the words rolled out as one, incomprehensible sound. Arman smiled, unsure of what to say. He patted Fred's shoulder, got up and left. He left the doors open an inch, enough to block out the world, but also enough to let a slither of clean air in to circulate.

Back at the house, he collapsed into an armchair and briefly slept. When he opened his eyes again, it was dark outside. He shifted in his chair, rubbing at his eyes to wake up properly. After everything that he'd been through recently, he was relieved that he hadn't had a nightmare. There was a tapping at his front door and his head snapped round to look in that direction, as if he might see through the wooden door to find out who was disturbing him this time. He had never been so popular. He ambled to the door, unfastening the latch and opening it widely. Violet Walker stood there in the rain, her hair tucked under a bonnet, a warm wool shawl wrapped tightly around her dress.

"Violet," he said.

"It's raining, Arman, can I come in?"

He didn't seem to hear her. He looked beyond her, as if expecting someone else. Seeing that she was alone, he asked, "What are you doing here?"

"Arman, please," she persisted.

He seemed to snap out of whatever daze he was temporarily in, holding the door open wider for her to enter. "Apologies, Violet. Come in."

"Thank you."

"How are you, Violet?"

"Wet," she said, "and cold. I've come to help."

"Help?"

"I've been in a world of my own, Arman. After the attack. The trial. The attempt at execution. I've just been...lost. Alone. I only just found out what they did to you and, Arman, I'm so sorry, this is all my fault."

He agreed with her, but didn't say so.

III

Violet covered her nose with her shawl when she entered the shed. She stopped just inside the doorway, letting the flickering orange of the oil lamp stutter dim light across the body of Fred, as he fidgeted under his blanket.

"He just left him on my doorstop," said Arman. "And I had hurt my hand and couldn't—"

"It's fine," interrupted Violet, her voice barely above a whisper. She looked around the shed, taking a mental inventory. She went back to the door, retrieving the largest part of a broken broom that was resting against the wall. She swept part of the ground, getting the hay and dirt and debris pushed into the corner. She dragged some sacks from the furthest wall and pushed them together, crudely making them into a makeshift mattress. "Let's move him," she said.

She moved behind Fred, tucking her arms under his as best she could. Arman moved to the feet, somehow manoeuvring Fred's legs into the crook of his arm, while protecting his bad hand. Violet lifted first and Arman followed, struggling to keep the legs in his arm. They all but dropped Fred onto the sacks. He landed with an "Oof" that was the first intelligible sound he'd managed since the poisoning. Violet retrieved Fred's blankets from the cart and laid them across him.

"We'll need to clean him up in the morning. Olive Kirby said she would visit with some medical supplies," said Violet. "I'm going to stay and help. Do you have room for me?"

"Stay at the house?"

"Unless you expect me to sleep in the barn?"

The congregation won't like that, Violet."

"I'm not welcome in the village, Arman."

He shook his head. "I don't understand. They can't blame you."

"Not to my face," she said, "but they whisper and they scheme. I offered to help care for the murderer of my husband and they agreed. Not one of them thought that might be inappropriate. Or unfair. They couldn't wait to get rid of me."

"I'm sorry, Violet—"

"I don't want your apologies, Arman, do you have room?"

"Of course. You can have my room. I'm happy sleeping in the living room."

"I don't want to..." she stopped, noticing him clutching at his wrist. "What happened to your hand?"

"Just an accident," he said.

"Let's go back up to the house."

At the house, she made him take a seat in his armchair. She knelt on the floor in front of him, moving the oil lamp closer so she could see properly. At her side, she had prepared a small bowl of water and a cloth. She took his hand, turning it over and holding it in hers. The sensation of her skin upon his made his hand tingle, as though the flesh had somehow become more delicate. Violet studied it. She could see it was swollen, badly bruised and with dried blood crusted around the knuckles and fingers. She took the cloth and dipped it into the cold water. She softly dabbed at his fingers, causing him to wince as she cleaned the stubborn blood away.

"I already tried to clean it," he said.

"Shhh," she interrupted. She held the hand close to her face to see it properly, working the cloth between the fingers and around the knuckles. As she moved it to see better, he winced in pain and she gave him a look, which silenced him, allowing her to continue. "When Olive comes, we'll get some bandages," she said, "and maybe some medicine to help with the swelling. I know I said this before, Arman, but I'm truly sorry I pulled you into all of this..." She looked up and saw that his eyes were closed and his head lilted to the side. He began to snore. She gently placed his hand in his lap and quietly got to her feet to leave him in peace.

When he woke, it was morning and he was disorientated. He looked around the room, taking a moment to register his surroundings. He moved forward and gritted his teeth as a pain in his back shot down his spine and lodged in his hip. He could hear the sounds of life in the kitchen. He got up and went through the doorway to find Violet at the cooker, swirling something unknown in his only pan. The kitchen seemed more ordered, the mess tidied away and the surfaces cleaned.

"How long have you been up?" he asked.

"An hour or two," she said. "I'm making porridge."

"You didn't have to clean."

"If I hadn't have cleaned then I wouldn't have found the oats at the back of your cupboard. Arman, what do you eat?"

"I get by," he said with a shrug.

"Will you take a seat. It won't be long."

He sat at the table, where a bowl and a spoon were waiting for him. In short time, Violet came over and spooned him some porridge into his bowl. She sat down opposite him as he ate.

"Are you not eating?"

"I had something earlier," she told him.

Arman took a mouthful, nodded in appreciation, then took another. He wiped at his lips with the back of his good hand and then laughed. "I'm not used to people watching me eat."

"I'm sorry," smiled Violet, "I wasn't watching. Just in a world of my own. Can I ask you something?"

Arman swallowed his food and put his spoon down before he said, "Yes."

"Do you believe him?"

"Fred Decker? Which part of his story?"

"All his story," she said. "The self-defence. He didn't have a knife. It was all just...some terrible accident? That he and Bernard were...that he..."

"—Violet," Arman said, "I can't answer that because I don't know."

"You don't know for sure, but you spent time with him. You listened to him. Did it make sense? Did it seem real?"

"Yes," he said. "It did."

"I thought you might say that."

"I'm sorry," he said. "I don't want to upset you."

"I just thought that Robert had no interest in...in...me...that way. I never really understood. That's why we never had any children." She looked at Arman as she said it, almost daring him to look away, but he didn't. She took a breath and continued, "I grew up being told I was pretty. I would catch the eye, that's what they told me. They told me my mother had been the same, but her looks withered with age, and with them, any interest from my father. But I am still young, Arman. I have not withered. Have I?"

"You have not withered, Violet."

"I was never much of a home maker, Arman, but I tried to be a good wife."

"Violet, you don't have to—"

"—and all that time, he was with Bernard Ogden. Is that what happened?"

"I'm sorry," he repeated again. "I honestly don't know."

"And Robert fought him, because he feared being caught? Is that what happened?"

"Violet, it's all just guesswork. We don't know that."

"And if that's true, then Bernard Ogden, let that man, Fred Decker, be accused of theft. Of murder."

"*If* that's true," said Arman. "'If', and that's a big 'if'."

"It's my fault, Arman."

"It's not your fault—"

"—I'm not like these people. I'm not from this background. Niall was right, I just married into it. I was never one of them. I come from a very different life." She held his stare for a moment longer than Arman felt comfortable with. Her lips were slightly parted, as if about to speak, though she remained silent.

"Violet, I—" he stopped when he heard a noise.

There was a bang at the door. He and Violet both went to it. Arman opened it while Violet stood just behind him. It was Olive, carrying a basket in the crook of her arm. She had a scarf around her neck. Arman guessed that she wore it to pull up over her nose when she had to face Fred once more. He smiled.

"Good morning, Mr Shaw," she said. "Mrs Walker."

Arman nodded. Violet returned the "Good morning".

Arman stood to the side, happy to let Violet take the lead as they went to the shed. He stood in the doorway as the women knelt either side of Fred.

"The smell..." said Olive, clutching her scarf tightly to her nose.

"We will clean him today," said Violet. "We struggled yesterday because Arman has injured his hand."

Olive stopped, turning to look at Arman, "What happened?"

"Nothing," he said, "just a little accident."

"Do you have bandages you could leave for him?" asked Violet, "Maybe something for the swelling?"

"Is it broken?" she asked.

"I don't..." he paused, then, "Yes, I think so."

"I'll take a look at it once I've dealt with him," said Olive.

Arman thanked her. He stood and watched as she administered some liquid between Fred's skewed lips. He wondered how Fred could trust her to let her put anything else inside him after what happened, but then he guessed Fred was in no fit state to fight anyone off. Olive felt Fred's forehead. She asked him to open his eyes, which he did, and to say if he was okay. He mumbled something that Olive smiled at. Arman didn't know if she understood or not. He didn't suppose it mattered.

"What will happen to him?" asked Arman. "Will he get better?"

"Perhaps," said Olive. "His breathing seems...improved."

Arman nodded, though he did so reluctantly since the loudest sound in the shed was still the rasping, wheezing efforts of Fred to breathe. "What can we do?"

"Keep him clean," Olive said. "Keep him warm, or as warm as you can. Try to sit him up soon, perhaps. Feed him. I'll return in a couple of days."

"Thank you, Mrs Kirby," Arman said.

"I can't imagine," said Olive, turning to Violet, "what it must be like to take care of the man that murdered your husband."

"We preach about forgiveness, and caring at every sermon, Olive, how could I not?"

"Of course," said Olive, though her smile quickly vanished as she turned away from Violet and got to her feet. She addressed Arman, "Let's have a look at this hand then." She went to him and took his hand, struggling to see it properly. "Shall we go out into the light?"

He agreed and she led him outside, moving a few paces from the barn, leaving Violet and Fred inside. She studied his hand, "oohing" and "ahhing" as she did. She looked up at Arman. "What are you doing, Mr Shaw?"

"What? What am I doing with what?" he asked.

"With Mrs Walker?"

"Nothing. She came to help with Mr Decker, that is all."

"People talk, Mr Shaw." She used her thumb, running it along the bones in his hand, feeling carefully as she went.

"Mrs Kirby, they dumped this man on my doorstep. They left me to fend for him. I can barely take care of myself. Violet came to help."

Olive said nothing. She ran her thumb over the same area on the back of the hand several times, eventually finding a spot and circling her thumb there for a moment. She pressed down hard, causing his hand to crack violently. Arman yelped, grabbing at the hand and pulling it away. "That should do it," she said.

"Keep it clean. Wrap some bandages around it, tightly, as tight as you can, and rest it. Is that clear?"

"Yes," he said. "Thank you."

"You don't have to thank me, Mr Shaw. Just be careful. Tensions are running high right now, but they'll soon calm down. Say goodbye to Mrs Walker for me."

Olive left, not turning back as she headed for the winding path down to the village. Arman watched her leave. As she was almost out of sight, Violet came out of the shed, carrying some bandages she'd taken from the basket.

"What's the verdict?" said Violet.

"Wrap it tight. Rest it. I can't remember if there was more."

"Did she mention me?"

"It was all a blur," he said. "I think she re-broke my hand."

Violet smiled, taking the bandages and beginning to wrap them round his hand. She pulled tight, and each time he winced. "A blur? I'm not sure when I became the villain in the congregation." She finished wrapping the bandages across his hand, then wound them twice round his wrist and tied them off. She turned to see the last of Olive as she followed the path out and disappeared behind the tree line. "She said she'll be back in a few days to check on him."

"Are you going to go back to your home, or will you be staying here longer?"

"I'll stay longer. If you'll have me?"

He was about to respond when he was startled by a loud banging noise coming from the shed. Violet took a step back. They both stared at the double doorway. From somewhere inside there was movement. From the darkness within, a lumbering form appeared. Fred Decker stumbled and fell against the doors, leaning on them with his shoulder. He looked up at them, attempted to speak, but instead collapsed onto the floor in front of them.

IV

Arman lifted the boiling pot of water from the stove and carried it through his house, careful not to spill it. He moved out through his back door to an extension built at the rear. A tin bathtub sat on four legs in the centre of the small room. The floor was stone, the walls and roof, wooden. Arman had built it for Mathilda but now rarely used it. Fred sat in the bath now, clutching his knees. The water sloshed around his feet and lower legs.

"Careful," said Arman.

He poured the water in at the bottom, careful to avoid Fred's legs. He put his arm in, swishing the water round, mixing the cold with the hot. He handed Fred a sponge, but it instantly fell from his left hand. Arman retrieved it from the water, taking Fred's right hand and putting the sponge in it. The fingers held it this time. Satisfied, Arman left, heading back inside and going to the front door. He stood in the doorway, looking off to his side, past the chicken coup, where Violet worked the water pump. Her hair had come loose from the bun it had been tied in earlier. Her dress had long sleeves, but she'd pushed them back, exposing her forearms. The mud peppered the lower parts of the dress as it skirted along the ground.

She had both hands on the handle, bringing it down with effort and then slowly controlling it as it returned upwards. The bucket underneath filled quickly. Out of breath, she clutched the handle one final time, taking effort to pull it down.

"Last one," Arman called out. He walked over, bending down to lift the heavy bucket up. "Are you well?"

"Do I not look well?" she asked.

"We'd probably have to tidy you up before we went dancing," he said.

She stepped back, lifting her arms to show off the true disarray of her dress. "You're almost certainly right," she laughed. "Maybe next time you pump and I carry and heat the water."

"Deal," he said, "though I normally just make do with cold. At the sink. Usually." He got a firm grip with his good hand on the bucket then headed inside with it.

He put the water into the metal pot, letting it slowly warm up on the stove. He looked out the dirty window, where outside Violet still stood by the pump, facing out, looking at the valley beyond. She was attempting to pull her sleeves back down to cover her arms. The wind was whipping at her hair, making it dance around her face. She ran her hands through it, holding it out of her eyes. Some mud had somehow spattered onto her neck and there was sweat glistening on her collarbone. She turned her head to look back towards the house, and Arman looked away, focusing on the pot. He thought he had seen her smile just as he looked away, but he couldn't be sure. Once the pot had heated, he carried it through and added it to the bath. Fred still shivered, the sponge still clenched in his hand. Arman took it from him, using it to wipe at Fred's face. He dipped it in the water and washed his back, his chest, his arms.

"This is a new experience for me," Arman joked. Fred didn't respond. Arman dipped the sponge into the dirty water, swirling it around. He washed Fred's lower half, hesitating just a second before he washed between his legs. When he was done, he dropped the sponge into the brown water where it floated. Fred used his right hand to wipe water away from his face. He looked up at Arman.

"Wha shid bey din h'me?" he asked.

Arman looked puzzled. "I'm sorry," he said. "Could you say it again?"

"He said, 'What did they do to me?'" said Violet, standing at the doorway, but looking away from Fred, towards a spot on the floor to her side.

Arman went to say something, to tell her she shouldn't be here, but after everything that had happened, it would feel hollow. He couldn't have done any of this without Violet. They were all in this together now. He wanted to tell her that, but he kept it to himself.

Arman turned back to Fred. "I don't have an answer," he said. "They tried to kill you, but they…got it wrong."

"Bu aay ill on a hi'me?"

Arman looked lost. He turned his head to look at Violet. She was struggling to pull her hair back, loosely tying it at the back. She briefly stopped to answer him, "He wants to know if they still want to kill him."

"Oh," said Arman, meeting Fred's eyes. "I don't think so. No."

Fred rested his head on his knees, his shoulders rising and falling with each torturous breath.

"Shall I prepare dinner?" Violet asked.

"Yes, please," said Arman. "And set an extra plate at the table."

Soon after Violet left to prepare the food, Arman assisted Fred out of the bath, helping him to sit on a bench against the wall of the bathroom. He dried him, and dressed him in some of his old clothes. Fred was bigger than Arman, taller, with broader shoulders. Even offering the biggest items he had, Fred's arms still kept going after the sleeves ended. The same with the trousers, which came to his shins, but not any lower. The top button on the trousers was undone to accommodate his larger waist. Afterwards, Arman wrapped his arm around his waist and helped him walk through to the kitchen. Fred went slowly, limping, uneasy on his left leg. As he got to the table, Violet left her position by the stove to help lower him into a chair.

"Later, I'll see what I can do with these clothes," she said, adding, "though I'm not much of a seamstress."

Arman took his seat to the side of Fred as Violet returned to the stove. She served them a vegetable stew, using two matching bowls and a different styled, shallower dish.

"We need supplies," she said as she sat down. "Ingredients. Some bits and pieces. I'll need fresh clothes if I'm going to stay and help. Will you get them for me?"

Arman, mid-slurp, lowered his spoon, swallowed his food and looked at her, "Me?"

"I can't go back there," she said. "Please."

He nodded. She rested her hand on his and said, "Thank you." She pulled her hand away and began to eat. Arman took a second, then resumed, stopping only when he noticed Fred struggling to hold a spoon. Arman leaned over, shifting the spoon from his left to his right hand. Fred's hand shook as he scooped the spoon into the stew, bringing it to his lips and slurping as he tried to eat. Some went down, some came out. He gritted his teeth in frustration, but continued, determined to do it.

"Serty," said Fred.

"Sorry, I—"

"He said," said Violet, "salty. The food is salty. Too salty. He's very probably correct."

"Wha und you nd?" said Fred, turning to Arman.

Arman immediately looked to Violet. Arman noticed a crinkle in her nose as she attempted to decipher the words. She seemed to make a connection, and asked, "Are you asking, about his hand?"

Fred nodded.

Arman brought his bad hand up from where it had been resting on the table. "How is my hand?"

"I think he wants to know what happened to it," Violet said.

"It's a long story," he said. He turned back to Violet, "What is it you want from your home?"

"I'll make you a list," she said. As she took a spoonful of the stew, her eyes fell upon Fred, his breath whistling through damaged lungs. He had found a rhythm and was eating the stew. His left hand was curled up into a fist and resting on the table. "How do you feel?" she asked him.

At first, it seemed like he hadn't heard. He carried on eating, taking in two more spoonfuls before he put his spoon down and looked at her. He tapped at his head. "E'r'ykin whurg zup ere—"

"-—Everything works up there," she said, "in your mind."

"Bu, cun mik orfer o'whurz."

"You can't...something...your words? Make order of your words?"

He gave her a 'close enough' shrug. "Bu behhr da beff'er."

"But better than before."

He nodded.

She pressed two fingers together, slowly tapping them on her chest, "And your chest?"

He laughed a slurred laugh that startled Violet. "I und'and yi."

"You understand me," she said, regretting making the accompanying gestures for her previous question. "I'm sorry."

"Bre'in har."

"Breathing is hard?"

Again, Fred nodded. Arman watched on, sipping at his stew, struggling to make sense of Fred and marvelling at Violet for understanding so much. He would've been happy with this arrangement, but Fred specifically turned to face him, a serious look on his face.

"Pee'pa whi ca."

Arman looked to Violet for help but she struggled. "People?"

"Pee'pa," Fred nodded. "Whi ca. Hi. Whi ca hi."

"People...will come here?" she asked.

Fred nodded. He pointed to himself, "My pee'pa."

"Your people? Your friends?"

"Pee'pa whi ca lhu f'mi."

"Your people will come looking for you?"

Fred slowly nodded. He looked down, taking his spoon in his right hand and continuing to eat. Violet and Arman watched him, waiting for more, but no more came. They exchanged a look, with Arman urging her with his eyes to push for more information. She gave him a look back that suggested she wasn't entirely happy with the proposed suggestion.

"How many people will come?" she asked.

Fred shrugged. Either he didn't know or he didn't want to say. He coughed, a deep whooping cough that made him splutter up his last mouthful of stew. He dribbled down his front, onto Arman's too-short shirt. He finished off his bowl, slurping loudly with the last spoonful, and using the back of his right hand to stop himself dribbling. He looked up and said, "Uh'y wo abbabba mi."

"You...they? They won't...?"

"Abbabba mi," he said it slowly, popping each 'b' as he tried to speak coherently.

"They won't abandon you," said Arman. He had finally understood.

Violet nodded. She stood, placing Arman's bowl inside her own. She reached for Fred's bowl but his right hand grabbed at her wrist, holding it in place. He was shaking his head, but she didn't know why. His brow furrowed and his lips pursed. He was already angry with himself for failing even before he tried to speak. But still, he tried. "I di'n ki'yon hubb'un. In wha'zza addiddun."

"My husband?" she said.

"Addidun," he tried again.

"It was an accident. Is that what you said?"

He nodded, "I di'n ki'm."

"You didn't kill him. It was an accident?" She nodded, flustered, pulling her hand away sharply and taking his bowl. She took them to the sink and noisily dumped them by the side.

Fred rested his right hand on the table and leveraged himself up to a near standing position. He leaned to his left, struggling to maintain his balance. "I um sawra."

With her back to him, she stopped moving, leaving the dishes where they were.

"I um sawra," he repeated.

Arman looked between the two of them, then to Violet's back he said, "He said he's sorr—"

She spun round quickly. "—I know," she said. "I know what he said. Could we not talk about this? Not yet."

Fred nodded, and sat back down.

Arman, keen to change the subject, but also wanting to revisit something that had been bothering him, asked Fred, "When you said people would be coming, that your people wouldn't abandon you. Should we be worried?"

Violet put down a cloth she had been using, waiting for an answer.

Fred winced, and said, "Har'd'exparr."

"It's hard to explain?" Arman was almost – almost – getting the hang of it. "Did you want to write it down? Is that easier? I can get you a paper and pencil."

Fred looked down at the table, shaking his head.

"Fred?" asked Arman, "Would that be acceptable?"

"He can't," said Violet. "He can't write. Can you?"

Fred looked up at her and said, "No."

"Should we be afraid?" she asked. "Yes or no?"

Fred looked at them both, studying them, but with a new, distant look in his eye, as if he had never seen them before. He ground his teeth together as a new pain hit him. He pressed his good hand against his ear, as if he may push whatever pain it was away.

"Fred," Violet persisted, "should we be afraid?"

Fred stopped pressing at his ear and stared at her, "Afwerd?"

"Afraid? Yes. Of your people?"

"Wha'perple?"

"You said..." but she stopped as Arman reached over and rested a hand on her forearm to stop her.

IV

Fred pressed against his ear again, lost in a world of his own. Suddenly, he turned to Violet and – as best he could – smiled, the lips curling on the right side but hanging limp on the other. The smile soon fell, and he said to Violet, as he had earlier, "I di'n kill'im."

"I know," said Violet, "I know."

V

Arman awoke in pain. He always seemed to awake in pain nowadays. He was losing track of days. Of time. He shifted in the armchair. At some point in the night, he'd tucked his legs beneath himself and now they tingled with a dull numbness. He stood, stretched and did an exaggerated yawn that would've been accompanied by a vocal accompaniment had he been alone in the house. It was still dark outside, though dawn was near. He trudged through the house, trying to find his boots. When he rediscovered them, in front of the fireplace where he'd left them, he sat back down and laced them up. The bedroom door was open, just a crack, but he went to it, looking through and just making out the sleeping form of Violet, wrapped in blankets, at peace with the world. She turned in her sleep and he took a step back from the door. When he realised that she still slept, he returned. She breathed heavily through a closed mouth, her cheeks silently puffing out with each breath exhaled. Her eyes flickered beneath her eyelids, a subconscious reality playing out just for her. He closed the door as quietly as he could. He wondered if he should check on Fred, outside in the shed, but decided not to. He wanted to get going.

The village of Hope lay covered in a veil of fog as Arman approached that morning after the long, winding walk down the path. He wished the fog was thicker. He wished it covered him. It wasn't quite dawn. He had hoped to make his visit back to the village brief and unnoticed. He had been tempted to come in the night, but was fearful that he would be discovered. It would seem like he was trying to sneak in and out and he didn't want any suspicion thrown on him for any reason. At least if he came early in the morning, he could argue that he was just up early. The streets were empty, just him and the still mist. The ground was soft underfoot, with morning dew wetting the grass. To his left, at the far end of the street, lived the oak tree. Just beyond, still standing though unused, was the shack they had built for Fred. The other way, the church stood quiet and empty. He headed in that direction, where Violet's house stood near the end of the street. He got to her gate, irritated when it squeaked as he opened it. He went down the path and opened her unlocked door. Inside, it was dark, with closed curtains blocking out the morning light. He opened the curtains and looked around at the tidy living room area. He remembered being here with Robert. The two of them had played cards and Arman had been thoroughly beaten. Robert had sat in the chair by the window and…he couldn't remember where he sat. It had changed since then. Everything had changed.

He pulled Violet's list from his trouser pocket, unfolding it and holding it up to the light to read properly. It was a small house, but she'd helpfully made a note of which room held which item. A few toiletries and kitchen items aside, it was mostly clothes from the bedroom. In some cases, he emptied entire drawers out (as instructed), placing all the items into a scuffed brown suitcase that was kept under one of the two single beds. He had to push down hard to close it, bringing his weight down onto the bed frame. The sudden movement caused a wooden cross, hung between the two beds, to fall to the floor. Arman bent to retrieve it. Part of the top section of the cross had snapped off. He went to hang it back on the wall regardless, but deprived of the top, it just looked like a wooden "T". He discarded both jagged sections onto the bed. He wondered which bed had belonged to Violet. What had she told him? That Robert had no interest in her, physically? Arman realised that there was so much he didn't know about his friend Robert. Had he been secretly meeting Bernard Ogden? How long had he been carrying that secret around? He wondered if Violet was a virgin, then shook his head of the idea, fearing he was going down a path that had an unsatisfying destination. Best to leave some things unsaid, unthought. He hoisted the suitcase off the bed, weighing it up in his arm. It was heavier than he'd hoped, and wouldn't be getting any lighter on the long walk back to his house. Satisfied that he'd gotten everything he came for, he hastily left the house. He made it to the gate before he heard the voice cutting through the mist.

"Are you moving in, Arman, or is somebody moving out?"

Arman stopped, his knuckle whitening as he gripped the suitcase hard. He looked up and saw Niall. With him, weaving in and out of his legs and jumping up and down, was his dog.

"Walking the dog, Niall?" Arman said.

"Otherwise he makes his mess in the house," said Niall, scruffing the black Labrador's fur behind his ears, "and we can't be having that, can we, Wags?"

"I suppose not," answered Arman for the dog.

"Moving house, are we?" asked Niall.

Arman shook his head, trying and failing to hide his rising anger. "Somebody decided that taking care of Fred Decker was my responsibility, Niall. That's why he was dumped, unceremoniously, on my doorstep. Violet Walker was the only offer of help I had and I jumped at the chance."

"People will talk, Arman."

Arman, tired of the weight, put the suitcase down by his feet. He rested his hands on his hips and looked off towards the church, as if it may give him some relief from his troubles, or maybe an answer to ward off Niall. It gave neither.

"Would you rather we killed him?" asked Niall.

"I believe you already tried that."

"And how is Mr Decker?"

"He warned us," said Arman, "that his people would be coming here."

"His people?" asked Niall. "So, he's talking now, is he? I was of the understanding that Fred Decker was knocking on the door, Arman. But now you're saying that you're all up there playing house, and he's threatening us with stories of revenge, is that right?"

"It's not like that."

"Then what's it like?"

"Whatever poisonous concoction Olive Kirby gave him, tore away at his insides. Every breath he takes is a struggle. A painful, loud, struggle. His left leg is lame, same with his left arm. His left hand is a dead weight. His vocal cords have been all but destroyed. He tries to speak, but what makes it out of his throat is mangled in his swollen tongue and lips."

"Then he shouldn't have killed Robert Walker!" shouted Niall. "Am I meant to feel sorry for this man? He gets to live, Arman. Does Robert Walker?"

"It was an accident," said Arman.

"Of course, yes, I forgot!" said Niall, his nostrils flaring as he became more animated, "A misunderstanding. A scuffle and then, inexplicably, Robert threw himself onto a broken wooden fence, was it? That stabbed him in the neck? Was that what happened, Arman?"

"It was."

"He's playing you for a fool, Arman. And now you've got the widow Walker involved in it too, living up there godlessly with two men. Do you wonder that people talk? I'm not entirely sure the village is done with this business yet."

"What does that mean?" asked Arman.

"It means, Arman, that you should tread carefully. There are some very vocal opinions that Robert Walker has not received justice while his killer walks freely, just down the path."

"And what do you think, Niall?"

Niall took in a deep breath, and puffed out a long, cold breath, then shrugged. "I wish we could go back to how we were. I just want it to be over."

"This won't last forever, Niall. Fred Decker will be gone when he is well enough. Will Violet be welcomed back? Will I?"

"As far as I'm concerned, Arman, you will always be welcome back in Hope."

"And Violet?" asked Arman.

"Yes," said Niall, though he seemed less sure. "Of course."

Arman bent and picked up the suitcase. "I need to get going?"

"Trying to avoid everyone, are you?"

"Wouldn't you? In the circumstances? We both share the same dream that this will be over, Niall. I just worry that we may have different ways of getting there."

Niall shrugged, though he seemed sympathetic. As Arman passed, Niall put his hand out to shake it. Arman put the suitcase down and shook Niall's hand.

"What happened to your hand?" asked Niall.

"Nothing that won't get better," he said. He nodded, and left, not looking back as he walked away from Hope, the fog seeming to clear a path, and cover his steps as he left.

He had to stop at several points on the path. He wished he could alternate arms, but it wasn't possible with his hand in the state it was. The one he was using was bad enough, with the rope burns and blisters still scored across his hand. He rolled his shoulder, as if that may magically massage his muscles and ease his burden. He hunkered down, lifting the weight and ploughing forward. He looked forward to a day in the future where he didn't have a pulled muscle or back pain. Finally, as he neared home, he took heavy steps up the inclined path and moved through the tree line. In a gap between the trees he could see his house, and it lifted his spirits. A few paces further along and he saw blurred activity between the house and the shed. He heard a thudding noise. He heard voices. He heard laughter. He ducked in between a row of trees, trampling fallen leaves and dirt to get a better look. On a stump outside his house, a block of wood had been crudely hacked. Violet, her dress clinging to her with sweat, the hem dirty, skirt billowing around her bare ankles with each sweeping surge of wind, her hair loosely tied to the side, stood with an axe clutched tightly in her hands. To her side, standing close, maybe too close, Fred stood, laughing, offering her advice. He leaned in, moving her hand further down the shaft of the axe. He said something to her which she didn't understand. He repeated himself and she nodded, widening her stance a little. She swung the axe over her head and brought it down crashing off-centre, splintering part of the log. She let out a squeal and laughed.

Arman moved aside some branches, getting closer with slow steps. Arman watched, surprised, as Violet held out the axe for Fred. Fred took a moment, hesitating, then took it in his right hand. He weighed it in his palm then wrapped his fingers tightly round it. Violet took a step to her side and Fred took her place in front of the log. A wind tore through the grounds, turning over a bucket by the door of the house and sending it off clattering. As Fred lifted the axe into the air, ready to strike, Violet's hair swept free of its knot and blew across Fred's vision. He dropped his shoulders, lowering the axe and looking at her in a way that made her laugh. Arman took another step closer, hoping to hear what they were saying. When he had left, they had both been asleep. He wondered what had happened in the past few hours that now made them seem so comfortable in each other's company, laughing and joking.

Fred swung the axe through the air with his one good arm, confidently striking the log in the centre and splitting it. Violet clapped enthusiastically at the achievement, though soon slowed, and stopped, looking down and away, as if suddenly aware of her own inappropriateness. Arman took a step back, then another, retreating back into the tree. He got back to the path, picking up the suitcase and continuing on towards the house.

VI

Violet and Fred were inside by the time Arman took the path round to his house. He stopped by the doorway, looking at the splintered and cut logs on the stump. The axe was laid across the top. He could hear laughing inside the house. He coughed, making noise as he opened the door and stepped into the kitchen. Fred was sat at the table and Violet, who was standing, took a step away from him when Arman entered. He grunted as he lifted the suitcase and put it on the table.

"How are you feeling?" he asked Fred.

"Mush bekker, thin ku," said Fred, sounding clearer and speaking slower.

"He said—" started Violet.

"—I got it," interrupted Arman, smiling. "Did you have a good morning?"

"We cut some wood," said Violet, "for the fire."

"That's great," said Arman.

Violet moved to Arman's side and undid the buckle on the suitcase. "Clean clothes!" she said as she swung it open, marvelling at its contents.

"And everything else on your list," he said.

She grabbed his arm, squeezing it and saying, "Thank you, Arman." She closed the suitcase again, and used both hands to drag it off the table.

"Do you'eed alp?" asked Fred.

"Thank you," she said, warmly. "I should be fine." With both hands wrapped around the handle, she took it away into the bedroom.

Arman went to the counter, pouring himself a glass of water from the jug. He sipped at it, letting it hit his dry throat. He was sweating still from the journey. He took his water to the table and sat down opposite Fred.

"You are making quite the recovery," said Arman.

Fred tried to smile, but his lip was still lop-sided, and it just contorted his face. He realised, and immediately softened the gesture, just curling his lips a little, giving an impression of a smile. "Certa'teli comper to duvva day. I'm learmin to spik slower."

"And the arm? You were cutting wood?"

Fred lifted his right arm, spreading his fingers out, making them into a fist. He then turned his head to the left. He tried to lift his left arm, and though it rose off the table, it wouldn't go any higher than that. The fingers, which had been curled inwards, slowly opened outwards. He moved the arm forward and put his shaking hand out for Arman's glass of water. He closed his fingers around it and lifted it an inch off the table. He went to lift it higher, but it slipped through his weak grip and slid back to the table.

"That's an improvement," said Arman. "You may yet make a full recovery."

"Ho'fully," slurred Fred.

"And Violet," said Arman, "how has she been?"

Fred looked at him with questioning eyes. "We 'alked earier. We cli th'air. She knowz I din ki'her hubban."

"You talked earlier? And...cleared the air?"

"Yesh."

"She knows...you didn't kill her husband?"

Fred nodded.

"And that's it?"

Fred's forehead furrowed, trying to follow Arman's train of thought. "Wha'do you min?"

"What do I mean? There's a big difference between not blaming you, and the two of you becoming great friends, isn't there?"

"I thin' she rea'ises that we are buff vi'tims."

"I...don't understand? You think...what do you think?"

They were interrupted by Violet, "She, meaning me, realises that perhaps both Fred and my husband are victims of a different kind."

"Wha'she sid," said Fred.

Arman turned to face her. She had changed, into a corseted, long-sleeve white top, with silver buttons running from waist to high on her neck, and a long teal skirt with a golden fringe. Her hair was neatly tied back, the usual wayward strands contained. She looked reinvigorated. She looked happy. Arman wanted to leave it alone, to enjoy her happiness, and Fred's recovery, but too much niggled at him and he couldn't seem to contain it. "Less than a week ago, you attempted to beat this man to death with a rock?"

"And it's a testament to him that he doesn't blame me."

"You don't hold any blame for what happened?" Arman asked her.

"Robert, like almost everyone in our village, was a deeply religious man. When we met, he told me I was living a sinful life. I won't go into the details, but he was earnest and confident and everything I needed at that time. He married me and his congregation took me in as one of their own. He didn't fulfil every duty you may expect of a husband, but he gave me a home. Food. Security. But he never let me forget my previous life. My previous sin. When he died, I mourned him. I feared for my future. I blamed Fred because I believed Bernard Ogden. But my husband was not free of sin. My husband was a sodomite, and his desperation to cover that up caused him to attack a stranger."

She rested a hand on Fred's forearm. Arman wondered how she could be so comfortable in her own skin. How confident she was with her touch. He was staring. She removed her hand and stepped away, saying, "Am I meant to blame Fred because my husband killed himself trying to protect his own sin?"

Arman shook his head. It was hard to disagree with her, but he couldn't shake the feeling that she seemed to have abandoned her empathy to Robert extremely quickly. As much as Arman felt that Fred hadn't killed Robert, there was a part of him that still held him accountable somehow. Maybe the problem, then, was with him.

"You are right, Violet," he said. "I apologise."

"It is fine, Arman," she said. She moved behind him and leaned forward, wrapping her arms around him from behind, resting her hands on his chest and pressing her head into his shoulder. He touched his hand against hers, leaning his head to touch hers, enjoying her closeness. She felt warm pressed against him. He basked in her attention but at the same time felt exploited, as if she were somehow manoeuvring him emotionally to a place he wasn't sure he wanted to go. He patted her hand, an unspoken signal. She removed her arms and stood back. He got up, finished off his water and replaced the glass back by the sink.

"I need to cut some more fire wood," he said. "Though I appreciate the two of your efforts, I don't think one log will be enough."

"You er almuss ou of'wud," said Fred.

"Something...wood?" said Arman.

"You're almost out of wood," said Violet.

"I'll finish up what we have and tomorrow, maybe the day after, I'll head out for more."

Arman left the two of them in the kitchen, happy to find some solace outside. A light drizzle threw cold arrows into his face. He picked up the axe and one of the remaining logs, resting it on the stump and swinging forcibly straight down its middle. The axe stuck deeply into the stump, and Arman needed to use his foot as leverage to pull it free. He put another log on the stump and lifted the axe above his head. He gritted his teeth and brought it thundering down, sending the two split halves of the wood in separate directions. He stopped, letting the axe rest loosely in his good hand. The bandage on his other hand was stained red. He must've opened one of the cuts without realising. He sensed movement behind him. Violet had come out of the house and had been watching him from the doorway.

"Did you hurt your hand again?" she called.

"It's nothing," he said.

She rolled her eyes, and closed the door behind herself.

"It's very muddy out here," he said, "mind your new dress."

"It's not new," she said, "It is just clean, though I didn't expect it to stay that way long around here." Her black boots, just visible from the bottom of her dress, sunk into the wet mud as she walked over to him. He turned to face her and she took his hand in hers. "We are going to have to change these more regularly," she said. "And perhaps we may consider less strenuous work."

"This from the lady that sent me to pick up her heavy suitcase! And less strenuous work is in short supply around here. My life, for long before you came here, was self-sufficient. You don't get that by sitting down all day."

"But still—" she said.

"—You're a woman, Violet, and you're being a great help, but I don't expect you to be out here cutting wood every day. And Fred is still half a man. We don't know if his left side will ever recover. We are all of us working at less than our capacity right now."

"I may be a woman," she said, "but I am capable of more than you think."

"I'm certain you are."

"And not just in the kitchen," she said. "I can care for the chickens. The sheep."

"I know," said Arman. "I'm very thankful to have you here."

"Even though you've lost your privacy? And your bed?"

"Even then," he said. He noticed that she had a distant, sad look in her eyes. A little girl lost. An innocence that seemed at odds with her usual confidence. Arman didn't know if Violet was opening herself up emotionally to him, or if it was all some kind of tightly controlled performance. He wondered, not for the first time, if she was somehow playing him, though he didn't know to what ends. Physically, he was aware that she still held his hand in hers, but he said nothing. "Where is Fred?" he asked.

"Inside. I believe he may have borrowed one of your books."

"He can read?"

She shrugged, "I did not ask."

"This can't last," said Arman. "Fred warned us that people would come. His people. He has never expanded on what that might mean, but it can't be good. We may not be safe—"

"—We are not their enemy."

"What if they don't stop to find that out? And I'm not just talking about these people that Fred spoke of. I'm talking about the congregation. About Niall. If they think Fred is recovering then maybe this idea, that he has suffered enough, will somehow ring less true. Perhaps they may desire to finish what they started. Cecil Garfield would leap at the chance to take his axe to him. Olive Kirby is due here any day now, perhaps tomorrow, with medicine. What if she reports upon his health? What if what she says is enough to rile the mob."

"The congregation is a mob now?"

"It felt that way when I was dragged out of the trial. Do not mistake these people's piety for anything other than a thin veil. Beneath it all lies a dark heart at its centre," said Arman.

"Perhaps we'd best go inside, get these bandages—"

He moved his hand from her palm and wrapped it tightly around her wrist, stopping her from leaving.

"Arman, you're hurting me—"

"—I mean it, Violet. I can feel it. There is a creeping darkness, coming from every side. I couldn't bear anything happening to you."

He didn't let go, but his hold lessened, enough for her to slip free if she wished. But she remained, her hand held in his gentle grip, his thumb softly pressed to the inside of her wrist. The axe fell from his good hand, falling to the floor at his feet. He moved his good hand to her face, tracing the back of his fingers against her soft cheek. She blushed as he touched her, but didn't stop him. Had he been judging her harshly? Did he really think she was so calculated? His fingers cupped her chin, her head tilting up so she was looking into his eyes. He could feel her warm breath on his face. She closed her eyes and he wanted to kiss her, to wrap an arm around her waist and pull her close. But he didn't. He stepped back instead.

Violet opened her eyes, "Arman, it is good, you don't have to—"

"—I didn't meant to," he said, though he had done nothing. He took another step back. Something in her expression had changed and Arman wondered if he had interpreted it correctly. The innocence had fallen, and a more predatory look had flashed across her eyes. He couldn't decipher it and it frightened him. Before she could protest, he turned and walked away, between the house and the shed, following a path around the back of the house that led to the animals. He cursed himself as he walked away, angry at himself for complicating an already complicated situation. He could almost feel the taste of her lips. He hadn't wanted to stop, to pull away, to leave so dramatically. He had wanted to kiss her. He thought of Mathilda. He hadn't thought of her since the nightmare a few days ago when he'd hurt his hand. He wondered what she'd make of the whole situation. What would she think of the trial? Of Fred Decker? Of Violet? He wondered if she might forgive him for everything he'd done. For everything he might do. It had been over a year since her death. He closed his eyes, to better conjure her face, but all he saw was Violet. Nowadays, all he ever saw was Violet.

VII

Arman stayed out until it was nearly dark, walking past his house, past the animals, across his land and beyond. The sweat he had built up from cutting the wood had turned cold against his skin. He tucked his hands under his arms to try and heat them up. He strode onwards regardless, as if some warm, secret place lay just over the next rise. He didn't see another person, or reach a destination; he just walked until he didn't. He stopped halfway across an open field. His shoulders slumped and Arman listened to his own breathing as the cold air swirled around him. He looked up at a starless black sky, feeling emptiness all around him. He didn't know how long he'd been gone. He wanted to lie down, close his eyes and forget about everything waiting for him back at the house, and back in Hope. He wondered what it might be like just to keep walking and never look back. He could find a new community someplace else, somewhere where nobody knew him. Perhaps after time, they may accept him as one of their own. He could take a new wife, start a new job and leave the mistakes and troubles of Hope behind him. He told himself he would do these things, one day, one day not too long from now. In truth, his thoughts of a new life never stretched beyond his dreams of Violet now. At some point, and he had been unaware of when, she had snuck into his soul and burrowed down. He thought of her at all times and at all times he felt a sadness wash through him because he felt her affections torn between himself and Fred Decker. Perhaps, once Fred had recovered, he may move on, heading back to his old life with the friends and family he must have had before this madness took hold. His fleeting temptation to keep walking waned. He would be leaving too much behind. Perhaps there may be a point in his future where that might be a possibility, but for now it would remain a dream.

He was shaken from his daydreams by a sound in the distance. Ahead of him, no more than sixty feet or so, a large, dark shire horse pulled a small carriage and a wagon behind. On the carriage sat an already tall man in a high top hat, giving him the silhouette of a giant. The man turned to look in Arman's direction and at the same time, pulled gently back on the reins of the horse and brought it to a stop. Arman considered turning back and going the way he came, but then the man called out to him.

"You! Pal!"

Arman hesitated. Turning and leaving may bring the man and whoever, if anyone, was in the wagon after him. Perhaps he could diffuse anything before it began. Perhaps, he had nothing to fear anyway. He took a slow walk to the wagon, stopping about ten feet from the man perched on the carriage. Up close, he could see the man more clearly. He had long charcoal grey trousers that flapped over whatever footwear he had hidden underneath. His shirt was pin striped, red and white, with a white neckerchief tied under the upturned collar. His face had patches of hair that didn't quite form a beard. His eyes were dark. He briefly tipped his top hat as a greeting, revealing a thick mane of dense black hair coiled beneath it. His wide smile presented a sporadic selection of teeth in various stages of decay. The smile remained, though the eyes seemed to survey Arman questioningly.

"You don't fear me, pal," the man said in a drawl that prolonged each of the vowels.

Arman tried, and failed, to place the accent. He guessed the man was from overseas, but couldn't be sure. He replied with, "Can I help you?"

"Stow yourself, pal," said the man, waving his hand in a gesture that Arman couldn't interpret. "Where's this all then, pal?" As if to emphasise his point, the man turned left and right, making a pantomime of searching his surroundings.

"Where are you heading?" asked Arman.

The man scratched at a patch of beard under his ear, seemingly considering the question, "Ah, where's he heading? Where's he heading? Something to eat. Something to sleep, pal, could you?"

Arman couldn't quite put together the broken English. Everything about the situation seemed wrong to him. Beneath the man was the carriage, which had a curtain drawn across the window. Arman could swear he saw it move aside a little. He asked, "How many of you are there?"

The man looked puzzled, glancing back towards the wagon at the rear. "How many? No more for you, pal. Sorry. Sorry. Can't help. Just me today. Just me, pal."

"You're travelling alone?"

"Just me. Where a town? Back your way?" The man leaned to his side, looking over Arman's shoulder, as if a town or village might miraculously form there. He seemed disappointed when it did not.

Arman looked back over his shoulder, more to buy himself some time than to actually look for anything. He thought back to Fred Decker, threatening that his people would come for him. But surely this was unrelated? This man was foreign and had made no mention of looking for anyone. Still, Arman was wary. He pointed to back where the man had travelled from and said, "Way, way back that way, the coast. The sea." He turned, pointing in the direction the man was facing and said, "That way, keep going and you'll come upon London if you go far enough."

The man stared at Arman. He stuck his tongue out and stretched his mouth open as he seemed to consider his words. He looked back over his shoulder and said, "Coast?" He then looked ahead and said, "London?"

Arman nodded and as he did, he again caught a flicker of the curtain in the carriage. He looked at it, waiting for it to happen again. Waiting for someone to show themselves.

The man clicked his fingers repeatedly until Arman looked up at him. "The horsey can't swim. The carriage and the wagon are grounded. I have no use for coast. And London? London, pal? All the way that way? All the way? Long way, yes? What about...back there?" he nodded over Arman's shoulder.

"Nothing," said Arman. He crossed his arms against the cold, shivering in the evening air. If they were here for Fred Decker then they would be prepared for violence. There could be a couple in the carriage. Maybe more in the wagon. If they'd just ask about Decker then he could lie.

"Nothing? Nothing back there? Where you came from?" The man swung his legs round, sitting on the side of his bench atop the carriage. He looked like he could jump down at any moment. He shook his head, laughing to himself and repeating, "Nothing."

"No."

"I'm no trouble, pal. Just want to eat. To sleep. What's back there ways?"

The shire horse whinnied, stamping two front feet down onto the ground. Arman jumped at the sudden movement. He took a step back. He was wondering how much distance he could travel before the horse drawn carriage caught up with him. Or if there were men in the carriage or wagon, how far could he get before they chased him down. Could he make it all the way back to his house? He knew he couldn't. He also knew he couldn't direct them to the village without running the risk that they'd come upon his house first. He would never have time to warn Violet. He decided to address the issue head on. "Are you looking for someone?"

"Looking, pal? I think I found someone but he won't help me."

"Have you lost someone?" he said, rephrasing his question. "A man? Are you here for a man?"

The man had a look of pantomime bewilderment on his face as he stared down at Arman. "I think, pal," he said, "that we aren't...whasstheword? *Communicating*? I've not got your man."

"You're just passing through?" Arman began to relax. The man seemed genuinely not to know what he was talking about. Maybe he wasn't here for Decker. Maybe he wasn't here to kill them all. His thoughts started to clear. He pointed past the carriage, away from his home in the opposite direction. "That way, not far, there's a village. I couldn't say for sure, but they may be able to offer you somewhere to camp."

The man briefly turned over his shoulder to look in that direction, then turned back to Arman. "That way, huh?"

As Arman said, "Yes," he saw a fleeting glance of eyes, peeking from around the curtain in the carriage. "How many of you are there?" he asked again.

"Just me, pal, remember?"

"Just you."

"Right. Say, pal, could you borrow a man a coin?"

"Apologies," said Arman, "I don't have any money on me."

"Sixpence, perhaps?"

"Sorry, I Don't—"

"—Thruppence? Perhaps?" The man smiled, but behind the smile was a stern face, threatening. He was perched on the edge of the seat. One good jump and he'd be at Arman's feet.

The curtain moved. Just an inch. Someone was lurking in the shadows of the carriage.

"I can't help you," said Arman, "I must go. I must..." He turned, calmly, walking back the way he had come. He looked over his shoulder, to nod a farewell to the stranger. Even as he felt threatened, he still stuck to social niceties.

The man mumbled some kind of farewell, but then laughed, from his belly up, roaring at something only he found funny. Arman quickened his pace, almost tripping over his own legs as he walked briskly away. He imagined the carriage door springing open and a man lurching out and coming after him. He pictured the blur of this man, garbed in black with a top hat that tipped off as he charged clear of the carriage. He looked back over his shoulder, and when the man and his carriage were no longer visible, Arman broke into a run. He didn't even know why, but he ran and he ran, the tiredness draining from his legs as he found a new burst of energy. Even as he began to put some distance between himself and the carriage, he could still hear the man's terrible laugh, deep and booming, echoing across the open land. Arman didn't dare look back over his shoulder for fear of slowing. Night was falling and darkness would give him the peace of mind he needed to feel safe. But his legs were becoming weak. His heart was thumping and his stomach churning. His thighs filling with lead, he still ran. His chest on fire, he still ran. Eventually he came faltering to a stop, losing his footing and rolling onto the soft grass beneath him. The night air stung his eyes. He lay on the floor gasping for air. He looked back but there was nobody behind him. He waited, as if a figure may emerge from the distance, coming out of the darkness to rob him. But nobody came. He waited, for a shire horse to bring a carriage containing his attackers. But none came. He wheezed and gasped for air, cursing his own cowardice. He stayed down, waiting to get his breath back. He didn't know what had spooked him. He asked himself if he had over-reacted. Or had he escaped from muggers? Had he shown Fred Decker's family the way to his home? He waited a further half hour, sprawled on the ground, shivering in the cold, waiting for the worst. Finally, when nobody came, he headed home.

VIII

Approaching the house, Arman saw a dim orange light glowing in the kitchen window. He got to the front door and wiped his muddy boots on a rock. He unlaced and removed his boots on the doorstep, then opened the front door and walked through to the kitchen, stopping in the open doorway when he saw that Violet was still up. She was stood at the kitchen sink, a bowl of water in front of her. She wore a sleeveless cotton chemise, revealing her slender arms. She had long wet hair, combed back, soaking the shoulders and back of the chemise. It clung to her skin and the flesh on her back could be seen through the thin material. She dabbed the cloth to her exposed neck and around to her collarbone, wringing the excess water off back into the bowl. She seemed lost in a world of her own, staring blankly out of the window as she washed herself. Arman looked back over his shoulder, considering a silent retreat. She didn't seem to have noticed him yet. They would both be surely embarrassed were she to notice his presence. But he couldn't look away. The candlelight gave Violet's skin a fiery glow. Arman's heart quickened and his mind clumsily raced through a multitude of variations of what may happen next. He wanted to touch her. To hold her. To go to her now. To kiss her. Arman shifted his weight, causing the floor beneath him to creak. Violet spun round, clutching the dripping cloth to her chest, as if it may cover her. She stared at Arman, not moving.

"I'm sorry," he said, but she didn't respond. "I can go..."

She shook her head; No.

He briefly turned to his side, seeing through to the parlour where Fred slept in the armchair. Arman picked up a half-full glass of water from the table and took a sip, his hand shaking as he did. "How has he been? Any mention of his people?"

Again, she shook her head. When she did speak, it was softly, "He has not spoken of it. I do not think he recalls saying it."

"Should we...press him?"

"He makes small errors. Repeats himself. Forgets small things as he is doing them. Earlier, I came upon him staring into the hot coffee I had made for him. He was lost in himself."

"What does it mean?" asked Arman.

"It may mean nothing. It may be everything. I would like to think that he was lost in the details."

"Is that a good thing?"

Violet smiled, "Always. There is a universe in the details, Arman."

Arman looked down into his glass, swirling the water, hoping to see the universe, but all he saw was water. He looked back up at Violet. "Do you imagine yourself returning to the village?"

"I hope so."

"One day, ask them about their lives before they came here. Let them speak of their sins. Of their mistakes. Let them tell you the reasons why they felt a need to start a whole new village."

Oh," said Violet, beginning to smile, "that sounds like a terrible idea. They'd be so mad." She giggled, trying to contain it, before breaking out into a loud, infectious laugh. Arman joined her, trying to agree with her statement but unable to get the words out. At one point, she indicated Fred sleeping in the parlour and tried to "shhh" them both, but she just burst out laughing over her own words. When it eventually faded, they were both left with wide smiles.

Arman looked away from her, back down into the last of his water. He took a final sip, finishing it. He took the glass to the sink, standing next to Violet as he placed the glass on the counter. He faced her, holding her stare.

"It is a wicked thing to be wanted," she said.

He turned, scooping his hand into the bowl of water and bringing it to his face, rubbing at his eyes. He was still wiping his face when Violet took a step closer, reached out and began to undo the buttons on his shirt. Arman slid his hand around her waist. He moved his hand to the small of her back and he drew her near. She finished undoing his shirt, pulling it open and stepping into him, pressing herself against him. He brought his bad hand to her face, threading his fingers into her hair and pulling her to him. He leaned down and kissed her neck. She tilted her head back, just a little, to expose the flesh. Her skin was still moist, though soft and wonderfully warm to the touch. He kissed her cheek, pulling back so slightly to rest his own cheek against hers. She moved her face around to find his lips and he kissed her. She responded to him, her lips parting, her tongue on his. He pulled the hand around her waist back and moved it to her stomach, tracing a line along the thin fabric to the underside of her breast, which he wrapped his palm around, squeezing gently as he kissed her. She undid the two buttons on the waist of his trousers and tugged them down. She took a half step back, coming down to her knees as she lowered his trousers. As they came to his ankles, he stepped out of them. As she stood, she took Arman's hand and guided it, pulling up the material on her flowing chemise and bringing his hand between her thighs. Arman used his free hand to pull his shirt off. He kissed Violet, his free hand at the back of her neck, keeping her close. It was the creaking floorboard that stopped them in their tracks.

They pressed together, Arman shielding her with his naked body. Fred stood in the doorway, his mouth open, but saying nothing. Arman didn't want him here. For the first time, he wished Cecil Garfield had brought the axe down upon this intruder's neck. He wanted Violet for himself. But he knew Violet felt differently. He knew what this ungodly bargain entailed. Arman felt caught, and remained speechless, unsure of what to do next. Violet stretched out her arm towards Fred. Arman turned his head to face her, and she held his stare, but she kept her arm outstretched to Fred the whole time. She leaned forward and kissed Arman and for a second he forgot about the third person in the room. But Fred responded to Violet's arm. He unbuttoned his own shirt and removed it, discarding it on the floor as he shuffled slowly over, his lame left leg dragging behind him. He came behind Violet, bringing his nakedness to her back, where he lifted up the front of the chemise, reaching round and taking her breasts in his hands while she kissed Arman. Arman pulled away for a moment, unsure what to do next. Violet took the bottom of her chemise in her hands and lifted it over her head and let it fall to the floor. Her hand reached behind her and found Fred, sweeping down his stomach, to his open trousers, between his legs, grabbing at him as he hardened and stroking him in her firm grip.

Arman looked at her and she could see his indecision, his fear. She turned her head back to Fred, though she leaned her head back over her shoulder to kiss him. Then she turned back to Arman, finding his lips, his tongue. They pressed tightly against her, one in front, one behind. She moved between the two men, kissing them in turn while her hands simultaneously worked each man. She took a step away, and moved to the table. Both men watched her silently, letting her go, enjoying her nakedness. She turned back to them and sat on the edge of the table, spreading her thighs and waiting. Arman moved first, approaching her, sliding his hands under her buttocks and finding the right position. He wanted to stop. He cursed his own willpower, painfully aware of his own weakness. He would pay for this, in the coming days. In the coming weeks. For the rest of his life. He slid into her easily and she exhaled loudly. She smiled, though it faded quickly, and her face became serious, focused. He found a steady rhythm, working between her legs. Fred was soon at Violet's side, running his hand along her stomach, her chest, up over her neck. His fingers moved around her throat, his thumb at her chin, tilting her head back a little. He stood over her, leaning down and kissing her hard. She grabbed at his long hair, briefly bringing him closer before breaking the kiss. Her lips parted and she took several short, shallow breaths in. Her back arched enough to lift slightly off the table as she pushed her hips back against Arman. Arman increased his movements, going faster and harder until eventually he stopped, grabbing at her thighs as he expelled himself inside her. He remained there, soft, satisfied. Violet's breathing, which had been growing in intensity, slowed and steadied. Arman thought he saw disappointment in her eyes. She seemed to sense his uncertainty so she reached out and stroked his face. Arman silently removed himself and stepped to the side. Fred switched places with him between Violet's legs. His hands clawed at her buttocks, and he clumsily shifted her position on the table. Violet propped herself up on an elbow and reached forward to help bring Fred inside her. He slowly began to find his own rhythm. Violet looked at Arman at her side and put out her hand. Arman took it in his own, and they held hands as Fred grunted and thrust himself inside her, again and again and again. Violet used her free hand to grab at Fred, finding his hip and clawing at it, trying to control his movements. She shifted her body weight, finding a better position for herself. Her grip tightened on Arman's hand and he squeezed back harder. He looked into her eyes but couldn't find any recognition. She seemed to be staring through him, to a world beyond. She looked feral. Arman was sure that in that moment, Violet would happily have taken a third lover. A fourth. Fifth. Violet's mouth was open and she seemed to be sucking in snatched breaths, moaning quietly at first, before becoming louder and filling the room. Fred, by contrast, was virtually silent. He was unsteady on his feet, his weakened left side causing him to lilt. Arman looked down at Violet. Was this revenge for her husband's infidelity? His *sin*, as Violet had called it?

Arman could see the effort it was taking Fred to co-ordinate his movements. Fred's brow furrowed, as if his tightened facial expressions could somehow keep him from falling. Arman tried to let go of Violet's hand but she felt him pulling away and she gripped harder. The fingers on Fred's right hand dug into the underside of Violet's thighs as he struggled to maintain his movements. Without missing a beat, Violet ground her hips back against Fred, moving them in a circular motion and bringing Fred to a place he was unable to reach himself. As with Arman before him, he held it for a moment, not wanting the moment to end. Violet lay back on the table, breathing heavily, and holding the hand of each of her lovers. A sheen of sweat clung to her skin, making her glisten and shine. Neither man looked at the other. Arman felt like Adam in the Garden of Eden, aware of his own nakedness and fearful of what might happen now that any pretence of innocence had been lost. He had taken a bite of the apple. Violet got her breath back and shuffled forward, off of the table and onto her feet. She looked at each man, unable to draw their averted eyes. They were hers now. Still with both men's hand in her own, she led them willingly away from the kitchen and towards the bedroom.

IX

When Arman woke, it was from a dream he had been having about Mathilda. In his dream, she was pregnant and they were planning a lavish christening in the village church. Now awake, he had a moment somewhere between sleep and awake where his realities blurred and he didn't know which was which. When his reality came flooding back, it brought with it a heavy heart. He was on his back. Violet's naked body pressed against him, on her side, her hand across his chest, her breasts pressed to his arm, her leg crossed over his, bent at the knee. She was warm and soft. Arman took her hand in his. She stirred but didn't wake. Her hair lay tussled and spread across the pillow. Behind her, Fred slept with his back to them, but his hand resting back against Violet's bare leg. Arman untangled himself from her embrace, placing her arm across his pillow where his head had just been, and extracting himself from her exuberant leg. He slid out of the bed, immediately feeling the frigid air upon his skin. He scratched at his chin, the first signs of stubble poking through. He looked at Violet and Fred and wondered if he had done the right thing or not. He had craved Violet, but having to share her with another was against everything he'd ever believed in. But everything had seemed so natural the night before.

He dressed in silence, adding layers as he knew he would be heading out into the woods. He foraged for his boots for the longest time before he remembered he'd left them by the front door. Before he left, he knelt by the side of the bed, watching Violet sleep, resisting the temptation to kiss her. He didn't want to disturb her. He snuck out the bedroom, then the house, stopping only to put on his boots and grab his axe. He swung by the shed to retrieve the cart. It would come in handy if he was going to be bringing wood back to the house. The sun was up.

He'd set off later than he'd hoped. His late-night activities had left him tired and groggy.

He retraced steps he'd made the evening before, only this time he branched off towards the tree line to the east. He was wary of coming across a camp site featuring potential hostiles. He took a well-trodden path, found a familiar spot, then settled in to work. He didn't notice the time going by. He worked diligently, cutting fallen trees and thick branches into manageable chunks then loading them up on the cart. He was working with his one good hand and everything was taking twice as long. He was in no rush to get back. He couldn't conceive of a world where he could step back into a room with Violet and Fred, knowing what they'd all done. What would he say? Would he act like nothing happened? The sun was high and he'd worked up a thick sweat by the time the cart was nearly full. He wasn't sure how long he'd been out there, but he was thirsty and he was hungry. His shoulders were tight and his neck felt stiff and sore. He knew he would have to return home. Dragging the cart as best he could, the wheels digging into the soft earth, he made his way to the path. As he cleared the edge of the woods and headed onto the opening field ahead of him, he saw someone up ahead. He slowly brought the cart down, letting it rest on the ground, and he waited.

The approaching figure covered the distance quickly, taking long, energetic strides. Arman soon recognised it to be Cecil Garfield, and in his hands he clutched an axe. Cecil waved, a friendly gesture that immediately threw Arman, who raised a hand in response, though quickly lowered it again. Cecil stopped just a few feet away, a smile spread across his large face, revealing uneven teeth. He arched his back, stretching, and let out a big sigh.

"What brings you out this way, Mr Garfield?" asked Arman.

Cecil nodded towards the woods, "Heading into the woods."

"There are closer woods," said Arman. "You've come quite out of your way."

Cecil, the inane grin never leaving his face, said, "I probably owe you an apology."

"You do?"

"You know I do. I acted badly. Let myself be led by anger. I hope there's no hard feelings."

Arman looked briefly to the sky, his mind replaying events; Cecil tackling him when he had tried to stop Violet attacking Fred. Cecil heaving him out of the church and flinging him to the floor. He spoke of "hard feelings" like they were detached from his actions. But then, Cecil made for an unpleasant enemy. Perhaps forgiveness offered a brighter future, should Arman ever plan on returning to Hope one day. "Emotions were running high," he said.

Cecil held out his free hand, holding it in the air, an offering.

Arman hesitated, but just for a moment, before taking the hand. Cecil's handshake was strong and confident. When he was released from the grip, he could feel the warm imprint of Cecil's fingers along the edge of his hand still.

"They gave you a thankless task," said Cecil.

Arman nodded, unsure how to respond.

"I hope you know, that when I dropped off Decker at your house, it wasn't my decision. I just pulled the short straw and had to wheel him there. You understand?"

"Of course," said Arman.

"At least you had Mrs Walker to help."

"I couldn't have done it without her."

"And Olive Kirby," said Cecil, "she came by a few times."

"Of course, yes."

"She – Mrs Kirby – came by your house earlier today actually, to drop off some more medicine. She feels so bad about what happened."

"I must've missed her," said Arman.

"Nobody answered. She got worried and looked through the window. Everyone was still sleeping. Except you. You must have left already."

Arman stayed calm, ignoring his increasing heartbeat, and tried to work out how much Cecil knew about what had happened. Had Olive really gone by? Had she seen Violet and Fred together through the bedroom window? Arman just nodded, desperate to appear calm. "Most probably," he said. Arman became aware of the axe that Cecil held loosely in his hand. In truth, if Cecil Garfield decided to attack Arman, then he wouldn't need an axe. Cecil towered over Arman. He had thick arms and hands as big as loaves of bread. He was intimidating even without the veiled threats of violence. Arman felt the growing silence push down on his shoulders and he stuttered to fill the void. "You never said why you were coming into the woods."

"Didn't I?" replied Cecil in mock confusion. When Arman shrugged, Cecil continued, "I'm just going to cut some wood."

"You said...that earlier, but I said there were woods closer to your home."

Cecil let out a small laugh, "I don't remember you saying about the woods closer to me. What did I say when you asked me?"

"It was just now," Arman felt a rising tension in his voice, his breathing becoming shallower, "and you never answered."

"Can I ask you something, Arman?"

"Yes."

"Do you think he did it?"

"Fred Decker?"

"Yes," said Cecil, "Fred Decker. I said before, how things had become heated, and perhaps I had let the emotion of the day sweep me up, and I apologise for that. But before you left that courtroom—"

"—I didn't leave, I was thrown out—"

"—you seemed pretty inflamed yourself. Am I right?"

"I just..." began Arman, unsure how to continue. "Nobody was listening to me."

"You were shouting and hollering and getting worked up because you didn't think people were listening to you? But somehow I'm in the wrong because I got riled up too?"

"No, I..." Arman's head dropped, his eyes resting on his shoes. "No."

Cecil rested a strong hand on Arman's shoulder and kept it there when he said, "I'll chop wood in whatever woods I want. Do you understand?"

Arman nodded.

Cecil removed his hand. He walked around Arman and headed into the woods. He stopped just before entering and turned back to Arman, who still hadn't moved. "A murderer. And a whore," he shouted back, shaking his head. With that, he hoisted his axe onto his shoulder and headed into the woods.

Arman stayed still for a moment, his mind racing, trying to decipher Cecil's words and actions. His hand grabbed at the handle to his full cart and wrapped tightly around it. But still, he didn't move. For the briefest of moments, he considered grabbing at the axe he had resting on the wood in the cart and going after Cecil. But he would fight, and he would lose. Most probably, Cecil would kill him. The handle of the cart slipped from Arman's hand and dropped to the ground. Arman moved away from it, heading back towards his home. He walked, but soon his pace quickened until he was running, running for his home, running as fast as he could. His chest heaved. His breathing was heavy and painful. His feet pounded the sodden earth as he headed across the open fields. Finally, his home came into view. His legs wobbled and he feared he may fall and be unable to get up again. Though his lungs burned, and fear pounded in his chest, his heart, his head, he shouted out, "Violet??" He finally slowed. He took heavy steps along the side of his house, having to press his hands along the wall to remain upright. He reached the front of the house and saw the door was ajar. He barrelled inside, shouting, "Violet? Violet?!"

He went from room to room, searching for Violet. The house was a mess. In the kitchen, the table was overturned and one of the chairs lay on its side. There had been a fight in here. Violet was not there.

He moved through to the bedroom, staring out the window, trying to think. The bedroom, like the rest of the house, was still and quiet. The bedsheets were strewn across the floor. Arman got his breathing under control, trying to calm himself and think rationally. Had Olive looked through this window and seen Violet and Fred together? Had she seen Arman too, or did she come later? He didn't know and he willed himself not to speculate. He reached down and gathered the sheets together. He made a futile attempt to make the bed, but gave up and tossed the sheets aside. He left the room and moved into the hallway, where the front door was open. For the first time, he noticed what looked like blood streaks across the lower half of the door. Just outside the front door were two, evenly spaced, indents in the wet mud. Not boots. He guessed knees. Somebody had knelt here, or been knelt here. That would explain the blood on the door. Had they beaten Fred here? Surely, not Violet? What had they done with them? He knew he couldn't stay here. Even if they didn't come back today, they would tomorrow, or the day after. He would never be safe in his home again.

Arman felt light headed. He rested a hand against the doorframe for balance. He closed his eyes, lifted his head and let the cold wind hit his face. His lips were cracked and dry. He was thirsty. He found a clarity in the darkness, as if the world may have reset itself while he had his eyes closed, and he would open them to a brighter day, without the events of recent times accumulated against him. But when he opened his eyes, the world came into sharp focus, and it was then that he looked over to the tree stump where he cut his logs. His mouth fell open. He walked to it, slowly, the only thing heavier than his feet was the leaden knot in his stomach. Fred Decker was knelt at the tree stump, his arms limply at his side, protruding from a shirt that was too small for him. His neck rested on the bloodied tree stump. His head was gone.

X

Arman had a choice to make. He hadn't noticed Fred Decker's body when he had first come home, and now he feared that if he explored the surrounding area, he may find Violet nearby. He was sure they wouldn't have killed her. Would they? Violet was one of the congregation. She was one of them. They would punish her. Maybe banish her. But they wouldn't kill her. He was sure of it. Positive, in fact. But he had to know. He had the outline of a plan, so tenuous, so lacking in detail, that he could hardly call it a plan at all. He would sneak down into the village, using a path other than the winding one he usually did. He would keep a lookout, in case they were closer than he thought. He would find a way to Hope and he would make sure she was okay. And then he would decide what he would do. But first, he had to find her.

Fleetingly, he had thought back to the previous evening and his run-in with the man on the carriage. Could he have done this? Were the wagon and the carriage with the restless curtains full of criminals? It seemed unlikely, but the thought lingered. Beggars and thieves and criminals roamed these lands looking for opportunities. Maybe they came upon the house and found a woman and a cripple and decided to take what they wanted. Had they killed Fred Decker and taken Violet? Arman shook his head of it. It was absurd. The man on the carriage had made him feel uneasy, but nothing more than that. There was nothing to tie him to this murder or Violet's disappearance. Fred Decker had had his head cut off by an axe and shortly after, Cecil Garfield had presented himself to Arman swinging that very weapon as he passed him on his way to the woods. The facts were clear. He knew who had done this and he needed to act.

Running alongside the main, twisting path down to the village of Hope, was a second, barely visible trail that led down.

Arman moved quickly, pushing aside brambles and wild grass, thorns and nettles, as he made his way methodically down through the dense thicket. The overgrown path found ways to scratch at his skin, swiping at his bare hands and his face and neck. He grimaced, teeth clenched, continuing on even as the path tried to stop him. Just over halfway down, he reached a wall of nature's chaos, with twirling thick branches of thorns covering the entire path. There seemed to be no way around. To his left was a bank too steep to climb, and to his right, a drop of around fifteen feet, into similar looking terrain. He considered going back; retracing his steps to find a way back onto the main path, just to get past the obstacle. He knew that time wasn't on his side. There were only so many places for him to hide. If they were looking for him, they would surely scour the paths between his home and Hope. He looked over the side of the path, contemplating what a jump down might be like. It wasn't an option. He would have to go straight ahead.

He tucked his trousers into his boots and tried to pull his hands back inside his sleeves. His bandaged hand snagged on the wool and somehow managed to get stuck. He had to bring it to his mouth to bite his way through the thread to tuck it inside. He looked around for a thick stick, something to pry apart the thorny wilds. He found nothing. He went forward, bringing his foot down hard into the branches, hoping to clear a path with might alone. The branches fought back, attaching themselves to his trousers, with thorns stabbing him through the material. His lips pursed together, he brought down his second foot, with the same result. Freeing his feet proved no simpler. It was like walking through thick needles. He pushed on, seeing a bend in the path and hoping it was clearer ahead. He was dragging some of the branches with him as he walked, the thorns deeply embedded in his legs, as far as his thighs. Near the bend, as he lifted his leg to plough forward, he became stuck. He had nothing to grab to give himself any leverage. He shifted the weight on the other leg, twisting his boot to give him a slightly wider stance, enabling him a greater balance as he tried to remove his stuck leg. When it pulled free, scraping dense sharp thorns as it did, his foot came free of his boot. He didn't have enough balance to hold on one leg, so as his bare foot pulled free, it slammed almost immediately back down into the thorns again. Arman couldn't help but cry out, though both his hands flew to his mouth to suppress his scream. Tears filled his eyes and his teeth ground together, hard. He still had a few yards to go, depending on what was waiting for him round the bend. If the thorns continued, he didn't think he could make it. He brought his boot down painfully, and before he could stop to think about it, he swung his bare foot ahead and slammed that down into the deep branches ahead of him. He could feel his skin tear, with sharp needles of wood and thorns embedding deeply into his feet, inside his toes, his heel and calves. He made the final two steps in equal pain and finally reached the bend, where the grassy wall at his side turned to hard rocks. He tucked his fingers as best he could into the rocks to pull himself clear of the branches. His legs and foot stung like fire but he somehow pulled free. The path, as it twisted round and down, was overgrown and muddy, but it seemed luxurious compared to the previous section. He fell to the floor, lying on his back, his hands pressed into the grass, trying to control his breathing, trying to ease the pain. He looked down at his bare foot and saw it was covered entirely in thick globules of red and black blood.

Each step onwards would be a horror story. He tried to relieve the pain as best he could by picking at the thorns he could remove. Some were too deep to get at, while others, though deep, had thick wide bases that he tried to wrap his fingernails round. He pulled a few free with relative ease, though each was followed by a new wave of blood as the open wounds bled heavily. Some had embedded under his big toe nail, and though he tried to pry at them, they wouldn't come free. He spent several minutes prying them loose and he built up a small pile next to his leg. He imagined eventually getting to his feet and accidentally standing in the pile. The thought made him laugh, albeit briefly. He managed to make it back onto his feet, though it was obvious that walking on the bad foot was going to be near impossible. Near, but not completely. He limped heavily forward, trying not to let the downward momentum of the path make him lose his balance. One slip and he'd be running head first down there into God knew what. Each time his foot came down, it felt like knives were stabbing everything below the calf. At least it took his mind off the scratches and cuts that peppered the rest of his legs. He went slowly, walking on the side of his bad foot and suffering each step on his way towards the village. Finally, on the outskirts, he took a wide, painful path through the undergrowth that led him round the back of the church. He limped into the rubbish storage area. It was lined on three sides by high wooden fences with an open wooden doorway leading in. Tucked into a hidden area behind the open entrance door, if anybody came by to drop off some more rubbish, he felt confident he wouldn't be seen. He took off his remaining boot and stretched his legs out in front of him. He panicked, hoping he hadn't left too obvious a bloody trail to where he hid. There wasn't much he could do about it now, so he just hoped that nobody noticed.

By the time it was dark, Arman had picked away at as many thorns as he could, pulling some cleanly out and leaving others half snapped off or still stuck into his foot. His hands were covered in blood, which he wiped across his shirt. He wanted to wait a while longer, until most people were in bed. As the evening wore on, a coldness consumed him, soon followed by rain which came down in a thick, penetrative downpour. He shielded himself as best he could with some pieces of long, flat, broken wooden sheets. When he felt the time was right, he moved to get to his feet. He hadn't counted on how stiff he had become, and moving his legs became a leaden chore. His thighs burned and he had to rub at his calves to get some feeling back into them. He decided to keep his one shoe off. He came out of the rubbish store, staying close to the church wall as he moved around the side. He stopped by the corner, crouching down and looking out across the empty village. Violet's house was close, just fifty yards across the front of the church. In better times, he would've sprinted the distance, but for now he'd have to limp slowly across and just hope that nobody noticed him. He waited, watching, looking for any sign of trouble. When he saw none, he made his move, coming out into the open and making his way across the front of the church. He'd barely made it ten yards before he sensed movement. He looked out and got a fleeting look at somebody moving near Violet's house. Arman looked back, judging which path was the safest to avoid being seen. His closest option was the church, and he stumbled towards it. He listened for two seconds at the door, but when he didn't hear anybody in there, he opened one of the doors and went in. His fingers slipped as he tried to close the door quietly, and it pulled away from his grasp and slammed shut noisily. He froze, his mind racing, trying to work out if he'd been seen. He would hide for now, and rethink his options. He pressed himself against the double doors, and through the small gap in the centre, he could make out the dark figure of someone approaching. He turned on his heel, moving down the aisle, his eyes scanning for hiding places. At the altar, he dove down, lying down and wedging himself in the small gap beneath the pew on the front row.

Arman tried to keep his breathing slow and quiet. His cheek was pressed to the floor. The underside of the pew grazed his ear. He heard one of the church doors open. He heard footsteps, moving across the floor, heading up the aisle. Arman waited, holding his breath as the person's dark shoes came into his vision, stopping near the altar. They seemed to stop there for an age before eventually moving away. He heard the groan of wood as whoever it was sat down somewhere out of his vision. Arman considered sliding out of his hiding place and making a break for the door, but he knew he couldn't be fast enough. As it was, he worried about any blood trail he may have left behind. His only friend was the darkness and the hope that it covered his tracks. With the church door open, a thin sliver of moonlight cut through the blackness and softly illuminated a small section of the altar.

Arman heard what sounded like someone moaning or crying. If he could've pressed himself further back against the underside of the pew he would've. Then the unmistakable sound of the door opening once more, followed by footsteps and a creak of the wood told Arman that somebody else had come in and sat down. Wasn't it too late for a church service?

"What did we do?" The voice, which Arman recognised as belonging to Niall, wavered as he spoke.

"What we had to," said the second, unknown, person.

"Do you believe her?" asked Niall.

"Violet Walker? No. Not at all. But…"

"But?"

"Decker had a trial and the verdict was death and death was what he got. It was not pleasant. Truthfully, it's the most horrible thing I've ever seen in my life. I don't think—"

Arman recognised the second voice as Cecil Garfield, but he was mumbling and Arman couldn't make out the end of his sentence. Towards the end, he recognised him say, "—need you to be strong."

Arman heard Niall sniff loudly, clearing his nose and composing himself. There was a pause and Arman panicked in case they had heard him, but then, Niall spoke.

"We can't let this infect our congregation. People will forget Decker. They won't forget if we turn on their neighbour. A widow at that. And after what she told us…"

"We could make an example?" said Cecil.

"We forgive Violet. We forgive ourselves."

"But we must—"

"—We heal," interrupted Niall, "we forgive. We have to."

"But—"

"—Enough! We heal. We must heal. We must heal."

As he spoke, the door opened and closed and Arman felt that Cecil had left. He waited, listening for something else, but all he heard was Niall, softly muttering to himself. The minutes stretched on and eventually Arman heard Niall rise and his footsteps head away. It sounded like he had left, but the door remained open. There was still the slim corridor of light running down the aisle. Arman waited. He had visions of climbing out from under the pew and finding Niall, or Cecil, just waiting by the door.

The floor was cold and his cheek was becoming numb. The base of the altar was sideways in his vision. A skirting board, which didn't quite touch the ground, was nailed across the bottom of the altar and spread off around the base of the stairs that led up to the podium. Arman feared rodents, scurrying from under the skirting. He looked into its darkness, half expecting to see small rodent eyes staring back out at him. What he didn't expect to see was a faint glint of light. He squinted, trying to refocus his eyes to the darkness. There was definitely something under the skirting, pushed back but just finding the corners of the dim light. Arman reached out, his fingers moving across the floor to the skirting and sliding beneath. His fingers probed the dark space, not finding anything but dust and dirt. He shifted his weight, sliding out ever so slightly from his hiding place in order to push his fingers in a little deeper. The bottom of the skirting board scraped along the top of his hand as he pushed it in further. With his hand in the way, he could no longer see the glint of light. He moved his fingers back and forth, terrified of meeting some furry inhabitant who would take a liking to his fleshy fingers. When he had finished moving his hand left to right and back again, with nothing found, he withdrew it. Surely, if somebody had been waiting by the door then they would have heard him and come to investigate. But there was no movement. No footsteps. Nobody coming to investigate. So Arman slid himself completely out from under the pew, but stayed on his front, sliding his arm once more under the skirting board to go deeper. His fingers touched upon something almost straight away. He teased at it with his fingertips, feeling it move to the side. He pressed himself tightly against the skirting board, stretching his arm in as far as it would go. His shoulder burned with the effort, but his second and third fingers managed to grasp at the object. It scraped its way along as Arman slowly pulled his arm free, careful not to scratch it on the underside of the skirting. With his arm free, he shifted himself round, off of his stomach and into a sitting position. He sat back against the altar to look at his find. It was a knife and it was covered in dried blood.

PART 3

I

Christmas came and went with no celebration. The New Year passed as any other day. Spring sprung in March and the flowers at the front of Arman's house bloomed in a multitude of vibrant colour. To the rear of the house, beyond the chickens and the sheep, lay an unmarked grave overgrown with weeds. Inside the house, Arman woke and stared up at the ceiling as the grim transition from the dream world to the real life took hold. He peeled back the sheets and swung his legs off the bed, pressing his bare feet onto the cold floor. He rose with effort, letting out a huge puff of exhausted air as he did. He shuffled through to the kitchen and dragged across a bowl of cold water that he had prepared the evening before. He leaned forward, bringing his hands down into the bowl and splashing water into his tired eyes. The thick, wiry beard that had grown back over the past six months was grey, with just the occasional dark hair that clung belligerently to a younger self. He scratched at it and it scratched back. He stood up and stretched, wincing as a pain shot through his left shoulder and ribs. He presumed he must've picked up a knock somewhere, but he couldn't remember when or where. His pale skin clung to him, almost translucent in places, as ribs and hips revealed themselves. He dressed in a once-white shirt and dark-grey trousers. The socks he pulled on were riddled with frays and holes. The big toe on his right foot was completely exposed. Arman laced up muddy boots and prepared to leave the house.

He opened the front door and stopped. He imagined Violet, forced to kneel in the mud having been dragged from the bedroom and beaten with enough force to cast blood onto the door. The blood had washed away, but Arman couldn't open his door without the image coming to him. It had gone before it had even taken hold. He shook the picture from his mind and left the house. He trudged over to the stump, where a small pile of logs lay gathered at its side. He had left it too long and had been persevering with the cold rather than come and cut the wood. The stump was stained with browns and reds and nightmarish memories. His axe was embedded in the centre, the wooden handle jutting up for him to grab. He pulled with his blistered left hand and the axe came free for him. He flexed, or at least he attempted to flex, the fingers on his right hand, but they barely moved. The hand had never set properly from its break. It was purpled, with an uneven structure to the metacarpal bones. The fingers were brittle and sore and naturally fell into a claw like stiffness. Arman struggled to use the hand, so mostly he didn't. He used his better hand about halfway up the base of the axe, and his weaker hand at the end, more for balance than power. His swing was weaker and it took several attempts to splinter each log into useable pieces. The wind was whipping up and the air had turned cooler. Arman raised his collar. He finished with the wood, finished feeding and cleaning the animals, and was inside by mid-morning. He had slumped into the armchair in the parlour following a light breakfast, and his eyes were becoming heavy, when he heard a sound at the door. He remained seated but turned his head in the direction of the door, waiting for more. A stirring wind howled outside and he convinced himself that the sound had merely been caused by that. He shut his tired eyes and quickly fell into a deep sleep that the elements no longer disturbed.

It was late morning when he suddenly woke, sitting upright in the chair and looking around the room as if it were a strange place. Normality soon clicked back into place and he let out a weary sigh. He heard a distant noise, rhythmically jutting its way through the otherwise quiet house. He pressed his hands down on the armrests and hoisted himself to his feet. Listening carefully, he recognised the staccato cluck of poultry and realised that one of his hens may have become free from the others. He opened the door to address the escaped bird and took an instant step back as the wind and rain swooped and swirled about him. The rogue hen, her "buck-buck" rising in volume, strutted across the front of the house. Arman wondered how such low intelligence creatures seemed capable of outwitting whatever fence or cage he attempted to contain them within. And then to flaunt the escape by parading herself in front of the house rather than fleeing for the woods. He considered, with a smile, that he may have been by himself for too long. It was then, as he braced himself for the onslaught of the weather, that he saw that something had been left for him outside his door. There was a letter, resting beneath a palm-sized rock, on his doorstep. He pushed aside the rock and picked up the letter, taking it with him into the house and hastily closing the door.

The rain had left wet spots on the envelope, though he could still read the beautifully scribed "Mr A Shaw" that had been written across the front in black ink. The last part of his name had smeared downward and left an inky wet smear. He turned the envelope over in his hand, looking for clues on the reverse rather than just opening and finding out what it was. He went through to the kitchen and rested the unopened letter against a teapot. Were they evicting him from his home? It belonged to the congregation and he had long since not been a part of it. Why had it taken them six months to punish him? Once he opened it, it would become real and he would have to act upon it. The worrying would start. The planning for what he might do next. He considered just putting the letter straight into the bin but knew that that would not stop him fretting over it. For the longest time he had been waiting for the repercussions of his actions. Perhaps finally he could put it behind him and start afresh somewhere new. He snatched at the letter and tore it open. He stared at the small sheet of notepaper inside. The dampness of the rain had penetrated the envelope and a runny black line trailed vertically near the far edge of the entire, short, message, with a smeared "a", "o", "e", "o" and a "G" blurring into one confused streak. But still, the message could clearly be read;

Mr Arman Shaw
You are invited to attend
The upcoming wedding of
Violet Cooper
And Cecil Garfield
On March 14th 1864 at 11am

Arman read it over. He stared at it, as if the various letters may reform into a different message. Violet Cooper, not Violet Walker? Arman presumed this was Violet's maiden name, though didn't know why it was being used rather than her married name. Perhaps they were purging everything to do with Robert and his death from their memories and this was a step on that path. Violet Cooper and Cecil Garfield. In a thousand years he never would have paired them. The man who killed the man, who killed her husband. There was a symmetry to Violet's life that Arman found absurd. Arman wondered if the sound he heard before falling asleep had been a knock at the door, and not just the wind. Who had come to deliver him this invitation? Was it Violet? Or Cecil? Which of them, if any had invited him? His mind was racing, trying to decipher a school of logic he could never possibly know from sitting there in his armchair. The 14th was just days away. If he didn't attend then his ties with the congregation would surely finally end. This felt like a last chance but he couldn't fathom a world where he could walk back into Hope as if nothing had happened. He couldn't imagine a friendly face greeting him upon his return. But he must return. He must.

The days that followed did nothing to ease his mind. He had hopes that perhaps an answer would fall into his lap somehow. But nothing. The silence and emptiness of his life funnelled him unwillingly towards his return to the village. There was no counter-point and there were no excuses. He would go to the wedding. They would accept him or they would not. Finally, with no more time to hide behind, he woke on the morning of the 14th and prepared himself. He bathed for the first time in a month. He trimmed and cleaned his nails. At the cracked mirror hung by the sink on the kitchen wall, he trimmed his beard. He had considered shaving it, but these last months had seen him lose a significant amount of weight, and he feared what skeletal horror may wait his smooth face. So he shaped it, to add volume to his face. He trimmed and plucked at the wiry hairs that refused to remain as orderly as the others. He tried to avoid his reflection. The haunted face that looked back at him had sunken eyes and pronounced cheek bones. It had deep furrowed lines and specks of brown liver spots. Arman laid the mirror flat, face down on the worktop. In his bedroom, he opened his wardrobe and pulled out his only suit. The jacket was dark grey, single breasted and came to mid-thigh. Beneath that he wore a white shirt with starched collar and a cotton waistcoat. His pleated trousers were of the same, dark grey. Thankfully, the trousers had been tight originally, so with his diminished waist they still just about fit him. Afterwards, Arman sat on his doorstep and scrubbed at his black boots. The stains were ingrained and though he tried, they would never shine in the way he envisioned. Even if they had, the walk to Hope would soon sully them before the wedding anyhow. He pulled them on and laced them up. He stood at his door, looking out across the empty land. His silence was disturbed by the clucking of the hen, still loose, who walked aimlessly in jittery steps to the side of the door. He had no desire to dirty his suit, so he granted the hen her temporary freedom, though he told her quite forcefully that she would be back in the coop when he got back. She took the information well, replying with a "buck-buck-buck" that Arman took to be an agreement.

II

Daffodils, primroses and early season tulips decorated the archway into Hope with an array of yellows, whites and soft purples. Flowers filled Arman's peripheral vision as he stopped briefly beneath it. The village was alive with activity, with groups of people laughing and talking and going about their various tasks on the streets. In the circular garden at the centre of the village, two local women were decorating the benches with bunches of flowers. Nobody had noticed Arman and he was hoping that it might stay that way for some time. He'd be more than happy to sneak into the church at the last moment and stand quietly at the back. Perhaps he could just smile politely and occasionally exchange a nod as people recognised his presence among them. That was presuming they'd want to look at him, or nod at him, or smile. He didn't imagine he'd have too many friends, if any, left in the congregation. It wasn't too late to leave. He could turn around and walk away and there was a chance nobody would notice. He had made a dreadful mistake in coming there.

"Arman?"

Arman looked up at the sound of his name. He crossed the rubicon into Hope and saw Herman Blyth striding towards him from the church side of the village. The last time they'd exchanged words, Herman had been ridiculing his plea for Fred Decker's innocence and making the pre-determined case for guilt. Arman expected the older man to continue where he'd left off, but instead, Herman's face broke into a smile and he strode forward with his hand out ready to shake. Arman took the hand and Herman pumped it hard, the smile never leaving his face.

"It's so good to see you, Mr Shaw," said Herman with genuine warmth.

"You too," said Arman.

"Nervous?"

"A little."

"Don't be," said Herman, shaking his head. "I'm glad I got to you. You looked like you were about to turn and run the other way!"

Arman laughed, nervously, then dismissed the idea with a simple, "No."

Herman, still clutching Arman's hand in his, took a step closer, almost pressing himself to Arman as he quietly spoke, "Nobody here thinks bad of you, Mr Shaw, I promise you."

"But after everything that happened..."

"Nobody," said Herman again. "Today is all about celebration. Today is about healing."

Arman nodded.

Herman gave Arman's hand one final hearty shake and then released it. He placed the same hand around Arman's arm, leading him away from the floral archway and into the village. "Niall will want to see you," he said.

"Of course," said Arman.

Herman squeezed the arm he was holding and let out a brief chuckle, "Of course! But not like that, Mr Shaw. Celebration. Healing." And he laughed once more.

Arman winced at the squeezed arm. He was sure it hadn't been done with malice, but Herman was a strong man, despite his age. There was activity by the church at the end of the road. He couldn't quite see from the distance he was, but a member of the congregation was up a ladder, fastening a sign of some kind to the outside of the holy building. Somebody else came out of the church with another ladder and climbed up the other side of the doorway. Between them, they unfurled an embroidered tapestry of swirling gold borders around a message that simply said, "Congratulations". Arman macabrely wondered if they might have a similar sign that read "Commiserations" that they used for funerals. A little girl crawled along on her hands and knees, decorating the path to the door with flower petals. A breeze came along and half of the good work behind her disappeared into the garden to the side, but she carried on, obliviously. Many of the doors of the houses running up and down the street were wide open, with the congregation mixing households as they got ready, preparing themselves for the wedding. Edmund Haynes and Nigel Vance stood opposite each other at their small garden fence, Edmund assisting his neighbour with his cufflinks. Arman guessed that their wives would be with Violet, flocking to the bride on her big day. Arman knew that Violet had always felt like an outsider. Perhaps today, as the congregation rallied round her, she would finally be accepted.

Violet. He had tried not to think of her too much, though she often found a way into his thoughts. His feelings. He was glad that she had found a way to become part of the congregation once more. As dire as things might have seemed in Hope sometimes, they were a thousand times better than anything the world outside might offer her. He would not have predicted her match with Cecil Garfield, but he recognised the allure of a union within the congregation. He was nervous about seeing her, though dismissed it. It was her wedding day. She would be surrounded by friends and well-wishers and, ultimately, at the side of her husband after that. If she thought ill of Arman, she would almost certainly keep it to herself. Arman was shaken out of his thought process as Herman steered him away from the church and further down the street. They arrived at Niall's house and Herman knocked. His hand had finally released Arman. Arman knew it had been a friendly gesture, but there was at least a part of it that made him feel like a prisoner.

Niall opened the door and the first thing that Arman noticed was how much he had aged. His hair seemed whiter, the lines around his eyes more severe, he had a stoop to the shoulders. But he smiled, and he smiled with affection and shook Arman's hand with the same gusto with which Herman had. He ushered him inside with a friendly arm around his shoulders. Arman and Herman sat at the small table by the window, looking out at the garden at the centre of their village. Niall presently joined them carrying a tray containing a bottle of brandy and three glasses. He laid the tray down and then disappeared briefly to retrieve a chair from the other room. He set it a little bit away from the other men, but still facing them. He crossed his legs and let out a long sigh, as if relieving a great discomfort.

"It's good to see you, Arman," he said.

Arman had a thousand questions, and almost all of them were to do with the morning he came home to find Violet gone and Fred Decker murdered. But he held his tongue. For now. Instead he said, "You're looking well, Niall."

Niall laughed, dismissing the compliment. With no warning, his dog came bounding into the room, excitedly scurrying around the legs of the guests as well as the table before he stopped to a dead halt, turned and leapt onto Niall's lap. Niall let out an exclamation and scrubbed the dog between his ears. "Forgive Wags," said Niall. "He is perpetually excited."

"Imagine that," said Arman.

"I know!" laughed Niall. "To be a dog!"

"Have you been well, Niall?" asked Arman.

Niall shrugged and said, "All is well."

"And the congregation?"

"The congregation?" mused Niall, sharing a look with Herman. "Good. Not good. We've had our share of ups and downs, Arman."

"We lost Bernard Ogden," interjected Herman.

"Mr Ogden?" said Arman. "He passed? What happened?"

"Poor Joan found him in the bath. His heart had given out. Joan was inconsolable for the longest time. Truthfully, I think this upcoming marriage is the best thing for her. She has taken over much of the planning and has been like a mother to Violet these past few months."

"I can't believe it," said Arman. "Mr Ogden was only a little older than myself."

"He has a plan, Arman," said Niall, by way of explanation.

The three men shared a silence. Arman swirled the brandy at the bottom of his glass. It had been many years since he had had alcohol of any kind and he could already feel the effects of the small amount he had drunk. He finished the glass off. He jumped a little as Wags barked, something grabbing his attention that none of the men could see. He bounded from Niall's lap and out of the room.

"You probably have more questions, but we might not have all the answers, Arman," said Niall.

Arman guessed this was a polite way of telling him to stay quiet. He was happy to comply for now. He had been nervous about his return, but so far, it had been pleasant enough.

"None of us feel particularly happy with how things turned out," said Niall. "But today is about celebration. Today is about healing."

The exact phrasing that Herman had used. Arman wondered if they had brainstormed these key words at a church service one morning. He wondered how many times he may hear the words said throughout the rest of the day. Arman had no time to object as Niall rose and poured him more of the brandy.

"It's a little early for me," objected Arman.

"Ha!" exclaimed Niall. "We are celebrating!"

Arman raised his glass and added, "And healing."

Niall's smile dropped, just a little, just for a moment, but it returned with vigour and he raised his glass. Herman did the same and the three men drank. Arman grimaced as the liquid burned its way down his throat. He made a silent promise with himself not to drink anymore.

"Are you presiding?" asked Arman.

"The wedding? Yes, I shall be performing the ceremony." He leaned forward and placed his half-full glass back on the tray.

"And will the bride be led down the aisle?"

Niall looked over at Herman, then back to Arman. He searched in his lap for the right response, eventually finding it, raising his head and saying, "We were hoping you might oblige, Arman."

Arman put down his glass and looked first at Herman, then at Niall.

"Now, before you say anything—"

"—'we' were hoping? Which 'we' are we talking about? Violet? The two of you?"

"I apologise, Arman, I blurted it out," said Niall. "So much has happened. We, and this includes Violet, felt that you giving her away may bring you back into the congregation somehow. Herman, help me out."

Herman shifted in his seat. "Give her away," he said. "I think, perhaps, in that moment, it may heal a rift that has been at the heart of this community since Robert passed."

Healing. Arman did not want to walk Violet down the aisle. He wanted to stand at the back and go unnoticed. He wanted to come back, but quietly, with no fanfare, at his own pace. "What does it entail?"

Niall suddenly laughed, though he quickly composed himself. "Always the worrier, Arman. You'll stand outside with her while we all take our seats. You'll say something comforting, like 'you look beautiful today', or 'Cecil Garfield will make an excellent husband', then you walk her to the front of the church and hand her off to Cecil and go and take a seat. Will you do it, Arman?"

Arman nodded.

Niall got to his feet and slapped a friendly hand against Arman's back. "Shall we join them outside. It is a day of celebration!"

Arman got to his feet, but Herman remained seated, looking stern and staring at Niall. Niall stood by the open door, unsure what his friend wanted from him.

Herman coughed. "And…the other thing?"

"The oth…." Niall trailed off as it dawned on him what Herman was talking about. "Of course." He gently pressed the door shut and dropped his head.

Arman, caught between sitting and standing, sat back down, looking between the two men. "What's going on?"

Niall attempted a smile, but it hung falsely on his face. "Violet is pregnant."

The colour drained from Arman's face. He looked from Niall to Herman, then back to Niall again, hoping that this was all some kind of macabre joke. Their grave faces were the answer he didn't want. They had not spoken of what happened during Violet's stay at his house. Arman did not know how much they knew and was wary of giving away too much. Surely if they knew that Arman had laid with Violet then they couldn't welcome him back. Cecil had called her a "whore" that fateful day. He had presumed that Violet and Fred Decker had been discovered together. He had hoped, prayed, that his own sin was undiscovered.

"How far gone is she?" he tried. Perhaps the child was Cecil's?

"Six months," said Niall. "She is sleight. It is barely noticeable. It is Fred Decker's bastard."

"And Cecil still marries her?"

"He is a good man, Arman," said Niall. "He will raise it as his own. In fact, as far as anyone is concerned in Hope, the child will be his. There is not one among us who intends to shame the widow. Today is an amnesty, Arman. What has gone before is forgotten."

Healing.

Arman nodded once more. He nodded his agreement that they would all live a lie. Nobody would speak of Fred Decker. His relations with Violet. His execution. Nobody would reference that Violet became pregnant before her marriage, and before Cecil had asked for her hand. The whole congregation would happily spend the rest of their lives with a veil of secrecy covering their eyes. And what of truth? The truth, that Arman was happy to remain hidden, that only he and Violet must know, was that Violet could be carrying Arman's child.

III

The world fell away. Arman accompanied Niall and Herman outside. They were immediately greeted by someone who shook Arman's hand and laughed about something before moving on. Niall laughed too but Arman hadn't heard what was said. He looked across to the garden at the centre of the town and saw Edmund Hayes and his sister, Esther, performing a song he didn't recognise. He heard the lyric *"healing in his wings"* and recognised it as a quote from the Book of Malachi. Did he hear it right? He tried to pick out more of the words, but they seemed to drift away on the wind and merge with the everyday sounds all around them. Another greeting. Merry Ramsey pumped Arman's hand and wished him well. Niall clamped Merry on the elbow, holding him in place as they shared small talk. Arman smiled and hoped nobody was looking at him too closely. A lead weight rested in his stomach. He wanted to lie down. Somewhere quiet, away from these people, away from the place. If he could just get somewhere quiet, he could stop and think. He could process what he'd been told. He was painfully aware of his breathing, with his breaths becoming faster, shorter, his chest tightening. He smiled, still, because otherwise they'd see the lie he carried around with him. Somebody patted him on the back. They were moving again. Another handshake. The Hayes siblings still sang their song, though it seemed far away now.

"Is that from Malachi?" asked Arman but didn't know if he said it out loud. Nobody answered him. He looked up and Terrance Everly was grinning at him and asking him how he'd been. Terence was squat, with a moon face and small mouth. Arman nodded and said he had been "well". Terence chuckled and continued speaking. Over his shoulder, the Hayes siblings kept singing. Arman looked to Niall and Herman and they were both looking at Terence, engaging him in a conversation that Arman struggled to keep up with. Arman couldn't get out of his own head. He could feel his tongue in his mouth and it felt swollen and clumsy as he swallowed. He blinked several times. His breathing, in and out, in and out. Overhead, a skylark flapped its wings, singing a sharp, high-pitched note at odds with the Esther and Edmund Hayes song. Arman wished he were a bird. He looked back down and Terrance was gone, but now Niall and Herman spoke with Roman Farley. He was laden with garlands and string and was half-turned away from the group as he spoke. Nobody seemed to notice anything different about Arman, or at least nobody said anything. He smiled, the great disguise, and it worked.

The sound of a loud crack ripped through the air and everyone turned to the supposed direction. Vincent Law, his arms full of bunting, one foot teetering on the top of a short ladder, desperately grabbed onto the broken tree branch of a small tree in the centre garden. As people rushed to his aid, the ladder tipped, the branch came free, and Vincent tumbled to the ground not too far below. Arman stayed rooted to the spot. It took him a moment to even notice that he was now alone and that Niall and Herman were both making their way hastily to the garden to assist. Arman took a step back, followed by another and another, until he turned and walked away. He kept his head down, moving away from the commotion, the village, and headed for the church. He passed by a few more people as they rushed by to check on Vincent Law, but they either didn't notice, or didn't care that Arman was going the other way. At the church, he moved round the side, sticking close to the wall. The rubbish at the rear had been cleared away, including the broken, bloodied fence that he had seen the last time he had been there. He kept going, beyond the church, heading out a little way until he reached a small plot of gated land. He lifted the string that tied the gate to a wooden post, going inside and closing it behind himself. The graveyard of Hope was small and already beginning to fill. They were only a handful of deaths away from having to expand the plot. The headstones were locally sourced stones, etched in the village and already, in some cases, beginning to fade and succumb to the weather. The newest grave, adorned with an array of flowers, was that of Bernard Ogden. The stone used was larger than some of the others and there was an ominous blank space under Bernard's inscription. He sidestepped Bernard's final home and moved between two others to get to the rear of the plot, where the village's first grave lay. It was a rounded stone, just under two feet hight, and bearing the inscription:

Mathilda Dinah Shaw
July 1834 - July 1863
Beloved Wife

Arman had not looked upon the headstone since the day it had been put in place. He stood before it, silently, staring at the stone, as if some secret meaning or message may present itself in the brief inscription. He sat down at the foot of the grave, leaned forward, and rested his hand upon the dirt which covered it. Under the headstone was a small bunch of wilting tulips, once yellow, now faded and wrinkled. He briefly asked himself why he had not come here before, but he knew the answer. He was ashamed. He carried with him the burden of her dying and it was a heavy weight. It hung upon everything he did. Every word he said.

"Morning Tilda," he said, quietly. He could not hear the noise of the village behind him. It was, thankfully, too far away to pick up. He revelled in the calmness of silence. His thoughts began to reform. The heaviness in his stomach melted away. The fresh, warm air caressed his face and he welcomed it. He wondered who had placed the tulips on the grave, but cleared his head of it. There was no mystery. Mathilda had many friends in the congregation. Perhaps the bigger mystery should be why there were not more. There was a line of small stones that ran around the perimeter of the grave. Arman moved onto his knees and began to put the ones that had come loose back into place. He sat back down and swept away the dirt from his knees. He wanted to plunge his hands into the soil, to dig away the dirt until he came to his wife. He wanted to pull her free and start his life again. The visit to the grave felt like the end of a journey. He couldn't imagine turning around and going back to the village. He didn't want to see Niall or any of them ever again. Their shame, like his own, clung to them, absorbed into every fibre of their being.

"Well, I suppose you've heard what's happened," he said, and then chuckled at the absurdity of everything. He waited, perhaps expecting a response of some kind, but none came. Even if she could talk to him, would she? He had killed her. She had begged him to help end her miserable life and he had wilted under the pressure and done it. He thought back over the time following the decision to go through with it. They had discussed ways he could do it and they drew a blank. It had almost become a joke and they had laughed, but it was a laugh laden with a bottomless sadness. It was Mathilda who had decided in the end. They had been in bed and she had talked him through what she wanted and how it should happen. She had told him that she would try her best not to try and stop him. She had told him that no matter what she did or said, he should end her life. He had done it. Against every better judgement in his body, he had done it. But at the end, right at the end, just as the last vestige of life left her body she had uttered that one word. That terrible word. She had said, "No," and he took it to mean that she wanted him to stop. But by then, he had stopped and it was too late.

At her grave, which he had been too shamed to visit in over a year, he whispered, "I'm sorry." But he could hear the emptiness in the word. It was meaningless. Sorry would not bring her back. Sorry would not forgive his sin. Sorry was a word you said when you spilled your tea, not when you assisted somebody's death. He was about to speak again when he became aware of movement behind him. He used the back of his hand to rub at his eyes. Still seated, he turned his head and was surprised to see Cecil Garfield standing at the gate, watching him. He wore his wedding suit, though it was ill fitting. The buttons on the jacket were undone and it looked like it would take more than a deep breath to do them up.

"I went to my window when I heard the commotion," said Cecil. "Then I saw you going the other way. I wondered, at first, if maybe you'd caused it." A small breeze swept across the ground. Cecil's hand went to his hair, patting it down. His usual unkempt appearance had been made over for his wedding and his wild hair was flattened and combed into a centre parting which he was clearly guarding against the elements as best he could.

"Is Mr Law alright?" asked Arman.

Cecil shrugged dismissively. He didn't know, or he didn't care.

Arman looked back at the grave, considering his next move. Mathilda would've told him not to be rash. Not to prod at Cecil. She would've advised calm. Reconciliation. But Mathilda wasn't there. Arman turned back and said, "I hear you're going to be a father?"

Cecil bristled, then regained his composure and nodded. "I am," he said.

"Of a kind."

"Something to say, Shaw?"

Arman shook his head and turned back to the gravestone. What possible gain could there be had in provoking Cecil? Absolutely none, thought Arman, and yet after everything that had happened, he found it hard to hold his silence in check. "You killed the father of the baby," he said.

"Did I?" asked Cecil.

Arman hadn't expected that, and it worried him. Was Cecil saying he hadn't killed Fred Decker, or did he know about Arman and Violet? Did he suspect that Arman may be the father? Or was it perhaps something else? Arman looked back over his shoulder to look at Cecil and nodded his head to indicate, yes, you did.

"You seem to know so much," said Cecil.

"What do you want?"

"I came here to ask you the very same question. Why are you here?"

"You invited me to your wedding."

"If it were up to me, Shaw, you would never be allowed to set foot in this village ever again."

Arman felt vulnerable, crouched on the floor as he was. Cecil was an imposing figure with a fiery temper. Arman told him, "I do not wish to stay. I will attend your wedding. I will give Violet away. Then during the evening's festivities, I will leave and not return." He had wanted nothing more than to return to the congregation. To live amongst the people of Hope once more. But too much had passed. It was a village that lived under an enormous cloud of lies and it was only a matter of time before the truth poured down upon them all. He would fulfil the obligations expected of him today, and then leave, just as he had told Cecil.

"Is that true?" asked Cecil.

"Yes," said Arman. He stared down at the grave, awaiting a response that wasn't coming. Eventually he turned, and saw that Cecil had gone. Arman turned back to the grave. He couldn't reconcile the fact that his wife lay beneath him on the soil. Arman took a handful of the dirt, letting it filter through his fingers. He rose, shaking his trousers free of the earth. He felt resolute. This would be his final day of Hope.

IV

By the time Arman got back to the church, a small group consisting of Niall, Joan Ogden and Alma Dryden were waiting outside, standing in a semi-circle. Niall grabbed at Arman's shoulders with both his arms and let out a relieved sigh.

"We were beginning to worry," said Niall.

"I was just..." started Arman, pointing his head back the way he had come. Without acknowledging where he'd been, they all seemed to understand.

"Violet will be out in just a moment, Mr Shaw," said Joan with a rare smile.

"Thank you, Mrs Ogden," he said.

She smiled again, though her eyes studied him, as if expecting some kind of trouble.

"Is everyone inside?" asked Arman.

"Everyone but us," said Alma, cheerfully. "Good luck."

"He doesn't need luck," said Niall turning to Arman. "You will be fine." He let go of Arman's shoulders but gave him a parting, friendly slap on the arm. "Tell her she looks wonderful. Wish her well. Walk a short distance and all will be well."

"I think that even I can manage that," said Arman, without believing it.

Alma took Arman's hand in hers, squeezed it, then threw herself into a hug, wrapping large arms around his waist. He let out a gasp and she released him, turning to head inside the church. Niall followed behind her, leaving just Joan Ogden and Arman. Arman watched them walk away. The church door was propped open and Arman could just about see Cecil standing at the front of the church. The pews were all full and the congregation seemed to take it in turns looking over their shoulder at the door, awaiting Violet's big entrance. Arman resisted the temptation to wave.

"This is a new start," said Joan, interrupting Arman's thought process.

"I am told that you have become very close with Violet," said Arman.

"It is true," she said, her voice softening. "A lot has changed these last six months. Sometimes in life, events happen which give you a new perspective. Sometimes you look in the mirror and see a different person from the day before."

He nodded, adding, "I was very sorry to hear of Mr Ogden's passing. He was a fine man."

Joan looked away, took a deep breath in and then returned to face Arman with a practised smile upon her face once more. She nodded and said, "Thank you." He thought she would go after that, but she lingered, considering her words before eventually adding, "Have faith. Things will work out." With that, she turned and headed inside the church.

By himself once more, Arman felt the urge to turn and run. He looked down the street which ran through the centre of Hope, to the decorated garden at the centre, and beyond that to the oak tree at the end of the village. It didn't feel that long ago since Fred Decker had been chained to it. Even then, the village had carried on. He wondered how strong the glue that held the village together was. He wondered how much more it could take. Almost as the thought entered his head, it was pushed aside by the sound of Violet's door opening. She emerged into the sunshine and stopped for a moment, turning her head to the sun and feeling the warmth on her face. It looked like she was glowing. She wore a white linen dress, with frilled lace trim that began under her arms and ran down the length of the sleeves. Joan had lent her a silk shawl that had a rose at its centre and a wool woven paisley border. She had a veil attached to a coronet of flowers; red and white roses interspersed with various coloured carnations taken straight from Alma's garden. She saw Arman and immediately walked in his direction. His heart raced as she approached and he deliberately slowed his breathing to try and ease his nerves. It didn't work. Violet stopped in front of him, her hands resting on her pregnant belly.

"It is good to see you, Arman."

"How have you been?" he asked.

"Accepted," she said. "The whole congregation seems to think their salvation lay in redeeming me. They've not said it explicitly, but..."

"Celebration. Healing," said Arman.

"You've been speaking to Niall," she laughed.

Arman could feel the stares of the congregation as he talked to Violet. "We had better get inside. I'm meant to be wishing you well."

Violet turned to the open door of the church and smiled at those inside, a big, broad smile that lit up her face. When she turned back to Arman, the smile remained, but the eyes looked tearful. "Why didn't you come for me, Arman?"

Arman looked between Violet and the people in the church. He said to her, "We have run out of time, Violet."

She shook her head: no. "Please help me, Arman. We can leave this place."

"It is too late," he said, his voice breaking. He hadn't expected this.

"Please," she pleaded.

"What would you have me do?"

"Meet me tonight at midnight. Here, at the church. Joan has arranged transport."

Arman took a step back, studying her face, unbelieving of what he was hearing. "Joan Ogden?!" he hissed.

"She has been like a mother to me since I got back. The only one who has shown me true kindness."

"You cannot trust her, Violet."

"Did they tell you what happened to Bernard Ogden?"

Arman stopped, a quizzical look on his face. "Niall told me. His heart—"

" — His *wrists*, Arman. Sliced. He died by his own hand. They told everyone it was his heart. The whole congregation — "

They were interrupted by Joan, stepping outside the church and standing by Violet's side. She looked between the two of them and asked, "Is everything well? Everyone is waiting."

"Yes," said Violet, "all is well."

Violet looped her arm inside Arman's and they turned to face the church doors. Joan hesitated, catching Arman's eye, just for a second, and then speedily going back inside. From the front of the church came the sound of music. On the threshold of the church, with them both about to enter and walk down the aisle, Violet said to Arman, "I wish you had come for me."

Arman didn't have time to respond before Mary Wheel, sat at the upright piano in the far corner, began playing as rousing a rendition of the wedding march as she could muster. Violet maintained a vice-like grip on Arman's arm as they walked down the short aisle. At the head of the church, with Niall waiting at the altar, and Cecil to the side, Violet removed her arm and Arman took a step back. Nobody had saved a seat for him at the front so he moved to the back of the church and found a space in the far corner. Violet's words raced through his mind as he sat down. What did she expect him to do? The ceremony had begun but he couldn't seem to follow it. At some point, everyone stood and sang. Arman stood alongside them, moving his lips in a pale imitation of song. He studied Violet but she daren't look in his direction. Her eyes were cast down, away from Cecil, who stared at her. At some point, Arman exchanged looks with Niall, but the moment was fleeting and Arman doubted it had any meaning. He sat when everyone else did. He looked around the congregation and wondered how many of them knew what had happened with Fred Decker. He wondered how many knew the intimacies of what had happened to Violet once she had been dragged from Arman's house that morning. Had the whole congregation made a conscious decision to ignore everything that had happened? Were they happy to talk of Cecil's baby and never reference the fact that it couldn't possibly be his? They would be happy to welcome the baby into the world once it was born, but they dare not mention it before her marriage. Arman imagined a world where he may stand up and demand everyone's attention. He would tell them, with his heart beating hard and fast in his ever-tightening chest, that Fred Decker and he had shared Violet that evening and that her baby could be *his* baby. His legs shook involuntarily, as if warning him that he better not try and stand. What had Violet said?

Why didn't you come for me, Arman?

Had she been waiting for him this whole time? They all stood for another song. Joan Ogden, sat on the front row, looked back over her shoulder and held Arman's stare for a second too long. Had what Violet said about Bernard Ogden been true? Had he taken his own life? Was it because of what happened with Robert? Why had they lied? The village seemed to be scrambling to keep itself free of the prevalent sin that was seeping in from all sides. Could Joan Ogden be colluding with Violet to get them out of the village? Where would they go? Violet was six months pregnant. They would have to start a new life and either marry, or pretend to be married. He shook his head of the thought. Violet would already be a married woman by then. Was he even considering fleeing with a married, pregnant woman? He could laugh at the lunacy of it all.

Why didn't you come for me, Arman?

He had planned to leave the village tonight anyway. Could he take Violet with him? Did he want to take her with him? He felt a responsibility to their unborn child. He couldn't leave it behind. He had tried for years to have children with Mathilda but they couldn't conceive. He hastily sat down, taking the lead of those around him. The singing had ended and now Niall was sermonising. Arman watched as soon, Violet and Cecil faced each other before Niall, looking into each other's eyes and reciting their vows. The wedding had the impetus of a runaway train. Arman couldn't stop it. All he could do was ruin it afterwards, and maybe hammer down the final nail in the congregation's coffin. With that, the congregation got to their feet and Arman was dreading having to stand awkwardly through yet another hymn. But this was different. This time the congregation was applauding. At the front of the church, Cecil held Violet tightly in his arms. Niall had a hand on each of their backs. Cecil released Violet from his embrace and kissed her. They were married.

Why didn't you come for me, Arman?

He wanted to storm to the front of the church. He wanted to grab Violet by the shoulders and look into her eyes when he answered her question. He wanted her to ask him again why he hadn't come after her six months ago. Because then he could tell her the truth.

He had come and she hadn't needed him.

V

With the ceremony over, the congregation spilled out noisily onto the streets. Amidst the bunting and flowers and decorative petals strewn across the ground, people formed into groups of two or three or more and chatted and laughed and cheered as Violet and Cecil emerged. Tables were brought out and placed in a line from the church to the garden and plates of sandwiches and fruit and cold cuts appeared on plates that parishioners quickly and quietly retrieved from their homes. Arman was alone, a fixed smile painfully etched onto his face, moving between the groups as his thought process did somersaults. He couldn't put one idea in front of the other. The people and the noise and the whole atmosphere were too overwhelming. He longed to be back at the cemetery, alone with Mathilda once more. He knew he would sneak away at some point, but it was too early, and somebody might notice. He had to put the time in first, socialise, eat, pretend to be a guest. He caught snippets of conversation, mostly about the weather, the food or the ceremony. Nobody mentioned that the congregation had tried, poisoned and beheaded a man not so long ago. They didn't mention Violet's pregnancy or Bernard Ogden's suicide. They were happy to bask in the sunlight and rejoice as a veil of darkness fell upon their sins.

Arman turned away from one conversation about the consistency of Freda Derby's ginger loaf, only to knock into the elderly Mary Wheel, who spluttered and spat out a well chewed ham sandwich as Arman barrelled into her.

"Mrs Wheel, I'm so sorry," he said.

She coughed, looked down at her empty plate, then back up at Arman, considering him a moment before politely saying, "It is quite all right. I'd finished it anyway."

The half-masticated sandwich on the floor told a different story but Arman didn't pursue it. He had not seen Mary since the trial, where she had made a half-baked job of taking notes. He decided to avoid that subject, and instead, he asked her, "Did you enjoy the wedding, Mrs Wheel?"

"I enjoyed her first wedding more," she said, in quite a loud voice. She leaned in close to him as she said it, as if they shared some great secret.

"Me too," said Arman.

From the church garden, Esther and Edmund Hayes began to sing Abide With Me. Mary's attention was drawn and she began to clap along. Arman sidestepped the food on the floor and moved through the wedding party. The Dryden boys, Bradley and Bertie, ran by. They were dressed in their Sunday finest, which was already giving way to loosened collars and rolled up sleeves. They fleeted and darted excitedly in between groups, over chairs and under the tables. Arman wasn't entirely sure who was chasing who, if either of them were chasing the other at all. The boy's parents, Alma and Philip, obliviously chatted in a small group nearby, never once checking on their wayward boys. Arman looked over at the wooden archway by the entrance to the village, wondering if it was too soon – *it was* – to leave yet. The crowd gasped and laughed, almost collectively, as a strong wind suddenly breezed through, flapping up table cloths onto the food and sweeping out almost as soon as it had arrived. Arman found himself at the far table, loitering at the edge, picking at some wafer-thin slices of pork. He'd considered the sandwiches but he wasn't hungry. These days, it took a lot for him to work up an appetite. Down the length of the assembled tables, between people's outstretched arms and piles of food, stood Violet, pouring herself a drink from a jug. She looked up and caught Arman's stare, locking eyes with him. The look was broken as someone further down from Arman reached across to fill his plate with more food. Then closer to Violet, a couple refilling their drinks leaned in front of her. Eventually, Arman merely stared at the space where he knew she was. He shook it off and turned away, looking down the village and off to the oak tree. He closed his eyes, imagining that when he opened them, the guests would have disappeared. That he would go to Violet and take her small hand in his and lead her away from Hope, under the wooden archway and somewhere far away.

But he couldn't shake the sound. The conversations and giggling and general murmur of the crowd brought him rushing back to reality.

"Are you with us, Arman?"

Arman opened his eyes. Herman stood opposite him, his hand extending him a drink, which he took.

"Thank you."

"You seemed a hundred miles away," said Herman. "Somewhere nice I hope?"

"No," he said, "right here."

Herman smiled, though his eyes probed, deciphering what Arman had just said. He shook it off, took a sip of his own drink and let out a long, weary sigh. Arman could see over his shoulder, where Violet and Cecil seemed pinned back by the church doors, exchanging pleasantries as different people came and went. He wanted to get to Violet. He wanted to talk to her. He wanted to find out if there was any more to her plan than merely running away. He wanted her to convince him. He turned back as Herman finished saying something that Arman hadn't heard.

"I apologise, Herman, I didn't catch that."

Herman studied him, a wry smile on his thin lips. "There's a lot going on behind those eyes."

Arman half laughed and shook his head. "I'm prone to getting a bit lost in my daydreaming sometimes. Would you excuse me, Herman?"

Herman obligingly took a step to his side and Arman moved past him. He headed in Violet's direction, contemplating how he may speak to her away from Cecil. Away from everyone. He moved past Merry and Ramsey Wharton, nodding and smiling as he did. Stepping aside Effie Hall, he swerved clear of Sylvia Farley, her mouth stuffed with a chocolate cake that left an unpleasant brown residue upon her lips. Up ahead, Cecil was engaged in conversation with Miles Faber, animatedly using his arms to express his point. Violet moved away, finding a home against the church wall and sipping her drink and surveying her wedding guests. She looked up and saw Arman working his way towards her. Her body straightened in anticipation of their coming together. He stuttered, as Olive Kirby approached Violet from her other side and, presumably, offered her congratulations. She embraced Violet in an affectionate hug.

Near the gate leading to the church path, he thought he caught Cecil giving him a side-eye and he briefly considered changing his direction and moving away from Violet, but quickly changed his mind and carried on. At the gate, Arman prepared to move through, but his path was blocked by Niall who planted himself across the gateway, blocking the only way in or out. Over his shoulder, Arman saw Olive move away from Violet, leaving her alone once more. To his side, Cecil still talked with Miles, but he still kept glancing sideways at Arman. Niall's lips curled begrudgingly at the corners, the thinnest smile possible before becoming a scowl.

"Arman, did you enjoy the ceremony?" asked Niall.

Arman turned his attention to Niall. "I think I was more nervous than Violet," he said.

"Walking down the aisle? I'm sure the bride appreciated it."

Over Niall's shoulder, Arman watched Olive return, handing a drink to Violet as they resumed their conversation. Niall looked back over his own shoulder, watching Violet and Olive for a moment before turning back to Arman. "I don't really know what happened out there," said Niall, "but whatever it was, if it was anything, it's over now."

Arman nodded. At that moment, there was a minor commotion, with Violet yelping loudly, that caused everyone around to turn her way. She had red wine spilled down the front of her dress and Olive was desperately apologising. Cecil rushed over, followed by a few others, all keen to help without offering any answers. Joan Ogden came through the crowd, desperately clinging onto a swilling jug of water and a cloth. Olive was on her knees, using the arm of her own dress to try and wipe at the growing red stain. Joan pushed past Niall and Arman and went to Violet, shooing Olive away as she did.

'It was an accident," cried Olive.

Violet was simultaneously trying to reassure her that she knew, while also fretting over her stained dress. With all eyes on Violet, Arman backed away, as he had earlier with Vincent's tree mishap. He took slow, backwards steps, against the congregation coming forward to check on the stricken bride. He got to the archway without a single eye falling upon him. He was through it and taking brisk steps onto the path out of the village when he noticed he was still clutching a glass of wine. He took a sip and then tossed the whole thing into a bush. Hope was out of sight by now, causing him to breathe a sigh of relief. He hoped Violet wasn't too upset about her dress.

The walk home was a long one. The sun was high and bore down on Arman's stooped back. He had to stop several times just to get his breath back. Before Mathilda had died, he would make this same journey two or three times a day, but now he struggled with each painful step. He thought of the congregation. If everything went to plan, he would never see them again. It felt like a big *if*. Joan Ogden had never given Arman any reason to believe he could trust her, but Violet said it was so. Perhaps all he needed to do was trust that Violet was right about it. Trust that she wouldn't let Violet down. Arman walked on, passing a winding section of the overgrown path where six months earlier he had been stuck barefoot in brambles and pain. He moved quickly onwards. An image of Mathilda appeared in his head. He remembered a day when the two of them had walked back from the village laden down with apples that Alma Dryden had given them. A couple of rogue apples had rolled free and over the side of the path. They had lamented their loss at first, before briefly discussing the ease of discomfort they'd feel if they tossed *all* of the apples over the side. Instead, they had walked with two baskets each and by the time they got home, their arms were leaden and painful. They had woken up the next day with sore joints that took days to heal. They had made fun of their own ails, and grossly exaggerated their weakened arms by doing less and less with them until eventually, they reached a point that evening where they both stubbornly refused to use their arms at all.

When he eventually did make it home, Arman wasted no time in packing a suitcase. He didn't know when he had made the decision to leave with Violet. He didn't even know if he *had* made the decision. Like so much of his life recently, he seemed to follow Violet's instructions, whatever they may be. He chastised himself for deflecting responsibility so cheaply. He didn't have to do what she said. He chose to. He tried to shake the thought from his head and concentrate on the job at hand. He packed light, not wanting to be weighed down when he travelled. He didn't have that many clothes to start with so choosing which ones stayed and which ones came with him wasn't too hard. He had lost so much weight in the last year or so that half the clothes no longer fitted him anyway. He went from room to room, checking to make sure he hadn't left anything vital behind. In truth, he didn't have very much stuff. Each room was full of memories and little more. He ended his short tour of the house in the parlour. On the mantle over the fireplace was the bloodied knife he had retrieved from the church six months earlier. He picked it up, studying it. The knife was folded into the wooden handle. There were no markings or engravings. No distinguishing marks except the dried blood of Robert Walker on the blade. He had meant to throw it away. He had wrestled with himself about the implications of its existence. He had told himself that the knife didn't prove guilt, but he didn't believe it. It made him question everything that Fred Decker had said and done in his house. It had caused him sleepless nights and he knew the best thing to do would be to rid himself of it, but he had failed, as he had failed at so many things in his life. He slipped it into his back pocket. It had lived above his fireplace all this time and now he would take it with him. Nothing else in the parlour was worthy of being packed away. He wished, not for the first time, that he had a photograph of Mathilda but they had never had one taken. Every day since her death seemed to make the image in his head fade a little further into the background of his mind. He worried that one day he would attempt to conjure the image of her and he would not be able to remember what she had looked like. He closed the suitcase and buckled it shut. He felt the weight and was happy with it. Afterward, he sat down on the armchair, exhausted, wondering how he would spend the 12 hours until he saw her again.

VI

When darkness came, it came slowly. The second hand on the clock perched on Arman's mantlepiece in the parlour flickered and stuttered and moved forward in long, heavy clicks. To fill his time, Arman went again from room to room, looking in drawers and under his bed and through cupboards and shelves and satisfied himself that nothing left behind was of any importance. Early, far too early, he said a goodbye to his house and he left it, never to return. The path to the village was quiet, as expected. The weather had turned colder, and Arman wore a thick, woollen coat with the collar turned up to shield himself from the whip of the wind. There was little sound but Arman's heavy boots upon the hard earth and the rustle of his coat, the arms swinging lightly and making the muffled sound of wool on wool. There was just enough light left for Arman to trace the well-worn path down. If he had waited any longer, then he would've been stumbling in darkness. He clenched his suitcase in his good hand, tightening and loosening the grip as he went to ease the burden as much as he could. His other hand was playing up in the weather. The brittle, badly set bones ached in throbbing waves, setting his teeth together and making him wince. He knew Violet would have a bag, possibly more than one, and they would almost certainly be heavier than his, and he would have to carry them for her. He pushed the thought to the back of his mind and struggled on. On the outskirts of the village, Arman stopped. He feared being spotted and he had no way of explaining himself. He moved into nearby long grass, keeping low as he went. The grass almost completely covered his hunched body as he stalked through it, and when he ducked down to a crouch, it covered him completely. He could just about make out the arched entrance to the village in the distance, but he was well enough hidden that nobody would spot him. Within the hour, the black of night had consumed him, and he could no longer see the archway. He sat on the damp grass, blind to the world around him, listening to the fluttering and crawling of the natural inhabitants. He got used to brushing things from his face, presuming them to be grasshoppers or moths. Up ahead, in the village, there were pockets of lights, but as time wore on, they went out one by one. Arman closed his eyes.

When he opened his eyes, he wasn't sure if he had slept. He didn't think so. It was late and he was tired. He pulled his pocket watch from his inside pocket and flicked it open, but it was too dark to read. He stared at it intently, willing his eyes to adjust to the light, or lack of it, and tell him the time. With a frustrated shake of his head, he snapped it shut and put it away. He'd have to get closer to the church, where there would be a light out front. He'd be able to read it there. He looked towards the village, but saw nothing but an icy cold darkness before him. He stood, clutching at his suitcase, and started moving through the long grass towards where he presumed the church would be. It didn't take long to break free from the moist grass. Only now, in the dry, did he realise how wet it had made him sitting in the grass. His trousers clung to his legs uncomfortably. He was on open ground now, exposed to the elements but hidden by the night. He moved forward slowly, with his knees bent to keep himself low. At the front of the church was a single oil light hanging over the door. He stopped at the corner of the church and removed his pocket watch once more. He was on the fringes of the light, but it was enough to tell him that he had judged it well. It was just a little before midnight. He looked into the village, not sure what to expect. Would Violet bring an oil lamp? A candle? Would she be able to get away from her new husband? He shuddered as he thought of Cecil Garfield. He tried not to imagine what the wedding night might have held. He told himself that Violet would've found a way to keep him at bay. Perhaps a feigned sickness, or an issue with the pregnancy? He told himself these things but he knew different. Her pregnancy barely, if at all, showed, and Cecil would not be daunted by a slight sickness. Arman tried to push the thoughts from his mind. It would do him no good to theorise upon such things.

Now with the benefit of a little light, he checked his watch again. It was past midnight. Just a few minutes, but enough to worry him. He thought he heard a noise, somewhere far off in the village, and it made his heart leap, but nothing came of it. Was he imagining things now? Another noise. A click? A door closing? Was this Violet? He waited but nobody came. He didn't want to check his watch again because he knew what it would say. It would say that she was late and he didn't know why. He began to wonder how long he might wait before he gave up and returned home. The path would be a death-trap at this hour and he would be one wrong step from falling into danger. His eyes, very slowly adjusting to the night, saw a flitter of movement further down the village. Arman took a backward step, away from the fringes of the light and into the nearby darkness. The figure was coming closer. He could hear their hurried footsteps.

A hushed voice called out, "Arman?"

Arman stepped forward, coming into the light. It was Violet and she was shivering in the cold. She wore only her nightgown and stockings, with a flimsy nightcap tied beneath her chin. Arman went to her and put his arms around her. "Where are your things?" he asked.

"Joan said she will prepare me a bag and provide me with a coat," said Violet, her teeth chattering together. "I couldn't risk packing a suitcase beforehand, and all my things, including my coat, are stored in the large wardrobe in Cecil's bedroom and to open it—"

"—We will find a way," he told her. Arman unbuttoned his coat, and after briefly protesting, Violet let him wrap it around her shoulders. It engulfed her, with the front ends overlapping enough to provide her extra warmth. She hugged it to her.

"This is madness," he told her.

"Arman, please," she said, "it is too late to stop now."

"You are married, Violet. You are pregnant."

"With your baby," she said, pressing herself to him.

Or Fred Decker's, he thought, though wisely chose to stay quiet. He reached down and picked up his suitcase. He reached for Violet's hand and she took it, holding it tightly.

Arman asked her, "What now?"

"Through the village, past the oak tree and onwards, through the woodland and we'll reach the river. We walk along the riverbank until we come to a road. It is there that a carriage waits for us to take us to London."

"How far is it?"

Violet shook her head, "I do not know."

Before Arman could respond, Violet pressed herself forward and kissed him. The feel of her soft lips on his fired his passion. He dropped the suitcase to the floor and wrapped an arm around her waist to keep her there. But she pulled away, breaking herself free of him. Time was of the essence. He reached down for the suitcase, but stopped just as he leaned to get it. He froze, staring at a light in the distance. "Violet," he said.

"What is it?" she asked.

He stood, squinting into the darkness. He heard a noise he couldn't recognise. "Something is wrong."

"What?" she repeated, "What is wrong?"

The noise grew louder. The light, so dim a second ago, was moving. It was joined by another. And another. Arman backed up, pressing himself against the church wall. Violet looked at him with terror in her eyes.

"They know," he said.

"What do I do?" she asked.

"Run," he said, then when she didn't move, he shouted it. "Run!"

She hesitated, but just for a moment, and then she ran, heading back towards the long grass that Arman had waited in earlier. Arman watched her depart until the night-time took her. Then he turned his attention back to the growing lights and sound. They were oil lamps, held by villagers, and they were coming for him. He felt at the back of his trousers and found the outline of the knife in his pocket. He considered running after Violet, but he knew she'd have a better chance of getting away if he could hold back the surging mob.

"Shaw!" the voice, unmistakably that of Cecil Garfield, pierced the night air.

Arman's heart thundered in his chest. He considered retreating into the church, but there was no other way out and even if he could block the door, he'd be trapped in there. His best bet would be to somehow get through the centre of the village and try and find a path back to his home. From there he could figure out a way to circle back round the other way and look for Violet. He needed to draw them away from her. The flickering, approaching lights converged on him, though he still couldn't make out any of the people yet. Had the whole village come out or was it just a couple? Even if it was just Cecil then he probably couldn't fight. He would have to try and talk his way out of it.

"Garfield?" he called. "Is that you?"

There was no answer. It wasn't too late to run. Just pick a direction and take off. If he could get free then maybe the darkness would be all the cover he would need. But still, to run was an admission of guilt and he didn't know how much they knew yet.

"Garfield?" he called again. His eyes blurred at the burning orange flames that came at him. A mob of about seven or eight people emerged from the darkness, and at their centre, in front and coming fast, was Cecil Garfield. His fist landed squarely in the centre of Arman's face. Arman staggered back against the wall. His ears rang so loudly that it blocked out every other sound. The pain that emanated from his nose was absolute. He felt it deep in his skull. He instinctively went to grab at his face, but he didn't get a chance before that fist came straight back in. Arman had never felt a pain like it. It was like running face first into a wall. His eyes watered and his vision blurred so much that he didn't even see the third punch coming. Thankfully, it missed his nose and clipped his cheek. He took a blow to the ear that unbalanced him, sending him veering to his side. He reached out his arms to his side and found the edge of the door. He half walked, half fell, to his side, coming back through the doorway and into the church. The darkness within was soon replaced by light as the mob followed him in. He took blows to his stomach, but the pain in his nose and face was so extreme that he barely felt them. The only thing he could hear was a sound like rushing wind firing through his ears. He swallowed hard, gagging as thick globs of blood went down his throat.

In desperation, Arman felt for his back pocket and found the knife. Through blurred vision, he swung wildly, hoping to repel the attack. Even in this most desperate moment, he knew it couldn't last. He couldn't hear. He could barely see. He knew he could hold them off for seconds at best, but like a drowning man holding his breath, he was doing everything he could not to succumb to the inevitable. He swung again, and again. Backing up, he hit something hard and guessed that he was back against the altar. There was nowhere left to retreat to unless he could make it to the back room and lock the door. Did it even have a lock? Was it to his left or right? He was disorientated; swinging his knife and fearful of the next attack. He used his free arm to reach next to him, trying to find a path to the back room. He sidestepped once, twice, unsure of his footing. He stumbled a little, though he couldn't imagine on what, though he managed to keep his balance. Through his blurred vision, he saw the silhouette of somebody approaching and he swung the knife to keep them at bay. But it didn't swing. It embedded in something and he didn't know what. He pulled it back to swing it again. All he could hear was that dull, rushing noise, like he'd fallen underwater.

"Stop!" he cried, but he didn't know if the words escaped his lips.

He was hit from each side, crushing him and making him lose his footing. Then something else piled into him, pushing him back. He went down, hitting the back of his head hard against the floor. He was barely conscious now, but knew it was over. He was down and there were people on him. Blows and kicks rained down on him and all he could do was take it and hope it would end soon.

VII

It was cold. He was awake but Arman kept his eyes shut because he feared what might happen when he opened them once more. At least with his eyes closed, they seemed to be leaving him alone. He knew it was the morning because of the light he could see through his eyelids but beyond that, he knew very little. The last thing he remembered was being held on the ground while he was beaten. He hadn't remembered a point where he had lost consciousness. He struggled to think beyond the beating, hoping a sliver of what happened afterwards may come back to him. He had no real concept of time passing. It wouldn't have surprised him greatly to have opened his eyes and still found himself in the middle of the attack. But it was dark then and it was light now so he guessed it was over. And it was cold. There was an icy prickliness in the air and it stung his skin. He must be outside. His clothing was torn or removed because he felt the prick of wind on bare skin where he knew he had been dressed before. He dared to open his eyes, though when he did, the thumping pain that accompanied it was almost unbearable. It felt like somebody had poured lead into his head. His face was pressed to the ground, with some loose mud stuck to his dry, cracked lips. He spat some free from his mouth, coughing as he did so. He took a deep breath in and a sharp pain stabbed him in his chest and side. He gritted his teeth and tried to take shorter, shallower breaths. There wasn't a single part of him that wasn't in pain.

He decided to make the effort to sit up, knowing that it would be one of the hardest things he had ever done. He ground his bare elbow into the ground, shifting his weight to it as he leveraged himself up. A pain tore through him, starting under his arm and ending at his ribs. He rose from his elbow and splayed his hand out, using that as balance but as he did, he felt resistance. He pulled his body forward and found it jerked back in response. He looked down and saw the chain that was looped around his waist. He grabbed at it, trying to pull himself free, but he couldn't get free of it. He bent his head round and followed the chain along the ground and around the large oak tree where it was tied tightly. He shifted his weight, finding a seated position. He was barefoot. He had on trousers but one leg was torn up the side from the ankle to the thigh. He had on a shirt but one half of it was torn so much that it just looked like a rag draped on his shoulder. The other side was more intact but the end of the sleeve was split and torn. His head was thumping. It hurt to breathe too deeply. He couldn't see, but he could feel that his face had suffered badly. It felt like someone was grabbing his nose and pushing it into his brain. His face was sticky with what he presumed was blood, though there seemed to be so much mud on him that it was hard to tell what wounds lay beneath. His back felt raw, but he couldn't get his hands round to feel it. He guessed that they had dragged him to the oak tree from the church. He still heard the sound of deafening, rushing wind in his ears, but beyond that he could hear distant sounds. He could make out the sound of someone approaching and he twisted round as best he could to see who it was.

"Get back, get back!" came a familiar voice.

Arman looked up as Niall approached him. He was waving off someone that Arman couldn't see, and for a second his attention was drawn that way. When he turned to face Arman, his face was solemn. He studied Arman a moment, looking him up and down and shaking his head. He moved back a few feet and stood there a second, contemplating his actions. Making his mind up, he squatted down to sit opposite Arman. His knees cracked loudly as he bent his legs. He reached down and picked up a twig, wiping it free of dirt and fingering it idly in his hand.

"Morning, Arman," he said, his eyes not leaving the twig.

Arman didn't say anything.

"I am not your enemy, Arman," said Niall. "*You* are your enemy."

Arman didn't immediately respond. So much of what had happened was a dark void for him, and he was wary of somehow making things worse for himself by speaking when he shouldn't. He willed Niall to say something about Violet but he didn't.

Niall threw aside the twig he had been playing with and stared at Arman. "Look at you," he said.

"I don't know what to tell you," said Arman, breaking his silence. His own voice rung in his head, though he wasn't sure at what volume he'd spoken. Niall sounded far away.

Niall looked at something, or someone, over Arman's shoulder. Arman turned his head as far as he could, but he couldn't see anybody else. He presumed there was an audience of some kind back there, though they were probably too far away to hear what was being said.

"If you were us, Arman, what would you do?"

"About what?"

"About you."

"I would unchain me," said Arman. "I would clean me and bring me fresh clothes. I would feed me and tend to my wounds. I would be the forgiveness that we preach." He put a finger in his ear, trying to pick free the source of the rushing sound. He was picking up most of what Niall was saying, but still dropping words here and there.

"Forgiveness? Do you even know what that means? You think forgiveness wipes your slate clean, Arman?"

Arman nodded. "It is a start."

"I wash my hands of you," said Niall, standing. He lingered, as if about to speak, and then changed his mind and began to leave.

"What happens to me now?"

200

VII

"I suppose that's entirely up to you," said Niall.

Arman wasn't sure what Niall wanted him to say. Would an apology be enough, or would he need some larger gesture? Did they want him to leave the village? He would be absolutely fine with that. He worried that once Niall left it would be a while before he got a chance to defend himself again. He called out, "I'll leave. I'll leave the village and never come back."

"I'm sorry, what?" asked Niall.

"I'll never come back," Arman repeated. And he meant it. He had planned to leave anyway, with or without Violet. In the months following Mathilda's death, he had dreamt of coming back to Hope. He would've given anything to have found a way back into the congregation, but now, he could never live among these people again.

Niall's face furrowed with confusion. He looked away from Arman, his tongue probing at the back of his front teeth as he sucked in a long breath. He held it for a moment and then let out a big sigh. Finally, he looked back down at Arman. "I don't..." but he trailed off, unable to finish his sentence.

"What do you want from me?" said Arman.

Niall, half-turned away, shook his head in disbelief and said, "After everything you've done, you still carry this gross sense of injustice, as if the entire world conspires against you, Arman Shaw."

Arman placed his hand either side of his head, hoping he could contain the horrendous pain that smashed rhythmically inside his skull.

"It hurts?" asked Niall.

"Yes."

"Good."

"You said it was up to me," said Arman, snarling through the pain. "You said it was entirely up to me. Tell me what you want?!"

"I think you misunderstood," said Niall. "You asked me what happens next and I said it was up to you."

201

"That's what I sai—"

"—No, Arman. I meant the choice was entirely yours."

"Choice?"

"The choice," repeated Niall. "Is poison or axe."

The air seemed to leave Arman's lungs and he sat, mouth agape, unable to breathe. He couldn't get his thought process to work properly. He fell over his words as he tried to respond, "What...what...are you serious?"

Niall nodded.

"I don't understand," said Arman.

"Poison or axe, Arman? Would it help if I came back?"

Arman tried to get to his feet but the chain around his waist jerked him back hard enough to cause him to splay back into the dirt, exasperating the injuries in his chest and ribs. He struggled to free his leg which had become wound in part of the chain. Throughout, Niall stood motionless as Arman floundered in front of him. Arman had to slow down his actions and check his breathing. It felt like something inside him was trying to cut its way through his ribcage. He stopped struggling, lying back and slowly unwinding the chain from his leg. He shuffled backwards and sat up, resting his back against the tree.

"Well at least you have your dignity," said Niall.

"I don't understand," repeated Arman, the desperation coming through in his voice.

"I'll give you some time to ponder. I'll come back by this evening for your decision, if you have one. Regardless, at sunrise tomorrow it won't matter anymore."

"Niall, wait—"

But Niall had turned his back on him. The conversation was over. He walked away, slowly but purposefully until he was out of sight. Arman could hear a murmur of voices somewhere behind him but he couldn't make out what they were saying or how far they were away. He hugged his knees close to his chest, wrapping his arms around them to try and stay warm. His head thudded with such severity that his vision clouded. It distorted and darkened and Arman struggled to keep anything in focus. They were going to kill him for attempting to run away with Violet? Fred Decker had murdered Robert Walker and even he had been given a trial of sorts. He looked down at his bare feet and wondered what had happened to his boots. If only he could remember some details from the night before. But then, what good would it do? The evidence against him wouldn't change. He had been waiting with a suitcase. Violet had come to him. He had no defence except to say that his punishment far outweighed his crime.

Arman felt the heat of the sun around noon, but it soon disappeared behind the clouds and the afternoon brought an icy chill and a prevailing wind. A light shower came around mid-afternoon and there was little shelter beneath the tree. Arman was cold and hungry and alone. The sounds of the village seemed far away, like listening through a wall. He wondered if the damage to his ears that he had suffered during the beating would be permanent. Sometimes, the loud rushing noise was replaced by absolute silence. Every now and again, three words would slink into his head without warning.

Poison or axe?

Even as the afternoon merged into early evening, he never seriously considered either option. To choose would be to condone. To choose would be acceptance that they would kill him in the morning. To choose to die by poison or axe was madness. And what of Violet? Did they have her? Were they punishing her too? He would ask about her when Niall showed up again. He had nothing left to lose now. He doubled himself over. He had a gnawing pain in his gut that he knew was a need to go to the toilet, but he couldn't bear to do it here, exposed as he was. He held it inside and he added it to his list of ailments and pains. He guessed that his body may override him at some point, but while he still had some semblance of control, he would not mess himself. Shifting in his position, he managed to manoeuvre around to press his face to the tree trunk and look back towards the village. There was nobody about and he didn't know why, except perhaps that the weather was cold and wet and they were possibly, sensibly, inside their houses. From this position he could see the garden at the centre of the village. Beyond that, the church. This was the village that he and Mathilda had come to with Niall and the rest of the congregation to start a new life. Everything had gone wrong since he had lost her. It was his fault. She was gone because of him and it was only now he could finally accept the punishment that he knew he deserved. Because he did deserve it. He had tried to find some salvation with Violet but he didn't deserve salvation. He didn't deserve happiness. Let them flounder in accusations of sin and adultery. He would take the punishment for what he had done to Mathilda and he would welcome it.

When Niall returned just as the light was failing, Arman was leaning back against the tree staring off into the distance. Niall waited to the side. Arman slowly turned his head to look at his old friend.

"Well, Arman," said Niall, "Have you deci—"

"Axe," said Arman. "I'll take the axe."

Niall nodded and turned to leave but stopped when Arman spoke again.

"We at least had the pretence of a trial for Fred Decker."

"Look how that turned out," said Niall. "You never should have defended him."

"At least he had someone to defend him."

"Poor Arman," said Niall. "Still the victim." Again he went to leave, and again he was stopped.

"Did you find Violet?"

Niall took a step back and faced Arman, looking incredulous. He waited, letting the silence linger longer than was comfortable, then he asked, "Did we find Violet?"

"Yes," said Arman, "did you?"

"Arman, why do you think you're here?"

"What?" Arman felt like he was walking into a trap. "Do you want a confession, Niall?"

"I'm serious. Why do you think you're here?"

"I planned to run away with Violet."

"You think we would sentence you to death for that? Arman, you weren't beaten and tied to a tree because of your sinful plotting. You are here, Arman, because last night you killed Violet and her unborn baby."

VIII

She had come back. She had seen the approaching mob and heard his screams and Violet had come back from her hiding place in the long grass. The mob had pushed Arman back into the church, backing him against the altar and descending upon him to beat him savagely. At their centre, the disgruntled husband, Cecil Garfield, had bloodied his knuckles splitting open Arman's face. Arman still tried to escape. He reached out for an exit. In desperation he had swung his knife at them to keep them at bay. She had gone to him, ploughing through the mob to reach him, to put herself between him and his aggressors. Beneath the altar, where her husband Robert Walker had bled to death, she received a knife to the throat. She fell and she bled and nobody could stop it. Arman had kept swinging, oblivious as he tried to save his own skin.

This is the truth that Niall told Arman. This is the reason he was tied to a tree and sentenced to die without a trial. What kind of trial could it be? He had struck Violet down in front of witnesses. What kind of person could ever defend that? Niall told Arman what had happened and then he had left, leaving Arman curled in a ball at the base of the oak tree. His hands were wrapped around his head. The headache he had been carrying all day had hardened into a dull weight. He didn't think he could lift his head even if he wanted to. Soon, darkness came, covering him and everything around him. He didn't know when he had begun to cry, but he couldn't stop. His sobs rocked through him and his body convulsed in shuddering anguish. At some point, the tears had dried up and he just lay there, his eyes open, staring into the nothingness that surrounded him. He couldn't tell you when, but his eyes detected an approaching light.

"Mr Shaw?" the voice was soft, calming.

Arman didn't move. An oil lamp had been placed nearby, and he watched as somebody settled themselves on the floor to his side.

"Mr Shaw?"

Arman wiped the back of his hand across his nose. He raised his eyes to see who his visitor was. Joan Ogden was sat on the floor beside him. At her side was a small basket, and next to that was the lamp. She had a shawl drawn tightly around her but she still shivered in the night cold.

"Are you hungry?"

He didn't answer.

"Would you like some food?"

"My ears..."

"Your ears? Can you hear?"

He closed his eyes, happy to have the darkness return. He was aware that Joan Ogden was saying something more but he couldn't make out the words. He seemed to only hear properly when he concentrated. His eyes snapped open and he interrupted Joan by asking, "Was it you?"

"I am sorry, Mr Shaw, what was that? Was what me?"

"That betrayed us," he said, barely above a whisper.

"No," she said, softly.

"Then who—"

"—I don't know. Violet, God rest her soul, was careless. She talked too much. She told me things that maybe she should have kept to herself. Who knows if she spoke to the wrong person, or maybe Cecil Garfield's not as big a fool as he seems to be."

Arman shivered as the icy wind hit his bare skin. His eyes found the food basket. Joan followed his gaze. She removed the cloth from the top and reached in. She pulled out some bread and tore off a chunk which she handed to Arman. He took it and nodded his thanks. He took small, delicate bites. His mouth was covered in cuts and bruises and it hurt to swallow.

"Do you have anything to drink?" he asked.

She produced a small flask from the basket, unscrewed it and held it to his lips. It was water, and most of it ran down his cheek, but a little fell upon his lips. He shifted his head and managed to swallow a little, though it made him cough, which in turn sent sharp pains across his sides. Joan dabbed at his lips with a handkerchief, wiping away the water he dribbled along with a trickle of blood from a freshly opened slice on his lower lip.

"She wasn't pregnant," said Joan, leaning in closer to his ear.

"What?" he couldn't hide the shock from his voice.

"When they came for her, all those months ago, she feared for her life. Did you know they beat her? She told them she was pregnant because she guessed that they were less likely to hurt her if they thought she was with child. She said that Decker had forced himself upon her. They executed him in front of her."

"There was no baby?"

Joan shook her head; no. "It kept her alive. After the execution, the congregation changed. It hung over everything we did, like a cloud. I think they saw Violet as their redemption. If they could forgive her, redeem her, then we were all redeemed." Joan shrugged, unsure of her own words. She took a sip from the flask and then said, "Cecil Garfield, more than the others, bore responsibility. He took it upon himself to make an honest, maybe semi-honest, woman out of Violet. What could she say? But she knew she would be discovered soon. So she invited you to the wedding. To save her from the lie. To take her away."

"But..." he struggled to speak, "I would've found out too."

"I suppose she thought it would be easier to tell you the truth when the time came, rather than confess to her new husband. Cecil Garfield is not known for his temperament."

"She...used me?"

"Perhaps you weren't entirely innocent, Mr Shaw," she said with a stern look. "Violet was a complicated girl. I only really got to know her these past six months."

"I killed her."

"I know."

"I didn't mean to."

"I know that too."

"I'm sorry."

"It won't bring her back, will it?"

"I deserve...to die," said Arman, tears rolling slowly down his face.

"All of us die, Mr Shaw, but that is up to the Lord, not Niall Terran and Cecil Garfield." She took his hand in hers and held it for a moment. When she let go, it was to reach inside the basket. She moved some items out of the way, and produced a small, corked, glass bottle with some unknown liquid inside.

"What's that?"

"A little something," she said. "It will help."

"Is it poison?"

"No," Joan said, shaking her head. "But it will make it easier." She pressed the bottle into his hand and closed his fingers around it.

'Thank you," he said.

"All this," she started to say, looking around her, "all this. Look where we've gotten ourselves. Look what we've done. You should never have agreed to defend him. I wish you had been stronger."

Despite the harsh words, Arman couldn't detect any malice in her voice. He just said, "I'm sorry."

"Did you want me to stay with you?"

His pressed his dry lips together. There was blood in his mouth which he swallowed. He tripped over his own words when he spoke, so he spoke slowly. "Thank you," he said, "but I will be fine. I was thinking...of making...a daring escape."

"Then I suppose this is goodbye," she said. She collected her things together. She left the flask of water by his side but nothing else. She groaned as she struggled to her feet, her old legs feeling the strain of being crouched down for too long. She gave him a friendly smile, probably the last he would ever see, and then she left him alone.

He slept. Somehow, he slept. He had imagined he would stay awake, contemplating his final night on earth, but he had fallen asleep in the early hours. When he woke, it was still dark, but he could feel dawn's presence. The sky was a deep, dark blue and there was a frozen stillness to the air. He moved his position to look back towards the village but a mist had drifted in during the night and laid a ghostly sheet over everything. It swirled and rolled like a living thing, leaving a ghostly imprint of what had been. Arman briefly made out the outline of the garden at the centre of town but even as he stared at it, it vanished from sight. The chain around his waist rattled and chinked as he stretched and yawned. His eyes felt heavy but he didn't want to sleep anymore. He imagined they would be here within the hour. He imagined the entire congregation turning out, holding hands, singing songs, celebrating his execution. He wished that anyone but Cecil Garfield would be swinging the axe. He moved his arm and the glass bottle that Joan Ogden had given him slipped free and rolled away from him. He scrambled around, dropping to his knees and lurching forward just in time to reach out and grab it before the chain yanked him backwards. He grimaced as the taut chain dug into his ribs. He moved back closer to the tree to give it some slack. He kept the bottle clutched tightly in his hand. He would take it at sunrise and hope it might give him some comfort. Why had she said that it would make it "easier"?

A noise from within the mist made Arman sit upright. He heard footsteps approaching. It was too early, surely? He looked into the stark whiteness and waited. The sound got closer and eventually a figure emerged from the fog. Cecil Garfield, in a thick winter coat that Arman recognised as his own, was walking towards him. He wore a bowler hat, tipped forward where it partially hid his eyes. Dangling in a loose grip in his right hand was an axe. Cecil didn't look at Arman. He walked right past him, around ten feet further on until he came to a knee-high stump. It was the same stump that Violet had sat on, all those months ago, and stared down and questioned Fred Decker who had been tied to the tree at the time. Cecil flicked up the back of his jacket so that he could sit down upon the stump. He looked up at Arman with a cold, emotionless face. He sat in silence for just over three minutes before he spoke.

"Shaw," he said.

"Is it that time?" asked Arman.

"Soon enough," said Cecil.

"I suppose you'll enjoy this."

"Not particularly," said Cecil. "All in all, I would rather be at home with my wife." He looked down at the floor, staring intently as though lost in his thoughts. He produced a small clay pipe from his pocket. He lit it and let it hang at the corner of his mouth, the smoke swirling upwards and escaping into the blank, morning sky.

Arman watched him, waiting, though he didn't know for what. What did it matter if he struck him with the axe now, or an hour from now? He studied Cecil's face. They were the same age but Cecil looked younger. His face was square. His dark hair short and curly with a fringe that was too high. His thick eyebrows seemed perpetually formed in rising anger. He had a gap between his front teeth. A perfect black rectangle. Cecil Garfield was straight lines and angry features. Arman tried to think back and wondered if he had always seemed so intimidating. He had been part of the first group that had come to the village. Even then, he had been alone. He seemed happy enough to live on the fringes of the congregation. Nobody had any reason to doubt his character or religious devotion, but somehow, Arman and Cecil had rarely spoken. Arman remembered that in his old life, Cecil had worked in insurance... was that right? Or a bank?

"You used to work in...insurance, was it?" asked Arman.

Cecil's head shot up, an instinctual reaction to the silence being broken. "Yes, that's right," he said. "Why do you ask?"

"I was just thinking back to when we first came here and I couldn't remember your old job at first."

"Insurance," said Cecil once more. "I spent my days having to decide if somebody was lying to me or not. After a time, it begins to prey on you. You end up seeing dishonesty everywhere."

"How could you tell," asked Arman, "if somebody was lying to you or not?"

"You just..." he paused, thinking of the right words, then added, "get a feel for it."

"And how—"

"—Would you mind if we just sat in silence?" Cecil lowered his head, staring down at the ground once more. He looked exhausted. He closed his eyes and Arman watched as his lips moved to some silent prayer. He had no interest in Arman. He was in his own world.

Arman struggled to his feet, unsteady and with a lean to his side caused by an injury in his ribcage which would never be diagnosed. He opened his palm and looked at the glass bottle. He unscrewed it and brought the bottle to his nose. It had no smell. He tipped it back, swallowing the small amount of tasteless liquid in one gulp. Now, he would wait. There was no sunrise. Just a lighter sky. A cold mist and a soft breeze. Morning had come, and it would be Arman's last.

IX

Arman watched as the congregation emerged slowly from the fog, some alone, some in pairs or groups. All their heads were down as they approached and passed by him. Nobody was ready to look him in the eye yet. People stood at a respectful distance, just beyond and around the stump where Cecil still sat, still eyes closed, still looking down at the ground. Some talked amongst themselves. Others found a fascination with the earth beneath their feet. Herman stood near Cecil. He wore a striped shirt with the sleeves rolled up and Arman wondered how he could stand the cold. He rested a hand on Cecil's shoulder, though the seated man did nothing to register the touch. Back far enough to almost be hidden in the mist, the ghostly figure of Olive Kirby stood with her arms clutched across her chest. He had not seen Olive since that morning when she had brought medicine for Fred Decker. She had fixed his broken hand that morning, though its subsequent recovery led him to believe that he may have fared better if she had left it alone. Arman knew that it had been Olive that had discovered Violet and Fred Decker that morning. It must have been a tremendous shock for her. He bore her no ill will. Olive had always been kind to him and Mathilda. He was glad, for both her and himself, that she hadn't had to make any more poison today.

Philip Dryden stood next to Edmund and Esther Hayes, though the musical twins weren't singing a song today. Arman presumed that Philip's wife, Alma, was at home with their two boys. Philip had a stern face, but had a gentle way. He tended to keep himself to himself and Arman admired that about him. He tried to find Philip's eye but Philip stared into a vacant point in the distance. Others came: Nigel Vance and his wife, Ottilie; Basil and Rita Hale; Miles and Lucille Faber; Phoebe Everly; Sylvia Farley and her husband, Roman. Merry Ramsey sat on the floor in a cross-legged pose that looked uncomfortable. Benjamin Hall and his wife, Euphemia, came arm in arm and stood to the side, at the fringes of Arman's peripheral vision. Vincent Law left the side of his eldest son, Dominic, to stride purposefully out and assist Mary Wheel as she walked slowly into view. He guided her to a nearby stump, where she clumsily flopped back into a seated position. Vincent returned to his son, who made a comment that made his father smile. Arman wondered if they were talking about him or Mary?

Arman felt a touch on his elbow and he jumped. He hadn't noticed Joan Ogden emerge from the mist on the other side of the tree. She had a dark shawl wrapped around her head which highlighted her pale face.

"Is there anything I can do?" she asked in a low voice.

He shook his head. "What did I take?"

"In the bottle? Nothing magical, Mr Shaw. It will just relax you. With hope."

He took her hand and held it, squeezing it and saying, "Thank you."

A few of the congregation shifted uncomfortably. Arman could feel their annoyance at somebody showing him kindness. Arman ignored them. Joan Ogden's hand was cold and sleight but he didn't want to let it go. He felt a swelling in his chest, rising, threatening tears. He fought them back, sucking in a deep breath that stabbed at his side. He let go of her hand and she moved away, finding a spot to the side by herself. Arman looked away from the gathering congregation and back towards the still hidden village. He had hoped the mist would lift so he could get one last look at Hope, but it wasn't showing any signs of clearing. A silhouette in the mist approached, slowly taking the form of Niall, dressed head to toe in black, with a broad-brimmed felt hat. In his hand he clutched a small Bible that Arman recognised, even from a distance. It was Robert Walker's Bible and it had been in the inside pocket of Arman's coat.

There was a murmur in the crowd though Arman couldn't make out anything anyone was saying. It seemed to get louder, as if Niall's presence was a signal for everyone to raise their voices. To Arman it was just a wall of sound, muffled and distant and that was fine by him. Niall stopped in front of him and, at first, stared down, but soon looked up and met Arman's eyes. He leaned in close, so their cheeks were almost touching.

"This is the way it has to be," he said.

Behind Niall, Cecil began to whistle to himself. Arman looked over Niall's shoulder and watched the burly executioner, still staring down at the ground. It didn't seem disruptive. He doubted Cecil even knew he was doing it.

"Perhaps, we should proceed," said Niall, giving a quick glance over his shoulder at Cecil, before turning back to Arman and offering what might best be called a sympathetic smile.

Arman's hearing seemed to be deteriorating with each passing moment. Whatever damage had been caused, was tearing its way through him. All he really heard was a low whine now. He had felt Niall's breath upon his face and the dull vibration of him speaking, but he couldn't really pick out the words. What he could hear, was Cecil Garfield's whistling, which cut through the air and hit him at a frequency that his ears accepted. He resigned himself to the fact that it might be the final sound he heard.

Arman felt unsteady on his feet. His head was light. He could feel his heart thumping in his chest. The headache, which had morphed into multiple forms since he had woken, swirled around his skull and settled behind his eyes. Blotches and specks of blackness peppered his vision. Ahead of him, Cecil rose to his full height and rolled his axe-wielding arm. He puffed up his chest and inhaled deeply. He tilted his head from side to side. Even through his blurry eyes, Arman could see that Cecil was in a world of his own. Cecil's lips still pursed together in a meandering whistle. He reached down and took a good grip on the handle of his axe and gave it a firm yank that drew it free of the earth.

Niall was sermonising, though Arman couldn't hear it. There was movement in the congregation, with Vincent Law and his son, Dominic, stepping forward and moving to Arman. They stood either side of him. Did they expect him to break free from the chain and make a run for it? Arman looked from side to side, at each of the men, but they didn't return his look. They stared straight ahead, their faces made of stone. Ahead of him, Niall read from the Bible and Arman wondered which part he'd chosen. Perhaps it was from the Book of Job, about a man who had been tested and lost everything. Perhaps it was from the works of Malachi, who warned God's followers that going through the emotions of worship couldn't hide their sins. Upon a cue he didn't register, Vincent and Dominic Law each rested a hand on Arman's elbows and guided him forward. The chain rattled and spun around his midsection and fell to the floor as he moved forward. Somebody must have undone it at the tree without him seeing. He almost laughed when he considered it may have been like that the entire time. He shuffled onwards, each step a painful journey in its own right. Cecil stood ahead of him, just behind the stump, still with his eyes down, rocking from foot to foot to combat the cold. Arman's bare foot hit painfully upon the edge of the stump. The men at his side moved their grip from his elbows to his upper arms, where they pushed him down. Arman looked to them for an idea of what they wanted before it dawned on him that they wanted him to kneel. He fell to one knee and then the other and went to lean forward to rest his head onto the stump but the two men either side pulled him back. Apparently, he was getting ahead of himself. He looked up at them and saw their attention was drawn over at Niall, who still passionately spoke, though he no longer read from the Bible.

Small stones at the base of the stump dug into Arman's knees. He shifted a little and as he did, the hands on his shoulders pressed down harder. He looked down at the stump. It was about as wide as his shoulders and coloured in earthy creams and browns and swirling lines that started at a single spot and spiralled out in ever increasing layers. He saw the lower half of Cecil's trousers, black and pressed. Beneath them his shoes were shined and Arman wondered if he had cleaned them especially for the occasion. Still the whistling, just at the right frequency for Arman's ears to pick up. If he strained, tilting his head a little, he could also make out a voice he presumed to be Niall's, though he could only hear the inflection, not the content. There was no anger in his words, or at least it didn't sound like there was. There was sorrow and pain and then, sadly, silence. There were no sounds. No visual clues. But Arman knew that the time had come. A change in the air. He could somehow feel the eyes of the congregation turn from Niall to himself. He saw Cecil's stance widen, just a fraction. He imagined the weight of the axe and the momentum it would gather on its short journey from above Cecil's head right down into the stump below. Cecil was whistling, though it was distant, between his teeth as he concentrated. Arman shivered as a numbing wind spun around him. The hands on his shoulders moved and he knelt forward, resting his chin upon the stump. This time, nobody drew him back. At this distance he could see the fine grain in the wood. At this distance he could see there was a universe hidden in the swirls of the tree.

X

Mathilda lay back on the bed, her arms outstretched and holding onto the sides of the bed frame. Arman's hands were wrapped around her throat, squeezing the life from her. He had tears running freely down both cheeks. He could see her fingers twitch. This is what she had asked for. This is what she had begged for. He looked down at her and her eyes met his. Her mouth flapped open and closed like a goldfish taken from his bowl. She tried to breathe in air that wasn't there and it took all her effort just to push out one word.

"No," she said. It came out in a breathless exclamation and the second she said it, she knew that if she'd waited a second longer, she wouldn't have been able to.

He let go. His hands flew away from her neck and he held them up and to his sides to show her. Her own hands grasped at her throat, as if they may massage the pain away.

"I'm sorry," he cried.

They hugged and they cried and they stayed that way until eventually they slept. The next morning, they had breakfast and there were more tears. More apologies. They went for a walk to help clear the air. Mathilda was present in a way she hadn't been in recent times. Arman noticed but didn't say anything. In the coming days, their life began to take on some of the lost joy that the past few years had taken. Still, at first, Arman didn't want to get his hopes up. Each day he waited for the moment when the darkness would return. He waited for Mathilda to look at him and not recognise him. He waited. He waited. But it never happened and they didn't know why. Days became weeks and slowly, steadily, hope began to blossom in both of them. Soon after, to both their surprise, Mathilda became pregnant. She and Arman decided to wait before they told everyone. They feared a return of Mathilda's illness or a related problem with the pregnancy. But morning sickness aside, the pregnancy passed with no problems. Youssef James Shaw was born in April and named after a grandparent from each side of his parentage. Mathilda wondered if the life inside her had somehow affected her illness. Somehow saved her.

On the day of his christening, the village of Hope was in bloom, with rich, beautifully coloured flowers decorating the fence outside the church and the small trees around the centre garden. A selection of lilies and chrysanthemum lined the church doorway. The congregation had all come out to celebrate the occasion, mingling outside the church before the ceremony began. Little Youssef was dressed in a white satin christening gown over his underclothes that had a cloak attached with soft pink ribbons. The lace cap he wore had a trim of cockades along the side of his head. Mathilda held the five-week old baby close to her chest, swaddled in a blanket. Youssef had his small arms pressed together and held tightly to his chest and stared up wide-eyed at his mother. Arman stood nearby, dressed in a dark frock coat over pin stripe charcoal grey formal trousers. At Mathilda's insistence, he had even shined his shoes, something he rarely did even on special occasions. He watched as members of the congregation flocked to Mathilda and their son. Mathilda's smile spread across her face and gave her a radiance he couldn't remember seeing before the birth of their boy.

He felt a hand on his back and turned to find Niall at his side, a grin on his face. Niall gestured, with an open hand at Mathilda and the baby, at the people around her, at the gathered congregation socialising together.

"This is the way it should be," he said, "with all of us together, celebrating new life. Celebrating each other. I'm so very proud of you, Arman. And Mathilda. You've overcome so much. You've overcome the impossible. And now you have little Youssef."

"Thank you, Niall," said Arman.

Herman came walking over, leaning to his side slightly to accommodate his bad leg. He shook Arman's hand vigorously and gave him a hefty slap on his shoulder. "Praise the Lord! You have a son! And how is Mathilda?"

"She is well," said Arman, "though because of Youssef, she no longer seems to sleep."

"That will pass," said Herman, "and everything that follows is a wonder."

Arman nodded, but his attention was drawn over Herman's shoulder, where Mathilda was talking with Joan and Bernard Ogden. Their relationship hadn't always been so, but in recent times, the two women had drawn extremely close, so much so, that along with Robert Walker, the Ogdens would act as Youssef's Godparents. Mathilda embraced Joan tightly, somehow managing to shift Youssef to her side to keep him from being crushed in the affection.

"Shall we go inside?" Niall asked Arman, and when Arman nodded, Niall said louder, to all, "Inside everyone, let's all head inside now, please."

The congregation funnelled through the gate and down the short path inside to the church. Arman walked at the back. Niall and Herman were just ahead of him. At each side of him walked Vincent Law and his son, Dominic. Inside, nobody seemed in any kind of rush for the ceremony to begin. Many still stood, talking to the person next to them, or in the row behind or in front of them. Arman went to the front, where Mathilda still spoke with the Ogdens. On the other side of the Ogdens sat Violet and Robert Walker. Violet was pregnant, though wasn't showing yet. Robert whispered something to her and she giggled. Niall had moved passed everyone and stood at the altar, though his attention was downward, on the Bible he had in his hand. His lips were silently moving, as he ran through his words. On the altar was a decorative silver bowl of holy water. To the side was a table and on it was a wicker moses basket lined with white linen. Niall stepped down from the altar and came to Arman and Mathilda.

"To begin, as we pray, we'll have little Youssef in the basket at the front," said Niall. He addressed Mathilda and said, "Then you'll take him as we start the ceremony, is that fine?"

"Yes," said Mathilda, beaming with pride.

"I shall take the little one once we bring the Godparents up, and once I've performed the blessing, I shall pass him back to you. Does that all sound good to you?"

"It sounds fine," said Mathilda.

"He is a handsome boy," said Niall.

"He is," replied Mathilda.

"Are we sure he's Arman's?" joked Niall, who subsequently burst out into hysterical laughter. He shook Arman's hand, as if reassuring him that he was just joking. His laughter trailed off and he turned back to Mathilda and said, "May I?"

Mathilda delicately handed Youssef to Niall, who cradled him in his arms. Niall stood there for a moment, his eyes locked with the baby, who gurgled quite happily in response.

Niall looked up and met Arman's eyes, telling him, "We live on through our children."

Arman nodded. He felt it too. He had felt, happily, his own time in the light fade and a new light shine upon his son.

Niall carefully moved Youssef slightly, bringing his blanket around him and making him comfortable, then he turned to head back to the altar. He arrived there and gently placed Youssef into the moses basket at his side. He looked around at the assembled congregation and, as if on cue, everyone began to take their seats. When he had surveyed those present, his eyes seemed to fall upon Arman when he said, "Will you kneel?"

The congregation shuffled to the floor in supplication to the Lord.

"Our Father, which art in heaven, Hallowed be thy Name; Thy kingdom come; Thy will be done in earth, as it is in heaven:

Give us this day our daily bread; And forgive us our trespasses, as we forgive them that trespass against us; And lead us not into temptation, But deliver us from evil; For thine is the kingdom, and the power, and the glory, For ever and ever. Amen." Niall looked up from the altar and stood in silence before the congregation.

Arman, smiling, proud, looked briefly over his shoulder and then returned his attention to the altar. But he stopped. Something felt wrong. He looked back over his shoulder and saw some spaces here and there in the seats of the congregation. Were there spaces before? Normally, the full congregation in church took up all the seats. He went to say something to Mathilda but changed his mind. He couldn't quite put his finger on it but he knew it somehow didn't matter. Looking further down the row, beyond Mathilda and Joan Ogden, he noticed that Robert Walker and Bernard Ogden were both gone.

Mathilda leaned into him a little and whispered, quizzically, "Do you hear that?"

Arman shook his head to indicate that he didn't.

"I'll see what's going on?" said Joan, rising from her seat. She shuffled sideways past Mathilda and Arman and headed back down the aisle towards the exit.

"I don't hear a noise," said Arman to Mathilda.

Arman looked to his side, across the front row of the opposite pew. Where there had been a full line of people, now there were just a handful. He turned to look over his shoulder again as, behind him, Alma Dryden's husband, Philip, got to his feet, said something to his wife and then disappeared down the aisle and out the exit. On the other side of the church, Edmund Hayes got up from his seat on the end of the aisle and headed for the exit. Arman turned to look back to the altar, where Niall still stood in silence. The only sound he could hear was the occasional creaking of the pews as people stood, and then their subsequent footsteps as they left.

"What *is* that noise?" said Mathilda, troublingly looking back over her shoulder.

"I don't hear anything," said Arman. He rubbed at his temples, unsure what was going on. He felt a tightening in his chest. It felt like everyone was in on a secret except him. He bowed his head and closed his eyes, hoping to gather himself. In his darkness, he could hear the creaking. The footsteps. The gentle movements of Youssef in his basket. He could hear Mathilda breathing beside him. He strained to hear more and thought, just for a second, that he could pick out something else, but it faded almost as soon as he had heard it. He felt someone brush past him. He opened his eyes and looked around. Mathilda sat at his side. At the altar, Niall stood silent. Youssef was in the basket. Arman looked around and saw the rest of the church was completely empty.

Niall stood down from behind the altar and began to head for the exit. He turned to Arman as he did, telling him, "I had best go and..." But he trailed off. He was gone before Arman could respond.

Arman turned to look at Mathilda. She stared ahead, at the large window that looked out behind the church, where you could see the far-off fields, or, closer to the church, the graveyard. She turned back to him and looked into his eyes. He marvelled at their detail. The small black pupil and then an explosion that formed the iris. Hazel eyes with tiny specks of grey and green that seemed to swirl before him. At this distance he could see there was a universe hidden within.

"Can you stay?" he asked.

She whispered a regretful, "No." She leaned forward and kissed him and then she stood up, walked past him to the aisle and then turned and walked out of the church. She didn't look back.

Arman sat facing forward. Everyone was gone but him and Youssef. Youssef kicked out with bent legs as his tiny arms reached up as if to grab something, but just hung in the air, lost, with no control. It was then that Arman heard it, or at least he thought he heard it. The sound. It was coming from far away but the more he listened the more he could hear it. Somebody was whistling. He cocked his head, listening intently as the sound changed. It was getting louder. It was coming towards him. It was then that little Youssef began to cry, a high-pitched shriek that seemed impossible from somebody so small. Arman desperately wanted to go to him but knew he couldn't. The whistling was at the door now. Arman briefly bowed his head as if in prayer, but he knew there was no time. The pew creaked as he stood up. He wiped at the thighs of his trousers, smoothing out the creases. He stood up and turned to leave, snatching the briefest glimpse of his son as he did. Somewhere, above the drill of the whistling, he could hear the sound of Youssef shrieking. The child's cries rung in his ears as he left the church.

**TOP HAT
BOOKS**

Top Hat Books

Historical fiction that lives

We publish fiction that captures the contrasts, the achievements, the optimism and the radicalism of ordinary and extraordinary times across the world.

We're open to all time periods and we strive to go beyond the narrow, foggy slums of Victorian London. Where are the tales of the people of fifteenth century Australasia? The stories of eighth century India? The voices from Africa, Arabia, cities and forests, deserts and towns? Our books thrill, excite, delight and inspire.

The genres will be broad but clear. Whether we're publishing romance, thrillers, crime, or something else entirely, the unifying themes are timescale and enthusiasm. These books will be a celebration of the chaotic power of the human spirit in difficult times. The reader, when they finish, will snap the book closed with a satisfied smile.
If you have enjoyed this book, why not tell other readers by posting a review on your preferred book site.

Recent bestsellers from Tops Hat Books are:

Grendel's Mother
The Saga of the Wyrd-Wife
Susan Signe Morrison
Grendel's mother, a queen from Beowulf, threatens the fragile
political stability on this windswept land.
Paperback: 978-1-78535-009-2 ebook: 978-1-78535-010-8

Queen of Sparta
A Novel of Ancient Greece
T.S. Chaudhry
History has relegated her to the role of bystander, what if
Gorgo, Queen of Sparta, had played a central role in the Greek
resistance to the Persian invasion?
Paperback: 978-1-78279-750-0 ebook: 978-1-78279-749-4

Mercenary
R.J. Connor
Richard Longsword is a mercenary, but this time it's not for
money, this time it's for revenge...
Paperback: 978-1-78279-236-9 ebook: 978-1-78279-198-0

Black Tom
Terror on the Hudson
Ron Semple
A tale of sabotage, subterfuge and political shenanigans
in Jersey City in 1916; America is on the cusp of war and
the fate of the nation hinges on the decision of one young
policeman.
Paperback: 978-1-78535-110-5 ebook: 978-1-78535-111-2

Destiny Between Two Worlds
A Novel about Okinawa
Jacques L. Fuqua, Jr.
A fateful October 1944 morning offered no inkling that
the lives of thousands of Okinawans would be profoundly
changed — forever.
Paperback: 978-1-78279-892-7 ebook: 978-1-78279-893-4

Cowards
Trent Portigal
A family's life falls into turmoil when the parents' timid
political dissidence is discovered by their far more enterprising
children.
Paperback: 978-1-78535-070-2 ebook: 978-1-78535-071-9

Godwine Kingmaker
Part One of The Last Great Saxon Earls
Mercedes Rochelle
The life of Earl Godwine is one of the enduring enigmas of
English history. Who was this Godwine, first Earl of Wessex;
unscrupulous schemer or protector of the English? The answer
depends on whom you ask...
Paperback: 978-1-78279-801-9 ebook: 978-1-78279-800-2

The Last Stork Summer
Mary Brigid Surber
Eva, a young Polish child, battles to survive the designation of
"racially worthless" under Hitler's Germanization Program.
Paperback: 978-1-78279-934-4 ebook: 978-1-78279-935-1 $4.99
£2.99

Messiah Love
Music and Malice at a Time of Handel
Sheena Vernon
The tale of Harry Walsh's faltering steps on his journey to
success and happiness, performing in the playhouses of
Georgian London.
Paperback: 978-1-78279-768-5 ebook: 978-1-78279-761-6

A Terrible Unrest
Philip Duke
A young immigrant family must confront the horrors of the
Colorado Coalfield War to live the American Dream.
Paperback: 978-1-78279-437-0 ebook: 978-1-78279-436-3

Readers of ebooks can buy or view any of these bestsellers by
clicking on the live link in the title. Most titles are published
in paperback and as an ebook. Paperbacks are available in
traditional bookshops. Both print and ebook formats are
available online.

Find more titles and sign up to our readers' newsletter at
http://www.johnhuntpublishing.com/fiction

Follow us on Facebook at https://www.facebook.com/
JHPfiction and Twitter at https://twitter.com/JHPFiction